TIDAL POOLS

Savannah ← → Rutherford ↑ Charleston → →

Poston's Landing

The Galeegi Islands

Marsh

Argeaux Bridge

East Cove

Galeegi River

Marina

Plantation Hwy.

Marsh

Amoyeli

Old Safari Road

Galeegi Island

Lighthouse

Pavilion Avenue

Monastery

Beach Pavilion

St. Agnes

N
W E
S

Pat,
Thanks for reading !
Hope you enjoy !

TIDAL POOLS

a novel by

LAWRENCE THACKSTON

Holladay House Publishing

Holladay House Publishing

Holladay House Publishing
1120 Bancroff Lane
Manning, SC 20102

First edition, first printing November 2013

Designed by Abby Sink
Author photo by Joni Thackston

Manufactured in the United States of America

Hardback edition ISBN 978-0-9900091-0-8

Trade Paperback edition ISBN 978-0-9900091-1-5

DEDICATION

For Joni

"He knew it. He could tell.

This one was something special."

ACKNOWLEDGEMENTS

They say no two novels ever come together in the same way. To that, I can definitely attest. Something happens between a writer's stab at ink and paper, and its final published form—something that is difficult to explain. Certainly hard work, good fortune, and good timing are often involved, but there is also a degree of publishing legerdemain, for lack of a better term, that helps a story find its way to print. I won't attempt to explain the elements of linguistic magic used in creating this novel, only to thank the many wizards and magicians behind it.

First and foremost, I want to thank Holladay House Publishing. Like a diamond that travels in stages from mine to market, this novel found its polished edges through the skillful hands of my editor and publisher, Holly Holladay. Her care and concern over the manuscript was evident upon our first meeting, and she was so good at responding to my many questions and concerns. With Ms. Holladay, I always knew my work was in good care. Mary Massalon and Ashley Cafasso with Holladay House Publishing were also invaluable to the marketing and promotion of *Tidal Pools*, and I truly appreciate their hard work and dedication.

I also wish to thank my friend and fellow author, Ken Burger. I don't think I'm overstating things when I say there would be no *Tidal Pools* if not for Ken. He was kind enough to read my first novel, *The Devil's Courthouse*, and bring it to the attention of others in the know. In a way, he led me back to the coast, and for that, I am forever grateful.

As for the novel's content, there are too many people to possibly thank for their contributions, but there is one I must mention. As a veteran policeman, my brother-in-law,

Phil Webster, has been extremely helpful in explaining all manners of criminal detection and law. The hours of interview he provided are evident on every page and left me with an even greater respect for him and his profession. Without question, there is no better lawman out patrolling our beaches, keeping our world safe from harm.

The support I have received for my writing has been overwhelming. I count endless new friends whom I have encountered in the publishing and writing game. Many in the business have been so kind in their willingness to accept both my work and me, and I have found the entire experience to be of a satisfying, yet humbling, nature.

I want to thank the faculty, staff, students, and former students of Edisto High School in Cordova, SC, my world for the past twenty-five years. They have been a continuing source of inspiration and support and are very deserving of my gratitude.

Close friends and family are also a major part of my support system. I shudder to think how my life, let alone my writing life, would be without them. They have been helpful in always pointing me in the right direction. I take great comfort in their love, concern, and understanding.

And finally I would like to thank you, the reader. I hope you find as much joy in reading this novel as I had in writing it. And please let me know what you think. I encourage you to visit the novel's website: tidalpoolsnovel.com and leave me your thoughts. Until then, thanks for reading, and may our paths cross again somewhere down the literary road.

"It is advisable to look from the tide pool to the stars and then back to the tide pool again."
-John Steinbeck
The Log from the Sea of Cortez

JUNE 1

6:00 AM

The alarm sounded just before dawn, but Jaja was already awake, lying on top of the covers, thinking about her—about that night so long ago. Her screams often tormented him. Her shrieks came straight from hell, always before light, wrenching his stomach, causing his heart to pound, and leaving his pillow soaked in cold sweat and warm tears. She haunted him relentlessly, always early in the darkness before the clock buzzed, always before he had to rise to face another day.

He threw his long legs over the side of the bed, and his feet landed flat on the floor. He rose and looked into a mirror hanging delicately on the door of an old chiffarobe, the only piece of furniture other than the bed in his tiny room. He blinked weariness from his eyes and stared into the looking glass. A tired old man stared back at him—a wrinkled black face that for too long had not felt the sun or salty breezes of home.

Soon, very soon, he vowed in silence.

Jaja bent down and opened the wide bottom drawer. His bony fingers rustled past a pair of baggy britches, a stained cook's apron, and a tattered white jacket. He pulled out a neatly folded blue suit, the same threadbare ensemble he wore when he arrived in Atlanta over forty years before.

He dressed quickly. His ride would arrive soon. He clutched the gold watch that management had given him the night before—a shiny Euro Geneve 14-karat piece with a thin leather band. The restaurant owner, whom Jaja knew simply as "boss man," had grabbed him by his arm and swung him around, while everyone hushed and watched.

"For meritorious service," boss man declared.

"But I jis a cook," Jaja replied in his thick Gullah accent, which drew warm applause and gentle laughter from the other cooks and waitstaff in the room. They gave him the best send-off they could, and he appreciated their efforts.

Now he was going home.

Unaccustomed to wearing a watch, Jaja slipped the time-piece into his front pocket for safekeeping, picked up his brown box suitcase, and returned to the mirror for another look. He shifted his weight from one side to the other.

Yes, enough time has passed. You must let it slip away.

10:47 AM

The Greyhound rumbled across Georgia over the state line into South Carolina and tracked two-lane highways southeast toward the coast. It stopped often in tiny towns—Salley, Wagener, North, St. George, Pinopolis—and each time the delay seemed to take forever. Jaja leaned his head sideways against the cool glass.

Soon, very soon.

The driver circumnavigated the flat, brown suburbs of Charleston to U.S. Highway 17 South. Gone were the sand hills, red clay, and monotonous rows of pines found in the Midlands. Jaja recognized the palmettos and mossy oaks and narrow rivers merging from brackish black and widening to salty gray. He noticed vast expanses of Spartina grass billowing like huge fields of wheat where rice used to grow. He inhaled the familiar scent of pluff mud at low tide—a sulfurous stench to most, a distinct aroma to Jaja. He welcomed the magnificence of the Lowcountry marshlands, dotted with numerous snowy egrets and a few tall, handsome herons—most of them white, a few grayish-blue. All confirmed what Jaja knew. Amoyeli was not far away.

Jaja was born on Amoyeli. This was where he learned to cast a seven-foot-wide, heavy cotton-mesh net for fish and shrimp day and night when the tide was right, until his fingers bled and his back was twisted like hammock rope. His grandfather had taught him everything he needed to know about life on the island. Jaja knew how to step gently on a redfish's head as soon as it landed in the bottom of the boat, so he could remove the hook, gut it cleanly, and slip it onto ice. He mastered the slow retrieval of chicken necks tied at the end of long strings to lure huge hungry blue crabs just within his reach. He could sweep the crab—bait, weight, and all—with a dip net in one hand while holding the line taut in the other. He could navigate across massive beds of oysters barefooted and rarely nick his feet. He learned to catch, fillet, soak, season, steam, broil, bake, and sauté these delicacies harvested from the sea. He made this his life's work: creating cuisine for thirty some odd years that fetched top dollar in one of Atlanta's Buckhead District's premier Southern-style bistros.

But Jaja reminded himself that his island home was also where he learned life's harder lessons—the distinctions that seemed to matter to most people. Land and sea. Black and white. Rich and poor. Love and hate. And very early in life, he learned the golden rule: that the lines separating each of these distinctions were never as clear as to the person standing on the wrong side.

4:15 PM

The bus slowed as it reached the south terminal of Land's

End Road in Rutherford, a town with run-down, roof-less sheds and shanties and dirt roads lined by scrubby trees and trash. Jaja peered out at a wasteland of failed restaurants, fly-by-night bars, cheap-sleeps, and red-dot liquor stores. He recognized none of the dark and forgotten faces of its inhabitants who stopped and stared as the bus thundered past. But they all looked the same to him. Jaja understood their hopelessness.

The driver turned right down a corridor of live oaks standing stalwart in a dense longleaf pine and hardwood forest. Spanish moss hung like cobwebs from oak boughs, casting a pall upon the riders as the sun tried in vain to break through. Jaja closed his eyes and waited.

The Greyhound emerged from the trees into the bright light of the Galeegi marshes; Jaja sensed the sun's rays and opened his eyes. Almost immediately a pair of gulls swept up past his window, dipped and danced in the light blue sky, and welcomed him back.

The bus bumped across a half-mile causeway and rumbled over the Galeegi River via the brand new Argeaux Bridge, its giant concrete shoulders and long blue-steel arms glistening. Jaja sat up straight and scanned the waters. He spotted a white wooden-hull shrimp trawler, its outriggers pinned back to the mast as it motored past the marina into the Atlantic. Except for the tall new bridge, the Galeegi looked like Jaja remembered it—deep, twisting and turning through the salt marsh, across massive oyster beds and into the whitecaps of the shallows where it collided with the open sea. The river had not changed since the day he was banished over forty years ago.

He remembered his grandfather's stories about the original human inhabitants of the islands — members of a small coastal tribe who named the river *Galeegi*, their word for "black snake." And like its water moccasin namesake, the river still held its viperous presence—unforgiving, dark, and deadly.

His grandfather once told him that the 206-mile black water river was the third longest of its type in the world. It gained its deep cola color from tannic acid created by the decaying leaves, branches, and roots of cypress and other hardwoods it encountered as it hissed and moaned through flatlands and swamps before emptying into the Atlantic. Not a year went by in Jaja's early life when some poor soul did not perish in the turbulent jaws of the Galeegi where river met sea.

Jaja felt sick to his stomach as the bus rolled onto the island proper. Repressed images and voices from long ago crept into his mind and stung at him like open wounds. He held his face down along this stretch of Galeegi's only highway. He dared not look at the high-gates of huge estates, their manicured lawns and miles of privacy walls that hid huge residences from the outside world; those whose inhabitants had established names and lived in established ways. Jaja pinched the bridge of his nose in a failed attempt to squelch the haunting memories.

The driver turned on Old Safari Road toward the marina and bus terminal on the west end. Jaja raised his head and looked out again without fear of the past. But he barely recognized this part of the island. Gone were the thick-leaved palms and primitive oaks that he knew so well. They had been unceremoniously replaced with stuccoed seaside condos, convenience stores, and fancy bars and grills. Galeegi was too busy now. Glitzy, like Atlanta.

What did you expect, Jaja?

6:11 PM

The bus pulled into the terminal and stopped. The passengers disembarked onto a sunbaked asphalt lot. Jaja emerged last, slowly toting his brown suitcase and looking around. He stepped over a low railing that surrounded the lot and walked a short way to the bustling public marina.

Dockhands in bright blue t-shirts and khaki shorts ran up and down the pier to help with the constant boat arrivals and departures. Jaja saw the dock master on an observation deck above the main building. The man, with a walkie-talkie in one hand and a cigarette in the other, appeared to be directing traffic. Pickup trucks with attached trailers lined up ten deep, their drivers waiting to use the two steep boat ramps.

Jaja walked behind the marina's open-air seafood market and climbed down to the sandy shore. He slipped out of his shoes and rolled up his pant legs. For the first time in forty-four years, he walked on the hard bottom and through the lapping waters of the Galeegi Sound. He closed his eyes and for a moment was his old self again—young and free of his enervating nightmares.

7:22 PM

An hour later Jaja rode the last ferry of the day from the main island to Amoyeli. He stood near the stern and breathed in the salty air. Two bottlenose dolphins rolled effortlessly behind the boat. They reminded him of the day he and his grandfather were returning from a fishing trip and counted thirty of them around their skiff.

Jaja walked to the ferry's bow and noted with near certainty drop spots he fished as a boy—old pylons and markers greatly weathered and leaning with the current. Soon he looked across the bow and saw Amoyeli, purple-edged and casting long red shadows across the Atlantic as the sun sank into the horizon. The same native tribe who had called the river "Galeegi" had also named Amoyeli, which simply meant "island."

Jaja's eyes measured the shore. He remembered the shoals and soft rows of island palmettos, and behind them, the thick pines standing tall. The palms danced and the pines swayed in the evening breeze, whistling Amoyeli's song.

At last, I'm home.

8:17 PM

No one greeted Jaja at the dock. The ferry crew just watched as the old man with a faded brown suitcase stepped off the boat and disappeared into the darkness. There were no streetlights on Amoyeli, but Jaja did not need them. He recognized the moon shadows and followed a dirt road until it morphed into a familiar path that crossed the dunes to the lighthouse at the water's edge. He walked up two stairs and the wood-plank deck to the side door of the station's main building. The black-and-white striped tower stood tall, silent, silhouetted by the rising Carolina moon.

The lighthouse was no longer active but remained open during daylight hours as a state historical marker and tourist attraction. During the summers of Jaja's youth, the lighthouse received hundreds of visitors. He would run down to the docks each morning as the herds arrived from Galeegi then strolled over to the tower. They gawked and snapped photos and quite a few climbed all one hundred eighty-nine steps of the lighthouse tower. It was Jaja's job to escort them.

As caretaker of the lighthouse, Jaja's grandfather greeted the tourists as they arrived. He smiled for photos all while carefully eyeing the visitors to determine if any might do the old landmark harm. They paid his grandfather directly for the brief tour—whatever each wanted to give him—which wasn't much. But Jaja remembered him saying that he had been dirt poor all of his life and needed little money anyway.

Now, it was Jaja's turn. He had accepted the position as new lighthouse caretaker; he was to make his grandfather's footsteps his own.

A faint yellow electric lamp hung on the station's outer wall near the door. Jaja slipped an envelope out of his pants pocket and removed a key, which he slid into the lock. However, the door was already open. Its rusty hinges squeaked as he pushed it in. Jaja flipped on the interior light and shuffled through a tiny mudroom and kitchen to the bedroom in the back. He placed his suitcase on bed springs in an iron frame. It was the same single bed on which his grandfather slept long ago. He smiled as he recalled tiptoeing into the room and then banging on an old pot to wake his grandfather for one of their sunrise fishing trips.

Jaja took off his coat and tie and laid them over a dusty chair next to the bed. He walked across the room to the narrow stairway, which led to the top of the tower. He flipped on the stairwell switch. The tower's cracked tabby walls, a composite of limestone and crushed oyster shells, glowed yellow in the artificial light. He began the climb, counting each step as he had many times before, until he reached the lantern room at the top. The heavy lens and ball vent remained in its lantern casing, and Jaja wondered if the aged mechanism still worked. He was tempted to see if he could stretch the light across the island as he had seen his grandfather do on numerous occasions. Instead he just stood in the middle and looked out through the spider webs and salt-stained windows at the great Atlantic Ocean.

Jaja then remembered the family marker. He stood tall and stretched his long right arm up over his head and slid his bony fingers alongside a thick heart pine rafter at the center of the dark room. Like a blind man reading braille, Jaja traced the lettering of his name, which he had carefully carved up there many years ago. He thought of his grandfather and his youthful days in the lighthouse—carefree, joyful times. But his memory soon took him to a dark place, and there was nothing he could do to stop it. Jaja thought about her again. He saw her face in the dusty reflection of one of the windows—her long, blonde hair blowing in the ocean breeze. He looked directly into her pleading eyes. A single tear streaked Jaja's right cheek.

Bury the past, Jaja. Bury the past.

Jaja looked through the reflection to the sea beyond and quieted his mind. He saw trawler lights rolling on the horizon, and he wondered as he often had when he watched the passing boats as a boy: *What are they doing out there in the darkness? Where are they headed?*

Suddenly the yellow light in the stairwell flickered twice and died. Jaja stood frozen in the dark, listening. He heard only the wind whispering inland past the lantern room at the pinnacle of the tower.

Jaja sighed and shrugged his shoulders. The lights often flickered in the tower, even on the gentlest of nights, all those years ago. He had hoped the South Carolina Preservation Society, which now owned the lighthouse, had upgraded the electrical system. The power outage indicated they had not, but Jaja knew exactly where to find the fuse box.

Jaja felt his way along the walls of the lantern room until he found the stairwell and carefully began his descent. He measured each step carefully as he pressed his back to the wall and counted them until he reached the watch area. He searched the wall near the stairwell with his fingertips until he found the switch and flipped it up, then down, and then up again to no avail. So he crept along, his right hand rubbing the circular walls, until he found the service room, where fuel for the light was once stored. Jaja smelled diesel and grease as he pushed open the heavy door.

He knew the fuse box was on the wall behind the door. He palmed the walls until he found the rusty metal cover, carefully removed it, and gently laid it on the floor. He reached inside the box and found four twenty-amp Edison fuses in a bottom corner. His grandfather always left good ones there just in case, and apparently the last caretaker knew of this trick as well.

He methodically worked his fingers down the panel pulling each old head and replacing it with a new one. Now all he had to do was replace the metal covering and pull up the handle switch. He leaned over and grabbed the cover. As he snapped it back into place, something moved behind him.

Jaja held perfectly still in the darkness and listened carefully. Again, the noise came. He felt a presence and slowly turned around.

"Who there?" he asked.

Silence.

"Who that?" he asked again, louder.

A bright light instantly blinded him. Jaja turned his head away and covered his face with his hands. He heard the familiar sound of a gun's hammer locking into place.

"Whatcha want?" He pleaded.

Jaja gagged as the intruder shoved the cold steel barrel into his mouth. He reached forward toward the bright light, trying to fend off his attacker. But he was not quick enough. The gun exploded with a loud crack. Jaja's head slammed back against the wall, next to the open fuse box, and his body crumpled. He sank to the floor, dragging a trail of blood with him.

Jaja's killer shined the light down the blood-streaked wall and onto what was left of the victim's face.

"Welcome home, Jaja."

JUNE 2

The Contender patrol boat cut across the Galeegi Sound through choppy, morning waves. The twenty-three-footer stood out from the departing fishing vessels with its sparkling white hull and a wide, blue Galeegi Police stripe on each side from bow to stern

Chief Fletcher Tate sat in the captain's chair at the middle console. He wore Ray-Bans in the early light to block the spray. His graying black hair flared in the wind as he held the wheel steady. The chief was tall, well-tanned, still strong and fit at the age of sixty-one. He wore the standard Galeegi Police uniform of blue pants, a blue visor, and a white, short-sleeved knitted shirt—a laid-back look—reflective of the islands themselves.

His nephew, Patrolman Tyler Miles, stood to the chief's right holding tightly to the console's rail. Twenty-four-year-old Tyler had joined the Galeegi Police Department less than a week before and was the youngest member on the force. Tyler favored his uncle in many ways. He had broad shoulders, dark hair, a deep tan, and the same even-keeled temperament, but at six feet, two inches, he was a little taller than the chief. Tyler also had a captivating smile that his uncle joked could disarm criminals as well as charm the pretty co-eds who flocked to the Galeegi beaches all summer long.

Sergeant Hank Johnson sat in the back next to the twin Yamaha 300s, his arms and legs crossed; head bent forward; eyes closed; double chin bouncing on his barrel chest. Hank Johnson was a thirty-year veteran of the Galeegi force. He was a narrow-minded man who took a cold-hearted approach to enforcing the law. He was about the same age as the chief, but he looked much older with his stout physique and thinning sandy hair. The bounding of the patrol boat seemed to lull Johnson into an even deeper slumber.

Tyler took a quick look back at the sergeant. "Should we wake him?"

"Naw. Let him sleep. Give us a few more minutes of peace anyway," his uncle said over the roar of the engines.

Tyler smiled, then nodded toward Amoyeli Island. "What time did you say the call came in?"

"Manu notified us around five a.m., but it happened late last night. Least that's what they're thinking anyway." He glanced over at Tyler. "You've been to Amoyeli before, right?"

"When I was a kid. Don't you remember? You took me fishing over there. It started raining, and we took cover in the old lighthouse."

"Right, right. I do remember that now," Tate said. "And from what Manu said on the phone, the lighthouse is where the incident took place."

Tyler raised his eyebrows and drew down the corners of his mouth. "I'll be damned—a suicide in the Amoyeli Lighthouse."

Tyler was excited about his first real assignment. He had been on the job for only six days. Two years ago, he graduated from Wofford College, a private school in Spartanburg, South Carolina, and entertained thoughts of going to law school. Instead, he worked at a firm in Greenville for a few months before deciding to become a police officer. He asked his uncle for a job with the Galeegi Police Department and enrolled in the S.C. Criminal Justice Academy. Upon graduation, he moved to the island and went to work. It had been a tough and busy time for him. And now, here he was on his first meaningful assignment—a dead body included.

As they approached the Amoyeli marina, Tate pulled back on the throttle and idled up to one of the floating docks. Tyler tossed the tie-line to an old dock worker who had sinewy arms, callused hands, and skin as black as midnight. "Sarge! Get up! We're here."

Tate cut the engine and spun around toward the stern. Hank Johnson popped one eye open, then the other, and momentarily scanned all about him. He sucked in a rasping breath and then forced himself to stand.

"Geez," he muttered.

The three Galeegi policemen gathered their gear, climbed onto the pier, and headed to shore. Another black man, Manu Ando, stood waiting. The early morning sun already angled down on Manu and beads of sweat glistened across his wide ebony brow.

Manu was Amoyeli's only constable although he looked nothing like a lawman. He was pear-shaped with skinny legs that bowed out as if he had been riding a horse his whole life. He didn't seem to fit the role of a policeman standing there in an old, red t-shirt with cut-off khaki shorts and a wide-brimmed straw hat cocked back on his head. His bulbous toes stuck out of the end of his cross-weaved sandals. He did not appear to be armed, and if he had a badge, he kept it hidden in his pocket. Only the serious look upon his face indicated that something was amiss.

"Hullo, Mistah Tate. Hullo, my ol' friend," Manu greeted Tate in a low, solemn tone. His accent was a typical island-opaque.

Tate held out his hand. "Hello, Manu," he said warmly. He then turned and pointed behind him. "This is Patrolman Miles, my nephew. And you remember Sarge."

Sergeant Johnson only glanced at Manu, but Tyler locked his eyes on the constable and nodded respectfully.

"Had some trouble out here last night, Manu?" Tate asked.

"For certain, Mr. Tate. Out to the lighthouse. New caretaker. He shot hisself, Mr. Tate. Shot hisself but good. Blood everywhere."

Manu lifted his hat and wiped the heavy sweat from his forehead on his sleeve.

Sergeant Johnson blew out a bored sigh that made his lips flap. "You found the body?"

Manu nodded. "Two night fishermen heard the shot and call me. I go out to the lighthouse." He paused. "I find 'um."

"Touch, anything? Any of your boys go in there and mess 'round with anything?" Johnson pressed.

Manu shook his head. "No, sir. Just me. And I ain't touch nothing. Too dark in there."

"Okay, Manu," Tate said. "We'll go take a look for you, but you know you gotta call the county in on this one. Like I told you on the phone this morning, Galeegi can't get involved in Amoyeli affairs."

"Already done called 'em. They say call Galeegi Police. They say call Mr. Tate. Colleton Sheriff be here this afternoon. Sancho'll drive you up there," Manu said, pointing to a pickup truck and its smiling driver in the sand-and-shell parking lot. "I go get witnesses, be 'long directly."

"All right, we'll meet you up there," Tate said. As the policemen walked toward the truck, Tate looked back and asked, "Manu, you said he was the new caretaker. Know anything else about him? You didn't say a whole lot over the phone."

Manu paused for a long time, forcing Tate to stop. "Oh, yes, Mr. Tate." He then wiped his forehead again. "We know much. Maybe too much."

"What do you mean, Manu?"

"It was Jaja, Mr. Tate. He done come back. It was Jaja up to the lighthouse."

"Jaja?" Tate swung around and stared at Hank Johnson, who appeared equally stunned.

8:34 AM

Despite a few failed attempts at small talk by the friendly driver, the short ride to the lighthouse was a quiet one. Tyler sat in the backseat of the pickup with Sergeant Johnson who merely stared out of the window. The name Jaja had caught his uncle and the sergeant completely off guard, but Tyler dared not ask about it at this point.

Sancho stopped near the entrance to the lighthouse, and the passengers got out. Tate led the way into the living quarters, through the kitchen, and into the tiny bedroom. The chief removed a palm-sized notebook and stubby pencil from his back pocket and jotted down some notes.

Tyler scanned the old building, as well. His memory of the place had failed him a bit as he did not remember the rooms being so small. He was anxious to get to the body. He had seen dead bodies in his situational training at the Academy, but something about death had always fascinated him. His own father had passed away when he was only six years old, which had left him with many unanswered questions.

"Okay, let's go up now," Tate said as he pocketed his notes, pulled his flashlight off his belt, and stepped into the darkened stairwell. Tyler and Johnson did the same.

"How old is this place?" Tyler asked as he shined his light on several large cracks in the structure.

"Pretty old," his uncle replied. "If I remember correctly, the state Maritime Commission built it in 1874—past the old slave days—but they got plenty of work out of the locals in its construction." Tate turned to look behind him. "It stopped as a functioning lighthouse in the 1930s. That right, Sarge?"

"Uh-huh," Johnson grunted as he struggled up the stairs.

They arrived at the watch area one hundred thirty-six steps later. The door to the storage room was open, and Tate led the way in. Tyler stopped in the entranceway and gagged.

"What's that smell?"

No one replied. The beams from their flashlights bounced off the walls until all three merged on the crumpled mass behind the door. Johnson moved toward the body and directed his flashlight up at the open electrical box. He reached over and lifted the side-handle. Light flooded the room.

The remains of Jaja Nayu lay on the floor against the blood-streaked wall. He appeared as a fallen scarecrow with straw-stuffed limbs. His right leg stuck straight out in front of him, and his right foot was oddly bent in on its side. His left leg buckled at the knee and pressed against his slumped chest. His left arm was twisted behind him, and his right arm crossed his lap. There, frozen in Jaja's stiff bony fingers, was a cold, black .45 revolver.

But Tyler dismissed all of that as he bent down and focused on Jaja's face, a chilling image that trumped any questions he had about the esoteric nature of death. Clotted blood from Jaja's nose and mouth covered his chin like a red beard. Lines of blood had streaked from his ears creating dried stains across both shoulders of his white button-down shirt. Jaja's eyes remained open, his pupils rolled back into his forehead, leaving an eerie, blank whiteness. The top and back half of his cranium had exploded and bits of bone and brain splattered the wall above the body.

Nothing in Tyler's police training had prepared him for this. The stench of dried blood, grease, oil, and post-mortem excrement sickened him. His eyes grew wide as the room began to spin. He felt his throat closing.

Tate, who had knelt down in front of the body for a closer inspection, saw his nephew's deteriorating condition. "Ty, you all right?"

Tyler nodded but caught a wave of nausea in his throat. He blew past Johnson and headed toward the stairs.

Hank Johnson rolled his eyes and mumbled, "Geez."

Tate rationalized, "His first time."

Johnson nodded but again grumbled something derogatory under his breath.

Tate stopped writing. "See to him for me, Sarge, will you?"

Johnson hesitated and then forced a half-smile. "Yeah, sure, I'll go take care of the kid. No problem."

As Johnson walked out, he stopped and looked down again at Jaja's twisted body. "Can't believe our luck, eh, Fletch? Jaja Nayu with his brains blown out." He smirked. "Long time comin' that's for sure."

9:45 AM

Beyond the lighthouse, Tyler found a cove between two dunes. He dropped to his hands and knees, wrenching up his guts among the reedy sea oats. A slight morning breeze blew in off the ocean. But Tyler's face remained flushed—more so from embarrassment than anything else.

Tyler shook his head, spit twice, and wiped his mouth with the back of his hand. This was not how he imagined his first investigation going. And as he saw Sergeant Johnson approaching, he knew it was about to get worse. Much worse.

"What's the matter, kid? You ain't feelin' so good?" Johnson's tone was gleefully sadistic. "Don't like a little raw bacon with your breakfast there? Don't care for a little ketchup on your grits and eggs?"

Tyler didn't move. Sweat streaked down his reddened face and neck.

Johnson bent over and grabbed his knees like an old quarterback in a huddle and got in Tyler's ear. "Listen, college boy, I ain't got time to hand-hold little pussies like you who can't stand the sight of a little blood. If you ain't cut out for this kinda work, then maybe you should drag your candy-ass back to where you came from and leave the police work to us real men."

Tyler rose, dusted the sand from his hands, and glared at Hank Johnson. "I can handle this," he said.

"Really? Because I don't think you can. You're only here 'cause your uncle gave you this job. But as staff sergeant, I determine whether or not you stay. You have one more screw up during your field training, and you're gone." He flashed his index finger in front of Tyler's face. "One more. Got it?"

"I said I can handle it."

Johnson reared back. "Ooohhh, tough guy, huh?" He paused. "You still got a little crud on your lip there, tough guy."

Tyler returned the sergeant's stare but held his tongue.

Johnson turned his back and made his way toward Tate who had emerged from the lighthouse. Tate threw on his shades and approached Johnson—out of Tyler's earshot. "How is he?"

Hank Johnson grinned. "Oh, the kid's fine. I told him not to worry about it. Told him it happens to everyone."

Tate nodded. "Manu and the witnesses just rolled up. Go see what you can get out of them."

Johnson's forced grin melted into a genuine frown. "Me?"

"Yeah, you know, find out what they heard last night and at what time."

"But why me?" Johnson cut his eyes over to Manu and the witnesses. "I mean, goddamn, Fletch, I never can understand a word them island coloreds is saying half the time anyway."

Tate slipped his fingers under his sunglasses and

rubbed his eyes. "Just do it, Sarge. Find out what you can. I'll be there in a minute."

"But..."

"Just *do* it," Tate repeated firmly.

Johnson shrugged his meaty shoulders and then headed toward the others. Tate walked over to Tyler and put his hand on his nephew's right shoulder. "Feeling any better?"

"Yeah, sorry about that. I thought I could handle it."

"Don't worry about it. Plenty of first responders lose it like that," Tate said. "My first year on the force, I spent half of my cases hugging toilets or running to the nearest trash can."

"Still," Tyler put his hands on his hips and flashed his thousand-watt smile, "why the hell did it have to be in front of the sarge?"

"But he's such a sweetheart of a guy. I'm sure he won't tell anybody about this or even speak of it ever again."

Tyler laughed. "We both know that's some bullshit there, Chief."

Tate chuckled but became serious again. "Ty, it looks to be a routine suicide in there, but believe me, this is gonna be far from routine. It's complicated as hell. There's a lot of history."

"I figured as much. Who is this Jaja person anyway?"

"That's gonna take some time. Years ago, the man lying dead in there came very close to destroying our little islands."

"How?"

Tate glanced out toward the ocean. "Like I said, it's complicated as hell."

Hammie Swantou cracked open the door to his mobile home, allowing a sliver of the Amoyeli sun to seep inside. The trailer was small—a quaint, one-man living quarters. Several rust colored stripes streaked from the roof, humbling the trailer's appearance and trimming the trippy, sky blue exterior.

A thyroid condition left Hammie's eyes wild and bulging. He shielded them as he opened the door just a little bit further. With a great deal of caution, the thin, black man pushed the door out until it hung half-cocked on its worn hinges. He stepped hesitantly onto his rickety, wooden stoop. He stood there in nothing but red-striped boxers, covering his brow with his right hand. He looked up through squinty eyes and measured the sun. Bright, white hot. *Nearly noon or close to it*, he thought.

Hammie reached back inside the trailer and grabbed a faded red beret from a wall hook by the door. He pulled it down snuggly over his bald head and shuffled down the wooden steps into his sandy front lawn. He stumbled around the yard a bit—a man on a mission. As he moved about, chickens scattered around him and a solitary peacock strutted and squawked out to the heavens.

He lifted several plywood "hurricane" boards leaning against a forgotten tractor. He grabbed a frog gig with two well-sharpened, barbed prongs. He took two steps back towards the trailer when his prey fluttered his way. With a single forceful stroke, Hammie speared the clueless chicken through the breast.

"Sorry 'bout that, Miss Gertie."

Hammie carried the dead chicken to the shady oak tree behind his trailer and rammed the tines into a shaved part of the tree's midsection, already riddled with prong holes. He dug a filet knife out of a surfaced, knotted root and wiped it clean on his boxers. He drew the knife down the breast of the chicken. Blood poured from the incision. Hammie stuck the knife back into the root and dug through the bird with his fingers, pulling out intestines and other organs. His right pointer finger had an inch-long, yellow nail that he used to examine the chicken's entrails. He stopped, looked again toward the sun, and furled his brow.

"Whatcha saying there, Miss Gertie? Huh?" He turned his head to the side. His sleepy eyes widened. "Whatcha mean storm coming to Amoyeli?" He dug around the viscera some more. He held it to his ear as if it were whispering to him.

"No, Hammie, ain't no storm. Darkness. Darkness coming." Hammie searched the innards again. "No, it ain't just darkness. No, sir," he whispered to himself.

His fingernail pierced the heart of the bird, and he took a closer look. "Black heart? Devil damn you black, Miss Gertie."

He dropped the remains of the bird to the ground and looked up at the clear sky as sweat ran from under his beret down every crease on his head. "Not just storm coming...not just darkness...hell be coming to Amoyeli. Have mercy...have mercy...hell be coming."

1:17 PM

Charles Wesly Argeaux sat at his table like an anxious king, drumming his manicured fingertips on the white linen. Condensation formed on the outside of his tall glass of bourbon and ice, creating a spreading ring at its base. His steely, blue eyes darted about the dining room, searching the faces of the diners seated around him. He leaned back in his fully cushioned chair until it creaked. He scooted the chair closer to his table—positioned in the center of the room—the center of his universe.

Time mattered to Argeaux, and he hated waiting for anyone or anything. All around him, young, black men in white jackets paraded heavy trays of iced tea and rose-shaped butter pats to the other guests in the spacious dining hall of the Cotton Seed Golf and Fish Club. The waiters kept their distance, knowing not to bring anything else to Mr. Argeaux until he was ready for it.

He folded his hands under his chin and perched his scowling face on them. Argeaux was the portrait of power and money.

He had thick, white hair for a man of eighty-three years and not a strand was out of place. He wore a Dolce & Gabbana woven, black button down—smartly pressed, tucked uniformly into his matching slacks. His tie, a refined cerulean color, suggested a hint of royalty. He wore black, Berluti loafers, but without socks—a Lowcountry custom for many. Everything about him indicated the epitome of culture, style, and refinement.

He whipped his wrist around and glanced down at his watch, a diamond-encrusted Cartier Pasha. He mumbled under his breath and reached for his drink. Patience was not this man's virtue.

Finally, his target appeared at the entranceway. Robert, the club's maître d', led a tall Latino man with broad shoulders to Argeaux's table. The man gave off a brutish vibe, as much a tiger to be reckoned with as Argeaux. His haircut, his walk, and even his demeanor suggested ex-military. But this was no ordinary hired thug. He was well dressed and well groomed himself, right down to his spit-polished footwear. A million dollar killer. A rich man's assassin. Robert stopped a few feet from the table and bobbed in the man's wake.

The man eased into a chair opposite Argeaux. There was no exchange of greeting or even a hint of recognition. He reached into his sports jacket and produced a white piece of folded paper. He slid it over to Argeaux's outstretched hand.

Charles Argeaux unfolded the paper and quickly scanned the message. He looked up and studied the tiger—claws out—posed to pounce. Argeaux leaned back in his chair and simply dismissed the man with a nod.

Argeaux took another sip and looked over in the direction of Robert, who had backed against the dining room's far wall. Robert straightened and in a flash came to Argeaux's table.

"Sir?"

Argeaux cut his eyes up at the tense, black man and held up his glass. "Robert, a fresh, Hirsch Reserve," he ordered. "And for once...move your sorry ass."

Robert dipped his head in servitude and then quickly disappeared from Argeaux's sight.

4:28 PM

Tyler Miles sat at the little table in the kitchen of the Amoyeli Lighthouse and rolled an empty plastic salt shaker back and forth across the sea-sticky table top. The heat and humidity continued to climb on the island, and the inside of the lighthouse felt like a cramped pizza oven. A large window fan near the kitchen stove pushed the dead air around, and Tyler positioned himself right in front of it.

He was alone. Chief Tate and Sergeant Johnson had gone back to Galeegi leaving "the kid" to wait for representatives from the Colleton County Sheriff's Office and Coroner's Division. It was his first official task: wait for the death experts and ride with the body back to Colleton Medical Center on the mainland. The sarge told him the process would take a few hours. He didn't care for the job, but he was the newbie so it made sense— even to him.

Tyler thought about the dead man in the watch area. His uncle did not have time to go into great detail about Jaja, only briefly explaining that he had been put on trial for the murder of the only daughter of a Mr. Charles Argeaux, a man of great wealth and power. He told Tyler that the months following the racially charged scandal were hard on Galeegi in every conceivable way.

According to his uncle, the fact that the guilty man had eventually gotten off scot-free nearly drove a stake through Galeegi's heart.

Tyler looked back at the stairwell entrance. It seemed strange to him that after all this time, Jaja would return home and suddenly feel enough remorse to commit suicide now. Tyler rationalized that it was just something the man tried to live with but couldn't. Perhaps he had planned this suicide for years. His instructors at the Academy had taught him that people will do odd things at odd times.

Tyler got up from the table, stretched his long arms toward the ceiling and yawned. *This waiting shit is for the birds.* He looked at his watch. *Good thing it's not a medical emergency.*

He leaned closer to the window fan and held his sticky shirt away from his sweat-soaked chest. The fan slowed for a second as the lights flickered. Suddenly everything went dead, and Tyler groaned. He went to the kitchen switch and flipped it several times but nothing happened. He walked outside to test the conditions. The morning breeze had long since stopped, and Amoyeli now cooked in the afternoon sun.

Tyler returned to the kitchen and looked at the still blades of the fan. He noted surface conduits for the lighthouse's wiring system along the ceiling and saw that all the lines led back toward the tower. *The wiring system must have been added after the lighthouse's initial construction,* he reasoned.

He went through the slider door and followed the lines upward until they branched off to the watch area. He realized that to get the fan started he would have to go back into the darkened service room with the dead body. Tate had admonished him not to go back in there, not to contaminate the crime scene. But he would be careful. He would not disturb anything.

Tyler slipped on his rubber gloves, pulled his Maglite from his belt, and inched through the watch area until he got to the service room. The stench hung heavy in the hot air and hit his still sensitive nostrils. He forced himself to breathe through his mouth and did not gag this time.

Tyler realized the wires emptied into a larger conduit tube behind the door, which then collected into the gray-paneled electrical box. As he moved forward, his foot bumped into the body, and he almost tripped.

Tyler hesitated and cursed his clumsiness under his breath. While holding still in the darkness, he suddenly felt compelled to take another look at the man below. He brought the light stream slowly down the wall until it rested on the scarecrow's harrowing face—blood-filled open mouth, white eyes from hell looking blankly back at him. Tyler momentarily contended with his dark, childhood fears. *He's dead. It's just a dead body*, he thought.

Resolved, Tyler leaned over Jaja, and as Sergeant Johnson had done earlier, he pulled on the box's handle. Nothing happened. He moved the handle up and down in rapid succession. Again, it remained dark. Tyler blew out a quick, antsy breath. He removed the metal cover and focused on the inside of the fuse box. He was no electrician, but he figured the odd-looking fuses might need to be replaced. He felt around the bottom of the box until he found the extra screw-in fuses. He held the light on each one to determine whether or not they were in good condition. Working quickly, he made the necessary changes. Afterwards, he replaced the cover, pulled the handle, and the lights sprang back to life.

Tyler took a step back from the wall and looked at Jaja. He tried to picture the remorseful man sticking the barrel of his weapon in his mouth, perhaps uttering a last-second, need-for-forgiveness prayer and then pulling the trigger. Tyler's whole body shuddered.

As he turned to leave, he stopped. Something about all of this didn't make sense. He looked at Jaja and then the electrical box and then back to Jaja.

So why the hell did you do that?

11:48 PM

Thunder pounded in his ears and brought more pain to his aching temples. He remained bent over, holding his head. He ran his fingers through his hair and felt the storm heat rising from his scalp. Sweat fell like rain from his forehead and poured down his strong back. The images flashed in his mind. *Power and dominance. Heat and pain.* It was the time of the ram, of lightning, of judgment.

His blood flow pushed the elixir deep into his system; it raced to all of his extremities. It was like a thousand swirling swords nipping and slicing into every nerve ending, every fragment of his being. It cut through his very soul.

Within minutes, it was over. The pain disappeared. He was there. The transfiguration was complete. He was in their world now, ready to administer his brand of justice.

It is my time.

Xevioso rose from his crouched position on the wooden floorboards and stood with his feet together. He raised his arms heavenward and flexed all the core muscles of his naked body. He felt calm now yet very powerful.

He walked god-like across the floor, taking slow, steady strides.

He emerged from the darkness into the golden light of his temple, the *Hounfour*. He noticed the *poteau-mitan*, the pole from where he could communicate with his disciples. It was centered in the room. Beyond the pole, twelve black cross candles awaited.

Twelve. They had been lit and appropriately stationed

in the right order. He nodded at the reverent attention to detail.

Xevioso moved to the altar, which was dotted with wooden idols, bits of skull and bone, dark beads and feathers. He opened a container beyond the candles and assuredly removed its contents. He untied two leather straps and discarded the black cloth in which it was wrapped, allowing the covering to fall freely to the floor. He took both hands and held the *Oshe* up to the candlelight. It was sharpened to within a hair of perfection. Its double heads glistened within the golden light. It was severe, cruel—an instrument of death.

Xevioso ran his finger over one of its curved blades, slicing his flesh. Blood swelled on the tip of his finger, ran down his outstretched palm and dripped onto the floor. He marveled at his hand washed in blood, the blood of a god. He breathed deeply and grabbed the axe again with both hands. He tightened his grip and raised the blade to within an inch of his face.

He closed his eyes.

He spun around and lashed out with the axe into the darkness behind him. Swift. He spun again and brought the head of the axe around with him slicing into the thin air, into nothingness. Powerful. He pivoted yet again, and with the precision of an assassin, swung eight maddening blows in quick succession. *Merciless.* He twirled the axe in his hand. The handle felt smooth, bone-like. With a viperous twist, he thrust the blade out once again into the imaginary form of his enemy. *Justice.*

JUNE 3

Fletcher Tate rolled his cruiser into his reserved parking space at the Galeegi Police Station. He hopped out with a copy of the Sunday *Post and Courier* folded under his arm and headed into the building. The station was a simple sand-colored stucco building with two palmetto trees placed symmetrically on the corners.

It was tropical in its appearance, natural, beach-like. Galeegi's city hall, fire station, and post office all followed with the same blend-into-the-background design. Even the Piggly Wiggly on Old Safari Road mirrored a spacious, island-style home, with only the parking lot and hand-detailed painted store sign to indicate its grocer status.

Tate brushed through the doors and headed across Control Central. Despite its grandiose-sounding name, the station's main hub was nothing more than a room of four cluttered desks, a bank of low-tech computers, and a long table with Styrofoam cups, discarded sugar packs, a stained coffee maker, and a filthy microwave. An American flag, the South Carolina seal, a littered bulletin board, and a stuffed marlin hung on dingy beige walls. Towering metal cabinets peaked out from an adjacent file room in the back. The Galeegi Police Department was a small agency, but it carried a lot of responsibility—most of that weight falling on Tate's shoulders. Besides Sergeant Johnson and several class three officers, who served only on beach patrol, Tate ran the show with just two other official policemen, one of whom was Tyler.

Robbie Cone, the other patrolman, sat at a desk, typing up the night report. A pudgy, two-finger typist with squinty eyes, Robbie made little progress. He seemed oblivious to Tate's entrance.

"Robbie, you seen Sarge this morning?" Tate asked.

Robbie swiveled in his chair. "Oh, good morning, Chief. No, no, I ain't seen 'im yet. But Tyler's in your office. Came in a little while ago."

Tate nodded and headed toward the back.

"Hell of a thing about that guy in the lighthouse, huh?" Robbie called out.

"Yeah, hell of a thing," the chief echoed dryly.

Robbie shrugged and turned back to his report. Tate shut the door behind him. Tyler sat on small couch against the far wall of Tate's office. He looked up as Tate entered.

"Hey."

"Morning, Ty." Tate moved behind his desk and sat in his squeaky chair. "Sorry to get you in here on your first day off, but, as you can imagine, we need to talk."

Tyler got up and walked to the front of the desk. "Did you speak with anyone in the sheriff's office?"

Tate spread the paper out on his desktop. "Yeah. And they thanked you for your observation. They're considering it. In fact, they have their crime lab unit out there right now. They're gonna do a thorough check—gun residue on the hands, shot angle, the whole nine yards."

"It just didn't add up. When we first went in the lighthouse, Sarge turned on the lights by simply raising the handle on the electrical box. But when the lights went out on me, I had to replace the fuses first." He stared at his uncle, awaiting a reply.

"So, Jaja either threw the switch himself to kill the lights before firing the weapon, or the fuses had already been replaced by the time we got there," Tate said.

Tyler nodded. "I can't imagine him going to the trouble of throwing the main power switch to shoot himself in the dark when he could have simply done that with a flip of the regular switch, can you?"

"Seems a bit excessive."

"Exactly. And if the Amoyeli constable is to be taken at his word, he was the only one who went in the lighthouse after the shot was fired. And he said he touched nothing. I'll bet you anything that Jaja was in that service room changing those fuses. So my question is... why? If you are getting ready to kill yourself, and the lights go out, are you going to stop to change the fuses? And then not even bother to turn it back on?" Tyler placed his fingertips on Tate's desk and leaned in. "That's weird as hell, isn't it? I mean, even for some guy unstable enough to commit suicide."

Tate nodded but held his tongue. He looked briefly down at his paper.

He then cut his eyes quickly toward his nephew, and leaned back in his chair.

"Wait, you did notice it, didn't you?" Tyler asked. "What was I thinking? Of course. You realized that too. You had to."

Tate simply nodded.

"So, why didn't you?" Tyler stopped. He plopped down in a chair in front of Tate's desk and rubbed his unshaven chin. "Because it's complicated as hell?"

Tate leaned forward, rested his elbows on the edge

of the desk, and clasped his hands. "There's a danger to speculating; to opening old wounds here, Tyler."

"Yeah, sure, but we have to pursue the truth right? No matter how hard this might be for us—for Galeegi—we have an obligation to find out if the man was murdered, right?"

Tate smiled at Tyler's innocence. "Of course, but in this case, we have to be cautious."

"Why?"

"So you won't lose your freaking job for one," a voice rang out from behind Tyler. Sergeant Johnson, his egg-shaped form filling the doorway, had several file folders cradled in his meaty arms.

Chief Tate leaned back in his chair. "Did you get all of it?"

Hank Johnson continued into the office. "Yeah, I think this is all of it. I mean, Jesus, look at all this."

"What is that?" Tyler asked.

Johnson dumped the files in his lap. "It's your Sunday reading, kid. Hope you weren't planning on hanging out at the beach today."

"The case files from the Katherine Argeaux murder," the chief said. "I thought it best if you got up to speed on everything that happened here that summer. Then maybe you'll see why we need to tread lightly."

Tyler shifted in his chair, trying to keep the files from spilling out of his lap. "You said the case was racially charged. That it divided the coast into black and white."

"That's right," Tate said.

"But this is 2012. The civil rights, the Sixties, the divisiveness are things of the past."

Tate shook his head dismissively as Johnson chuckled and added, "You're just fooling yourself, kid. It ain't never that simple when you're talking race." He leaned his weight against Tyler's chair. "Now, don't get me wrong. We have come a long way, so to speak. The coloreds and us may go to the same schools, eat in the same restaurants. There may even be one of 'em sitting up there in the White House pretending to be president, but some things don't change. Galeegi is still Galeegi, and Amoyeli is still Amoyeli. And the water separating the one from the other is deep and wide."

Tyler shook his head. "I still don't get it. A man may have been killed, and we're cops for crying out loud. It's our job to find out."

"Let me ask you something, Ty," Tate said. "Let's say for the sake of argument that Jaja was murdered, and you were heading up the investigation. Who would head your list of suspects?"

Tyler frowned. "I don't know. I guess whoever had something to gain from his death, or just wanted him dead maybe."

Tate sat back and waited.

"The trial. I guess it all comes back to the trial," his nephew continued. "Those who hated to see Jaja get away with the murder of the Argeaux girl—the Argeaux family mainly."

"And there's your problem," Johnson said. "You getting it now? They control everything and everyone on this island, everyone—including the people who sign our checks." Johnson leaned over the chair and forced Tyler to look up at him. "It was Charles Argeaux's kid for Christ's sake, his little girl. It nearly destroyed him. And now you want to shake up that old hornets' nest— piss that man off all over again? Better to leave this as a suicide."

Tyler dropped his gaze to the files. "I still don't see why. I know they're a powerful family, rich and all that, but they're not untouchable. If they had something to do with Jaja's death, they need to be held accountable. And the sooner we…"

"Geez, kid, you got a lot to learn about how the real world works," Johnson interrupted.

The sarge then turned to Chief Tate. "I'm outta here. Got morning patrol."

The door to the office closed behind the sergeant. Tyler looked back up at his uncle "Are you really gonna let this whole thing slide? I just can't believe you of all…"

Tate held up his hand, forcing Tyler to stop. He reached inside his belt and pulled out his observation notebook. He flipped it open, found the page and pushed it across the desk so that Tyler could read it. There were shorthand notations about the time of day of their investigation, Amoyeli, Constable Manu Ando, and the lighthouse. Under the description of the crime scene he had written: "Electrical box—fuses replaced?" And on the bottom of the page he had written and circled "Argeaux."

Tyler smiled. Tate leaned forward again and whispered, "When you're going after big fish, you keep the line as still as possible."

9:18 AM

Needing space to spread out and analyze the files, Tyler drove over to the Lucky Shark, a popular bar and grill near the marina. The Shark served coffee to Galeegi's fishermen in the morning and cheap beer and Jell-O shooters to a younger crowd at night. It was nothing fancy, a converted warehouse with boarded windows. A cartoon shark over the front door welcomed patrons.

Tyler sat in his booth and flipped through the files. He occasionally glanced around the smoky room. He noted an unplugged jukebox adjacent to five Joker-Poker machines with posted disclaimers: For Amusement Only. Hundreds of bleached shark jaws decorated the walls amid lighted Budweiser, Michelob, and Coors signs. Yellow and green neon colored placards posted throughout the bar announced the upcoming play-dates for the rock band Blue Dogs and solo artist Bryson Jennings. Tyler looked to the back at an open door that led to a party deck overlooking the west side of the marina where most of these summer performances were held.

Tyler noted the Lucky Shark's barkeep and owner, Yancey Holland, behind the wide oaken bar. A retired insurance salesman from Chicago, Holland fell in love with the warm weather, excellent fishing, and the easy-living coastal lifestyle during one of his earlier tours through the South. Ten years ago, he said goodbye to the Windy City and her cold lake winters, divorced his wife, sold all his properties, moved to Galeegi, and bought the Lucky Shark.

Affectionately known now as Poppa because of his graying, Hemingway-like beard, he was a genial man most of the time calling everyone "Babe," "Sweetie," or "Buddy Boy." But he showed a fierce temper if anyone messed with his business or his customers. It was always done Poppa's way inside the Lucky Shark.

Holland had a pudgy belly, which he covered with one of his many darkly colored barber smocks. He was fond of Tareyton Cigarettes and Inver House Scotch—

never far out of his reach. Tyler smelled both on his breath as he brought over a pot of coffee.

"Need some more joe, Babe?"

Tyler threw his hand over his cup. "No, I'm good for now. Thanks, Poppa."

The old man held the pot by his side and looked at the files scattered over the tabletop. "What the hell you reading there, anyway? What's all this?"

"Just work." Tyler laughed. "It looks like I got it cut out for me, huh, Poppa?"

Poppa hacked a guttural, smoker's laugh. "It sure does, Babe, especially this being your first week, and on a goddamn Sunday too? You'd be better off telling them to stick those files where the sun don't shine."

Tyler smiled then diverted his eyes, cutting the conversation short. Reading file after file wasn't the ideal way to spend his Sunday morning, he thought, but the old case fascinated him. And its ties to Jaja's death were too strong to ignore.

Katherine Argeaux, the sixteen-year-old, and by all accounts, beautiful daughter of the scion of Galeegi's oldest and most prominent family, was found bludgeoned and floating in the marsh two miles from the sprawling Argeaux estate. She was face down in the black water, naked—her hands tied behind her back with baling cord.

The family reported that on the day she died, one of the gardeners saw her heading out beyond the giant oaks of the backyard and through the back gates toward the estate's elaborate docking pier. A quarter mile of marshland separated the lush lawn of the Argeaux mansion and the Galeegi River. It was well known that on late afternoons Katherine often went down to the dock area to enjoy the sunset on the meandering river.

When nightfall came and she had not returned to the main house, family, servants, and neighbors made a quiet search of the extended area. By late that evening, the police had been called to investigate. And because of the girl's important social status, all of Galeegi soon was involved. Early the next morning, the crew of a fishing vessel found her body, and the missing persons operation quickly turned into an intense search for her killer.

A sweep of the grounds turned up nothing until they came to the plantation's old thrashing shed, which the Argeaux family had in modern times used for storing their lawn service equipment. Matthew Haynes, chief supervisor of maintenance, escorted several police officers inside. The police thoroughly searched the whole shed until, at last, they looked in the millet storage bin and found the young man, Jaja, sobbing and shaking, hiding under bags of seed grain.

Katherine Argeaux's murder brought a horde of media attention to the little island, but that was only the beginning. Up and down the Carolina coast, the case became a source of great contention during that long, hot summer.

During the troublesome sixties, racial tensions increased in the South, and the Argeaux murder became a standoff for all types of racially charged issues. South Carolina's most notorious lawyer, Leonard O'Dell, took up the defense for Jaja, enflaming the volatile situation even more. O'Dell was a Yankee transplant, a social-radical, a political liberal, and to the horrors of most South Carolinians at that time, a member of the ACLU.

Those on Galeegi believed O'Dell used the case as his own vendetta against all things Southern, white, and conservative. Accusations from both sides started the second after the funeral and continued in the time leading up to the court case. The attacks from all parties worked public opinion into a boiling frenzy. It was a circus trial—a daily source of gossip and rumor about the Argeaux family, the wild-eyed Katherine, and the mysterious island boy, Jaja.

Despite all the build-up, the case never made it to a jury. O'Dell convinced the judge that the prosecution had failed to prove any motive or provide any key evidence against his client—that everything was circumstantial and hearsay. O'Dell called it a "one and done." The fact that the police found Jaja hiding on the property didn't mean there was just cause for murder. To the surprise of almost everyone, Judge Edwin Burns, a reputedly staunch adjudicator, agreed and set Jaja free.

But the Galeegi folk knew better: that black boy killed that girl. He raped her, beat her in the head, and dumped her body in the river. They would not let Jaja or anyone else say anything different. At some point, amid the fallout of the trial, Jaja slipped out of town and was never heard from again. Most folks eventually forgot about him.

Until now.

3:22 PM

Tyler was drained as he made the short drive back to the station. His head ached, and his eyes still hurt from reading the yellowed, dog-eared files. He somewhat understood the need for a cautionary approach to all this. However, he still believed that if Jaja had been murdered, then no matter who killed him, his killer needed to be brought to justice. And if some of the island's bigoted, contrary faction happened to implode because of it, then so be it.

He was also not as convinced of Jaja's guilt in the murder as everyone else at the police station seemed to be. He agreed with the defense lawyer's assessment that while Jaja may have been there and may have even witnessed Katherine Argeaux's murder, there was no evidence that he committed the deed.

Tyler walked into Control Central with the files and headed to Johnson's desk. The sergeant glanced up at him before jamming his thumb in the direction of the records room.

Within minutes, Tyler was stuffing files back into the old pull-drawer cabinets. He fanned through a stack and then stopped when he came to the personal file on Katherine Argeaux. He opened it up and scanned through the few documents on the sixteen-year-old. He took another look at her attached photograph—a black and white proof photo from her high school yearbook.

She was smiling, radiant—her hair pulled back with some kind of wide headband. She posed slightly turned in profile. Her eyes were beautiful, yet there was something more. They were wise looking—the eyes of someone who had seen much in her young life, and maybe not all of it so innocent. Tyler became lost in her image—the smooth curve lines of her cheek, the slight flare of her nostrils, the long lashes, striking lips, perfect hair....

"Beautiful, wasn't she?"

Tyler looked up. His uncle stood in the doorway. "Yeah, she was. She could've been a model."

Tate nodded and then quickly switched gears. "The crime unit called. They're shipping Jaja's body to the Medical University in Charleston for a thorough autopsy. The initial findings were inconclusive. But the revolver appears clean. No other prints and no serial number."

"A man about to kill himself wouldn't give a damn about a clean piece," Tyler said with increasing assurance.

"Agreed. And that's not all. They found blue fibers from his suit pants all along the wall of the stairwell to the lantern room."

Tyler's eyes lit up. "Maybe he was up at the top when the lights went out, then backed his way down the darkened stairwell wall to get to the service room—to replace the fuses."

"Well, yes, that's possible, I suppose."

"Maybe the lights didn't go out by themselves that time. Maybe the killer knew that Jaja was aware of the lighthouse's electrical problems—that the electricity went out from time to time. Just like it did on me."

He paused as it became clear to him. "It would have been a great way for Jaja to be tricked into the room. Do you think it's enough evidence to start a murder investigation?"

Tate put up a cautionary hand. "Whoa, now, hold on. No one is saying that, but the sheriff said the investigation would be left on-going."

Tyler shut the filing cabinet drawer. "Well, at least that's something. What do we do now?"

"Officially, we can't do anything. It's Amoyeli's problem. Not in our jurisdiction."

"And what about unofficially?"

Tate laughed. "Easy, Inspector Miles. All things in good time."

6:47 PM

Tyler left the station and returned to his small apartment off Shore Breeze Street near the marina. It was part of a no-frills complex on the west side of the island, far away from the grand estates and high-end, private beaches. Most of these stacked tenements housed young people who worked the docks and local restaurants during the summer as indicated by the number of piled pizza boxes in the dumpster outside the building. It was a small step up from the college dorm experience for Tyler, who was just glad to be on his own and that he could afford the rent.

As soon as he got home he went for a run on the beach. He came back, showered, changed, and grabbed something to eat. He then sat at his kitchen counter, turned on his laptop, and opened an ice-cold beer.

The Argeaux case was still picking at his brain, so he Googled as many of the principal players of the case as he could remember. Besides a rather large database for Charles Argeaux and his enterprises, the most hits came back for the lawyer, O'Dell. But there was little online about the case itself. Tyler began to feel that the Katherine Argeaux murder had certain discussion limitations. It was just like with his uncle, Sergeant Johnson, and even the Amoyeli constable, there seemed to be an air of unspeakability about it.

His cell phone buzzed, and Tyler answered quickly. It was his co-worker, and at this point and time, only friend on the island, Robbie Cone.

"Hey, Robbie. What's up?"

"Just hanging. How are things?"

"Quiet. Surfing the net. Doing nothing really," Tyler said as he shut down his laptop.

"Want to come over here? The Braves are playing the Phillies tonight, and I've got plenty of beer."

Tyler laughed. "No. I'm good. I think I'll keep it a quiet evening. I've got to work patrol with Sarge in the morning."

"Ouch. Feel for you there, buddy."

"Yeah. I'm going to need all the energy I can get to-morrow. To be honest, I really can't stand that son of a bitch."

"Nobody can. I'm just glad you're here now, so he'll stop hassling me."

"Oh, you're very welcome," Tyler joked. "Makes me wonder why my uncle has kept him around all this time."

"He's like stink on a shrimp boat. Once it gets in there, you can never get it out."

Tyler laughed and then paused, looking at the blank computer screen. "Rob, what do you know of the Katherine Argeaux murder?"

"Not much. An old case obviously. It's out there, but not something I really think about."

Tyler scratched his cheek. "You think Jaja killed her?"

"Of course."

"How can you be so sure?"

"I'm not, Tyler, but I'm a cop. As far as I'm concerned, they're all guilty. Every scumbag we throw behind bars.

And I'm sure it was the same way the cops felt when they arrested Jaja Nayu a long time ago."

"Shouldn't we worry about justice being done?"

Tyler heard Cone laugh on the other end of the line.

"Are you kidding me, Tyler? Why do you think God made that vile creature called a lawyer in the first place?"

11:22 PM

The quarter moon played hide and seek with the tall palmettos on Amoyeli Island. The light filtered in and out, but it was enough to see—enough to make passage through the island's dense forest. Fifteen islanders, all elderly men and women, walked the trail up from Crossing Cut, the main road through the interior of Amoyeli, to the top of Wachasee Hill.

Only the Amoyeli Lighthouse was a higher point on the island. From the top of Wachasee Hill, one could look down across the slope and see distant East Cove and the tip of the lighthouse. The first church on the island had been built on Wachasee Hill during the post-slavery era called Reconstruction. It was destroyed in a fire years before, but a number of the markers of the accompanying graveyard remained. Many of the islanders, especially those who had now gathered, still revered the hill. They stood near the solemn headstones speaking to one another in hushed tones.

"It is bad news, yes?" asked one of the women.

Hammie Swantou stepped forward. "It was Jaja. He returned to take his grandfather's place."

"Lord Almighty, no," another woman said. "If Jaja's dead, what will happen to us?"

"You know what will happen," the first woman said.

"Perhaps we should gather our families and leave," said yet another.

Hammie shook his head. "Ain't gonna matter. You will be found. Can't run from this. Can't run away."

"Then what we do?" someone else asked.

Hammie shrugged. "Ain't nothing we can do. Best allow what's to happen to happen. Best not stand in its way. Keep quiet, keep still, and pray." His eyes widened as he spoke and the others moved closer. "Hell coming," Hammie said.

Xevioso remained in his hidden position, having heard everything the elders had said. After they left, the god stood and ran the blade of the Oshe down the back of one of the old tombstones, drawing sparks everywhere the sharpened edge of the blade made contact.

Tiny sparks tonight. An inferno tomorrow.

JUNE 4

6:59 AM

Tyler parked his Ford Ranger in the station's lot and headed inside. He signed in and checked the duty board. He grabbed a cup of black coffee and took slow sips, hesitating for as long as possible.

God, I do not want to do this.

He eyed the wall clock, summoned all of his will-power, and then went back out of the station. He saw the patrol car. The engine was running, and Sergeant Johnson was at the wheel. He opened the passenger door of the black Ford Crown Victoria and slid in.

"What are you doing?" Johnson asked with mock surprise.

"I'm with you today. I'm scheduled to go on patrol with you."

Hank Johnson scowled. "Yeah. But not until 7:30. It's 7:25 right now."

Tyler searched the man's eyes to see if there was even a hint of jocularity behind his words. He saw none. "So, what am I to do for the next five minutes?" he asked.

"I don't know, and I don't care. But our patrol doesn't start until 7:30."

The words weighed heavily between them. Tyler just shook his head in disbelief and opened the door again. He got back out, shut the door, and stood next to the idling patrol car. He crossed his arms over his chest and waited.

Minutes later, Tyler opened the car door again, slid

in, and looked over at Sergeant Johnson. "Ready now?" he asked in his most pleasant voice.

Johnson leaned up and threw the car into drive. "Yeah, I'm ready, but you're fifteen seconds late." He flashed him his watch and tapped the face. "I'm gonna have to put you on report for that."

Tyler leaned back into his seat as the car pulled out onto the street and thought to himself, *This is going to be the longest day of my life.*

8:47 AM

Manu Ando drove his truck up and down Crossing Cut. He periodically stopped as his fellow islanders walked by and asked them about their morning. He nonchalantly threw in a line to see if they had come across anything unusual. A suicide on Amoyeli had been upsetting enough for the constable, but the fact that it involved Jaja Nayu forced Manu to be more vigilant.

The islanders, however, reported nothing out of the ordinary. They went about their routine of living off the land and sea. Many of the islanders busily prepared for the tourist trade that the morning ferry would bring, setting up to sell their wares of seashell jewelry or simple sweetgrass baskets.

Amoyeli had retained its pristine social environment over the years. Unlike neighboring Daufuskie, it was too small for real estate development. There were no condos or golf courses forced upon its shores. Besides the lighthouse, an elementary school, and an island-centered emergency shelter, outside agencies had constructed very little on Amoyeli. It was a protected island, a lost way of living that remained simple, un-rushed, and peaceful. Manu hoped to keep it that way.

He parked near the lighthouse access trail and await-ed the first group of tourists from Galeegi. The morning ferry was due at any minute. He rolled down the truck's window and allowed the ocean breeze to seek out the perspiration on his skin. Two elderly women carrying lawn chairs, boxes, and homemade baskets, slowly set up their wares near the trailhead. Manu climbed out of his truck and walked over to them.

"Good morning to you, sisters," Manu greeted them.

The women nodded but did not offer any words. Manu placed his large hands on his large hips. "Gettin' ready for the day, I see," he tried once more. But again there was little response. He picked up one of the sweet grass baskets, feigning interest.

"You know we had to close the lighthouse. The white people coming can still take photos, but they cannot go inside for a spell just yet."

One of the women lifted her hand in a pacifying ges-ture. "As long as they still come this way."

"Yes, well, good luck to you then." Manu turned away.

The other woman, who had a bluer, darker tone of skin and flat, gray hair, called out to him. "We know what happened here, Manu. Hammie say what will happen, will happen."

"Tattiana!" the other woman admonished.

"He say, hell coming to Amoyeli," Tattiana added.

Manu paused, taking in the woman's words. "Might be, Sister Tattiana. Might be." He returned to his truck and as he opened the door, he turned and said, "Let us hope this time, Hammie Swantou is mistaken."

1:45 PM

Tyler brought the oyster po' boy baskets out to the patrol car. Sergeant Johnson had held out as long as he could and finally decided to take a lunch break. As Tyler predicted, the morning had moved painfully slow with Johnson taking him through the routine procedures of patrol. They had combed the streets, checked the empty rental houses along their route, and made inspections of the beach access areas for illegal parking. It was basic island patrol course of action, processes and methods of which Tyler was already well aware. But Johnson took great delight in explaining every action in excruciating detail to the new recruit. Tyler was relieved when they pulled into the Lucky Shark, giving him a chance to stretch his legs and rest his ears.

Tyler reentered the car and handed the food to Johnson who tore open the wrapper and immediately took several quick bites. He then looked over at Tyler. "Where's the tea?" he asked through a thick mouthful of the po' boy.

Tyler winced. "Forgot. Sorry, I'll go get it."

"Damn right you will," Johnson said through a menacing grin with remnants of the sandwich squishing between his teeth.

Tyler went back in and paid for the iced tea. As he hustled back, he noticed Johnson had gotten out of the cruiser and now stood face to face with a stranger. Tyler held back and watched their interaction. The other man was physically intimidating—tall, muscular with a dark complexion. He had a crew cut, military style, and continuously pressed his finger into Johnson's chest, forcing the sergeant to lean back against the patrol car.

Tyler hesitated for a moment more and then decided to intercede. The man noticed Tyler's approach and quickly turned away. He hopped in a silver Lexus LFA and drove off, the tires squealing on the pavement. Johnson let out a held breath—obviously upset.

"Everything okay?" Tyler asked.

Hank Johnson straightened up, glared at the rookie cop, narrowed his eyes, and drew down the corners of his mouth. "Yeah, everything is okay. Who are you? My fucking mother? The guy was just asking directions."

Every muscle in Tyler's body tightened, but he managed to control his temper. "Here you go," he said and slid the cup of tea across the hot roof of the Crown Victoria to Johnson's waiting hand. "Don't choke on it," he added under his breath.

6:49 PM

As the day drew into the early evening hours and the tide retreated out to sea, most of the local fishermen and recreational boaters returned to the marina. It was one of the busiest times of the day for Dock Master John Cane and his crew. Fish and shrimp needed to be unloaded, hulls cleaned, and a myriad of other docking related operations performed. Most days they went off without a hitch.

But this day was not like most.

"Got a vessel breaking the lanes, John," dockhand Amos Carlton's voice filtered through the tower's com system—his words swift and a bit garbled.

Cane sat up in his chair and doused his fortieth cigarette of the long day. He grabbed his walkie-talkie. "Say again, Amos."

59

"An eastbound vessel cutting the lanes. Heading directly at the marina. Looks like it might be the *Witch Doktor*."

Cane picked up his binoculars and scanned the Galeegi Sound. "Damn. That is the *Witch Doktor*." He refocused the binoculars and took a closer look at the fishing vessel. "And look at Anatu's speed. What's that crazy son of a bitch doing?" He swiveled his chair to the right and snapped his fingers at the tower's radio operator. "Raise the *Doktor* for me and hurry."

"Jesus!" Carlton's voice blasted again from the walkie-talkie.

Cane turned back toward the Sound just in time to see the *Doktor* slam the bow of a sixteen-foot Boston Whaler, rocking the small boat and throwing its captain into the water. The *Doktor* did not slow at all and kept its deadly trajectory toward the marina.

Cane hopped up and headed for the stairs. "Call 9-1-1 now!" he shouted. Cane leaped five steps at a time and hit the bottom of the stairwell hard. He got up and ran towards the dock area—his chest tightening with each stride.

Everyone on the pier immediately sensed the danger, and they rushed to clear the dock area. The bulky *Witch Doktor* continued cutting a heavy path through the water—incapable of being stopped. It plowed a warning buoy and was now only a hundred yards from the tip of the dock.

Cane kept his struggling pace toward the pier. "Get clear!! Get the hell outta there!!" As the last of the blue shirts made running long jumps onto the bank, Cane stopped just a few yards in front of them and watched in horror as the boat rammed his pier at 18 knots. There was an ear-piercing screech followed by the sickening sound of popping metal and splitting timber.

The secured boats at the tip of the pier, mostly forty-foot pleasure cruisers, broke their ties, rocked up against the *Witch Doktor*, and bounced off to the side. They looked like struck bowling pins spinning up and out of the frame.

The sea sent a collapsing wave on shore as the *Witch Doktor* came to an abrupt stop. Its bow stuck ten feet into the air atop the smashed pier.

In a flash it was over, and almost immediately it became strangely quiet. Only the fizzle of broken mains streaming pressurized water into the air could be heard. Cane held his position; his swollen heart pounded in his chest.

Cane's eyes jumped about, trying to take it all in. His sense of relief rapidly turned to anger as he scanned the destruction. Amos Carlton appeared beside him, his chest still heaving with excitement. Blood from a long gash was running down his leg.

"My God, John, did you see that? They wouldn't stop. They just wouldn't stop." He craned his neck to look for movement on the wrecked craft. "What in the world got into the *Doktor*?"

"I don't know, but if everybody on that rig ain't stone-cold dead, they're gonna wish they were when I'm finished with them."

7:03 PM

Tate made the typical ten-minute drive from the station in less than five. He jumped out of his cruiser and ran down what was left of the pier to the wreckage. The boat's impact severed several of the wooden trusses of the dock, and ankle-deep water now submerged the entire end portion.

With the help of several dockhands, Cane climbed down the *Witch Doktor* and back onto the wrecked pier. Tate moved quickly towards him.

"John, is everyone okay? An ambulance is on its way," Tate hollered.

Cane turned to Tate. He was whey-faced. His hands shook, and he shot an unsteady look at the chief. "No need," he said—his voice barely audible.

Tate looked hard at Cane. "What do you mean?"

"Ain't no need," he repeated. Cane stumbled a bit as if he were about to faint. Two of his dockhands grabbed him by the arms.

They looked at Chief Tate.

"Get him to the shore. Get the paramedics to check him out once they get here." Both men followed Tate's order and ushered Cane down the pier.

Tate turned to Amos Carlton who was still taking it all in. "What happened?"

Amos pointed out at the sea. "She came in on all full. A bat outta hell. No radio warning. No nothing."

"Whose boat is this?"

"It's an Amoyeli trawler, Chief. The *Witch Doktor*. Anatu's the captain's name. They come here for fuel and supplies every now and then. But we ain't never had problems with 'em before."

Tate slid past the confused dockhand. He looked at the *Witch Doktor*. It was an older fish trawler, twenty-nine feet in length. There were several cracks in the hull, extensive damage to her boom arms, and the diesel engine coughed out a continual line of deathly black smoke. Even before the wreck, she had seen her better day.

Tate then looked back to Amos. "Get all these people out of here. No one is to come out this way unless I authorize it. Understand?"

Carlton nodded.

"But when the rest of Galeegi Police gets here, send them directly to me."

Tate used the same attached swing ladder that he assumed Cane had used to get aboard. Within seconds he climbed over the rail and onto the *Witch Doktor*'s deck. The boat was at such an angle that he had to hold onto the side railing to keep his balance. He inched his way up to the bridge cabin and its open door. Tate paused for a moment when he saw blood leading from the entrance and running down the edge of the cabin's housing. He could see that it collected on the aft deck near the base of the boat's winch. Blood in any accident of this magnitude would be expected, but this didn't strike Tate as being the case. It was too much blood, and it had pooled too soon.

Tate let go of the railing and seized the frame of the cabin door. He held his position and scanned the inside of the bridge. "My God," he whispered in shock.

Tate could not believe the slaughter before him. Five bodies, Amoyeli fishermen all, had been savagely attacked. The chief's eyes drifted over the entire scene. It had been a blood bath—the likes of which he had never before encountered in his thirty-five years of law enforcement.

Two of the fishermen in the back of the cabin were angled face down in inch-thick blood. Their arms were outstretched—dead birds tossed to the ground after the madness of a swirling storm. The two other mates were each tied to a console station that centered the cabin and which held the *Doktor*'s emergency position-indicating radio beacon and sonar devices. They sat with their arms behind their backs, heads slumped over, and a giant gash ripped into their chests—their white t-shirts stained a bright red.

The body of a man that Tate figured to be Anatu, the captain, was positioned in front of the pilot's chair; his hands and arms tied to the boat's steering wheel. He too had a massive rip across his chest. His blood and a portion of his entrails spilled out from his chest cavity and onto the navigation console.

Tate moved into the soiled cabin. He approached Anatu and got into a position where he could see his face. The trawler captain had his eyes squeezed tightly, and he had bitten down on his protruding tongue—his final act in bracing for the onslaught.

Tate donned his gloves and looked at the bindings on Anatu's arms. The killer had strapped his hands and arms to the wheel housing so that there was no way the ship could have veered off course from its deadly path.

And then Tate noticed something else. As he positioned himself around the steering wheel, he looked to the back of the bridge and saw something the killer left behind.

His own blood grew cold. A shiver crept down the center of his spine.

8:45 PM

Tyler floored the accelerator of his Ford Ranger 4x4 en route to the marina. After he had left the station that afternoon, he had gone back to his apartment and fallen asleep on the couch. Jaja's death, the associated old case, and his long day with Sergeant Johnson had worn him out. It had taken several calls from Robbie Cone just to rouse him. But now he was wide awake.

He drove the truck into the marina—still crowded with on-lookers and lit up by the flashing lights of the emergency response vehicles. He hopped out and headed for the pier. A yellow police line and Johnson's imposing frame awaited him.

"Well, lookie here. Glad to see you could join us," Johnson hissed.

"What happened here, Sarge?"

Hank Johnson turned and took a quick look at the wreck behind him before turning back to Tyler and glaring at him. "What do you think happened, genius?"

Tyler moved past him with a shake of his head. Johnson called out, "Going up there, boy? Be careful...lot of blood. Wouldn't want you to lose your supper too."

Tyler blew out an angry huff but managed to keep his cool. He kept his back to Johnson and continued on, sloshing through the water to the end of the pier. He reached the ladder and made his ascent. Like his uncle had done before him, Tyler carefully pulled himself along the railing toward the bridge.

He slowed as he came to the swirl patterns of red dried on the deck. Summoning his courage, Tyler moved towards the cabin. An EMT suddenly emerged out of the cabin door—his gloved hands covered in blood. He shook his head and whistled.

"Brutal."

Tyler walked past him and then slipped into the cabin. Chief Tate was still in there. He now had the station's

DSLR camera, a Nikon D-80, and was getting shots of the scene. He looked up at Tyler and then around the entire cabin. "Breathe in through your mouth and be careful where you step, okay?"

Tyler nodded, then focused on the horror before him. The stench overwhelmed him, but his gag reflexes held for the moment. He moved into the cabin—conscious of his feet sticking to the bloody floor. "How did this happen?"

Tate bent forward and framed the camera under Anatu's body and snapped a shot. "I don't know. This is as bad as I've ever seen."

"What do you think? Robbery? A drug deal gone bad? Some kind of rage?" Tyler tried to process it all, tried to think like a cop, and desperately tried not to think of his rising nausea.

Tate flashed his camera again. "It's rage all right—in its purest, darkest form," he answered. He slowly stood and looked around again. "But I'll tell you this: it was rage with a calculated, personal touch. Whoever did this, wanted to make a statement beyond the brutality."

"What do you mean?"

"Well, not only did he butcher them all in the same way, but it appears the attacker left us some kind of message as well."

Tyler followed his uncle toward the back of the bridge. On the wall space underneath a cabin window, Tate pointed to an odd representation drawn in the fishermen's blood. The crude drawing seemed to bleed right through the wall. It was insidious enough to give Tyler the same cold chill his uncle had felt before.

It was circular in shape with two flaring points leading away from the center. The circle also had an open end with a thin rectangle emerging from the opening and a double-headed square attached to its end.

"I can't make heads or tails of it. What does it look like to you?" Tate asked.

"Trouble," Tyler responded. "It looks like trouble to me."

11:42 PM

Tyler sat in a wooden, Adirondack-style chair on his Uncle Fletcher's back deck. It was a clear night with the temperature remaining in the low eighties. A last-quarter crescent moon shone through the grove of tall sycamores that dotted the yard edged by a creek. The pungent odor of the marshy creek hung in the warm, wet air, and the Lowcountry no-see-ums were out in full force.

Tyler rapped his fingers along the side arm of the deck chair—waiting. He could see the old catamaran that Tate had hanging in a makeshift lift under some of his sturdier sycamores. It had been dry-docked back there for as long as Tyler could remember. Uncle Fletcher always promised he'd have it finished by the next summer and that Tyler would be the first to sail on her. But it never happened. Something always seemed to get in the way.

Tate finally emerged through the sliding glass door of his modest home and walked over to his nephew, handing him a Bud Light. "Here you go. Sorry it took so long, but I didn't want to wake Marie."

Tyler grabbed the bottle. "She's used to your strange hours by now, I imagine."

"You would think that," Tate replied with a soft laugh. He paused, then leaned over and toasted his nephew with a clink of their bottles. "You sure picked an interesting week to start down here, huh?"

Tyler smiled. "I can just hear Mom now: 'You should have gone to law school like I said.'"

Tate smiled back and took a swig from his bottle. "Well, you're certainly smart enough. And there's still time." He laughed again as he thought about it. "Of course, a couple more weeks like this one and I might want to go to law school with you."

"Mom doesn't understand why I wanted to be a policeman in the first place."

"If I remember it correctly, she questioned my sanity when I signed up as well."

"Yeah, but she says you were always a badass. Even when y'all were young. You were cut out to be a cop. But me? She questions whether or not I have what it takes."

Tate grinned but shook his head dismissively.

They paused in silence for a moment.

Tyler straightened up in his chair. "Do you think it's possible that all of this is tied together—Jaja's death and now these new killings?"

Tate pursed his lips. "Tied together? I don't see how."

"But, it couldn't just be a coincidence, could it? I mean, when was the last time you heard of a murder over on Amoyeli—let alone two incidents like this?"

"Granted, murder on Amoyeli is rare, but it has happened before. And don't forget there is still no official word on Jaja being murdered anyway. It is still listed as a probable suicide."

Tyler was about to respond but paused when the sliding glass door opened. With squinty, sleepy eyes, his aunt Marie stepped out onto the deck. She was dressed for bed with only an old, faded Atlanta Braves jersey draped over her long, thin form—a triangle of pink underwear showed from beneath the jersey. Her arms were folded over her chest, and she walked gingerly towards them. Tate looked up. "Oh, sorry, honey," he said. "We didn't mean to wake you."

Tyler turned in his chair and gave her a wave. "Hey, Marie."

Marie rolled her fingers in his direction and tried her best to muster a smile. "Hey, Ty. You guys hungry? Want me to fix y'all something?" she asked in a sleepy voice.

Tate raised his bottle. "I think we got what we need. You go back to bed."

She closed her eyes as if falling asleep and then made a kissing gesture at her two boys. She turned and stepped back inside.

Tyler smiled. He had always liked Aunt Marie. A beautiful, sexy woman, Marie was younger than his uncle by fifteen years. And she was always fun to be around. He had fond memories of coming to Galeegi in the summer with his mother and then hanging out with Marie most of the time. She would take him to the beach or to the arcade at the pavilion. She was always vibrant and flirtatious, and she teased him about how the girls would soon be all over him. Tyler understood well what his uncle saw in her. She was someone to build a life around. The fact that Marie and Fletcher had never had any children together always seemed a shame to him though.

"That's one great lady," he finally said.

Tate took a quick sip of beer but remained quiet. He seemed suddenly distracted, staring out into the yard.

Tyler picked up on his uncle's silence. "Chief? Everything okay?"

"What?" Tate asked, finally looking at his nephew. "Yeah, sure, everything's fine. Just thinking about what happened at the marina." He looked at his watch. "I think I'll head back to the crime scene now and relieve Sarge. SLED detectives should be here on the island within the hour, and I'm sure the FBI will be here before too long."

"Oh," Tyler said, jumping out of the chair with renewed interest. "Do you want me to come with you?"

Tate slapped him on the shoulder. "No. Go home. Get some rest. At least one of us should be semi-alert through all this." He flipped his beer bottle into a trash can at the bottom of the deck.

"Just get back early. We're going to need your help."

Tyler nodded and then headed down the steps of the deck. He stopped as he thought about it for a second. He turned back to his uncle. "Jaja was murdered. Just like the men on the boat. And I can't help but feel it is somehow all tied together. I don't know how I know, but I know. I just feel it."

Fletcher Tate smiled at his nephew. "My sister's wrong. I've got a feeling you're gonna make one hell of a cop."

JUNE 5

The morning tide brought heavy rains, and the investigation into the fishermen's deaths continued as a soggy affair. The marina at Galeegi remained a confused combination of a slow-working port and a fast-moving crime scene. Fishing trawlers and shrimp boats periodically exited into open sea with their sailors staring intently at the wrecked *Witch Doktor*. Members of local and federal law agencies danced about the daily happenings, alternating between documenting evidence and scratching their heads. Emergency personnel removed bagged bodies from the *Witch Doktor* one at a time, lowered them into waiting ambulances, and shuttled them off the island to nearby Colleton Medical Center.

Decked out in an orange rain slicker, Tyler stood positioned behind the yellow crime scene tape. He blinked the weariness from his eyes as he checked the crowd, keeping unauthorized persons away. The past few days had been tough. Tyler found that trying to mentally escape from the madness was a dubious process.

Tyler noticed his uncle talking to a group of his fellow professional investigators, those outfitted in the jackets of the FBI, US Marshal's office, and SLED—the State Law Enforcement Division. Chief Tate had been there all night, and his frazzled condition showed it. His broad shoulders slumped, and his face was ashen.

Eventually, Tate made his way over to his nephew with two other investigators in tow. "Ty, I'd like you to meet Special Agent Kasko of the FBI. And this is Lieutenant Dupree of SLED from their Colleton office in Walterboro. They've both been assigned to this case. They'd like to talk to you about it."

Tyler shook their hands. "I'll be happy to tell you what I know."

He took a good look at the men before him. Miller Kasko was not what Tyler thought of when he pictured the typical FBI agent. The Bureau's Special Agent in Charge of its Atlanta office was lean and athletic enough, but he also had a craggy face, droopy eyes, and featherweight hair that he wore slicked back. He was an older man, perhaps even older than Tyler's uncle. And he had a forced grin as well as a quick handshake. He struck Tyler as more of a used car salesman than policeman.

Howard Dupree of SLED, on the other hand, was the picture of a hardened cop. He was a tall, black man with broad, football shoulders, focused eyes, and a powerful grip. He was more reserved than his federal counterpart—quiet in his manner and approach.

"I understand you went aboard the *Witch Doktor*?" Kasko asked with a detectable Texas twang. "What was your impression, young man?"

Tyler looked at his uncle and then back to the FBI man. "Impression? It was a bloody mess if that's what you mean."

Kasko grinned—all wrinkles and thin lips. "What do you think about the style of the attack?"

"I saw no style, sir. It was just a brutal attack. But we do think it was purposely done. Not some random act of rage."

"And what makes you say that?"

"The blood drawing on the cabin wall."

Kasko nodded quickly, talking over him. "Yes, yes, of course, let's talk about that. What was your impression of that drawing, Patrolman?"

"Sir, I don't know what to make of it."

"You ever see a representation like that before?"

"Never."

"Think hard, now. You've never seen that kind of drawing before?"

Tyler slowly shook his head no. Kasko moved a little closer and flashed a bit of his ghost smile. "I understand you just started working here, Patrolman Miles."

Tyler confirmed again with a simple nod.

"Well, let me give you a piece of advice." Kasko moved even closer and lowered his voice to a whisper. "Don't mention what you saw on that boat to anybody. Got it? Nobody needs to know. Nobody. Not your grandma, your girlfriend, or your pet goat, Gully. Are we clear on this, son?"

Tyler stood there, looking perplexed.

Kasko's smile broadened. "We just don't want any of this getting out into the community, Patrolman. Only the killers and us know the details. Let's keep it that way. Okay?"

"Besides, the good folks of Galeegi have enough to worry about," Dupree added through his own grin.

Tyler well understood that and again nodded.

"Good," said Kasko. He turned back to Tate. "Keep the lines open, Chief. And remember, we'll need those support patrols by this afternoon."

Tate signaled that he understood and watched as the two men walked off back toward the *Witch Doktor*. Tyler sidled up beside him.

"Support patrols?"

"The waterways. We're to keep a sharp eye out for anything suspicious on the river and here in the sound while the FBI takes a look around the islands. With any luck, they'll catch this bastard sooner rather than later, and then we can be done with all this."

As Tate moved away, leaving Tyler alone to guard the line once again, a far off rumble of morning thunder sent Tyler's eyes searching the sky. He shared the same hope as his uncle but not the same conviction.

We aren't done with this. Not by a long shot.

8:41 AM

Emil Rutherford, her slight, aged body clothed in a robe of pink satin, sat at her wrought iron table with a glass inlay in the rose garden behind her ever-shrinking estate. A green and red Monet print umbrella served as protection against the gray skies and misty rain. It was Emil Rutherford's routine to have breakfast served to her at this very spot every morning, and she was not going to let a little rain stop her today.

Ira, an elderly, black island maid, who had served the Rutherford family for decades, brought her a tray of oatmeal mash, biscuits, and coffee. As was also customary, she included a single rose in a Waterford cut glass vase along with the folded morning newspaper at the top of the silver-plated tray.

Emil dipped a sourdough biscuit into the gruel and took a small bite. "Ira? Is Collin stirring this morning?"

Ira remained expressionless. "Not so far as I know, ma'am. He come in late again last night."

"Stone drunk, I imagine. Drunk as Cooty Brown."

"Yes, ma'am."

"Always drinking. Always. Just can't leave the bottle alone." Emil sighed. "Can't blame him though. It's his father's fault he's turned out this way. His father didn't love him. He just never showed him any love." She took another small bite. "His father never showed anybody much love for that matter...even me."

"Yes, ma'am." Ira had heard it a million times.

"He was a good man, hardworking, but he just didn't know how to express love." She looked wistfully away into her garden. "It's the way Southern men are, Ira. Something in their makeup, I guess. Heredity. Got to be heredity."

"Boys a lot like they daddies," Ira confirmed.

"Of course, he was a whole lot better than that low-down snake, Charles Argeaux. My husband's been dead cold in the ground for eight years now, and he's still a right smart better than that egomaniacal jackass across the way."

Ira forced a smile. She heard footsteps and looked back toward the main house. "Mr. Collin up now, ma'am. He headed this way."

Emil sat rigid, staring blankly, taking a delicate sip of coffee.

Collin Rutherford swung his gangly frame into the seat opposite his mother. An opened robe showcased a rude meshing of stained t-shirt and wayward-fly boxers. He was unshaven, swollen, and red-eyed. His thin hair, cropped closely, sprang out at all angles.

"Morning, Ma. I see you're up at the crack of dawn again."

"Why, Collin, it's nearly nine o'clock now. The day has begun in earnest and is already leaving you far behind."

"Yeah, like I give a shit," Collin mumbled. He leaned back in the chair and stretched his arm out into the rain. He gathered some of the moisture, rubbed his palms, and applied it to his puffy face. "I tell you, Ma. I don't know why you do it."

"Do what, Collin?"

"Come out here every freaking morning—rain or shine. Sit here like the queen of Galeegi and piss your time away looking at that weed-infested garden of yours."

Emil turned her nose up to her son. "Custom, Collin. I am accustomed to it." She took another bite of the gruel-sogged biscuit. "I am accustomed to it like you are to your bottle, I suppose. By the way, where were you last night? Ira said you didn't come in until all hours."

Collin glared at the Rutherfords' maid. He clasped his hands behind his head and leaned back in his chair. "I don't know. I don't remember the gory details. I was just out, okay? I mean, Jesus Christ, I'm a forty-two-year-old man, Mother."

Emil put her napkin thoughtfully to her chin. "Collin, are you homosexual? Is that why you act the way you do? You can tell me."

"Christ...yeah, Ma, that's it. I'm one big homo. I really like it up the ass. *Jesus.*"

"Then what is it, Collin? Why are you so unhappy that you feel you must drink yourself half to death?"

Collin's face soured. He hopped out of his chair and pulled his robe together. "I ain't got time for this." He headed back toward the house.

"Collin, where are you going? Collin?" Emil Rutherford turned in her son's direction and caught Ira's stare. She slowly turned back to the table and allowed her eyes to drift down to her plate. "Ira," she called.

"Yes, ma'am."

"I think I'm finished," she said in a suddenly frail voice.

10:13 AM

About a mile east of Rutherford and just before the main island, the black waters of the Galeegi swirled and frothed under the concrete bridge at Poston's Landing. Daily traffic swept over the bridge as commuters made their way to and from the islands.

Unbeknownst to the travelers above, giant red eyes stared up at them from the river's murky depths. They remained fixed on the surface for only a moment and then slowly sank into the water's darkness.

2:23 PM

Tyler Miles sat on the top of the captain's chair of the Contender patrol boat with his right bare foot propped up on the steering wheel. The boat was idling but drifted quickly with the tide up into the reaches of Galeegi Sound. The morning rains had ended, and the sun had now made a powerful return. Tyler peeled his shirt off. He scanned the reedy islets with a pair of Steiner Binoculars; his ever-present Costa Del Mar's hung around his neck.

As he imagined, there had been very little for him to see—a few non-descript boats—some with folks casting shrimp nets and others heading up the sound. Almost everyone seemed oblivious to the happenings of the past few days. *The world stops for no one,* Tyler thought. *Not even for some crazy-ass killer.*

He mainly stuck to the left bank as he made his way up river. He noted several pipers, terns, and a large, black skimmer darting in and out of the marsh banks. As the tide continued to rise, Tyler drifted into the high marsh. He found a break in the grass and made his way into a thin inlet. It led to a more open estuary. He raised the twin Yamaha engines, took out the boat's reach pole, and punted through the reeds to the open area.

The sun's rays caught the shallow waters of the estuary and reflected back at Tyler like exploding fireworks. For just a moment he was blinded, but then he saw it—a boat no more than twenty feet from his own. It was a brand new, twenty-eight-foot Bayliner 285 Cruiser, white with hunter green trim. Beautiful as it was, it seemed odd to Tyler that it was sitting back in this cove, especially since there did not seem to be anyone stirring on deck.

Tyler pushed the Contender alongside the Bayliner. He held onto its rail. "Hello?" he called out. He waited and then tried, "Galeegi Police...anyone on board?"

Again, silence greeted him.

Tyler whipped the tie cord on his boat to the Bayliner's rail. He strapped his weapon to his side and then leaped over onto the other deck. The boat rocked a bit, but again nothing stirred. There was evidence of life on board, however. Two wet towels lay balled up on the white cushions of the fore deck, and a Diet Coke can was in a cup holder next to the console. Tyler reached out and slid his fingers down the outside of the can. It was hot to the touch, having baked in Galeegi's sun. He spun around and took note of a discarded t-shirt and khaki shorts stuffed under the captain's chair.

Tyler made his way down to the galley. A light was on in the foreroom, and he saw several metal containers crammed in there. An open container held glass tubes, six-inch stick sensors, some type of pesticide test strips, and unmarked solvents. He also noticed a spilled open carry-bag with several unidentifiable clothing items.

Tyler backed out onto the deck, checked around the engines, and then did a 360 around the boat's perimeter. Satisfied that he had surveyed the entire area, he decided to call in his findings and let Control Central dictate his next move.

As he turned to go, Tyler was unaware that someone had eased aboard the stern and that a loaded spear gun was now pointed directly at his back.

2:45 PM

Manu Ando drove his old truck down a bumpy section of Crossing Cut. Special Agent Kasko rode next to him. Dan Sheridan, the Colleton County Sheriff, sat with Lieutenant Dupree in the back.

"I dunno whatcha men is looking for," Manu stated defensively. "We ain't got no killers here on Amoyeli."

Dan Sheridan, a thin man of forty with angular facial features and wavy brown hair, leaned forward. "It's like I told you, Manu. These detectives figure the man who done in them boys on the fishing boat might be a hiding out here on the island. They ain't accusing anybody of anything...yet."

"The sheriff is correct, Mr. Ando," Kasko said. "We're just very concerned for the rest of your island citizens.

We must process this case and that includes checking out any potential witnesses or potential suspects. I'd like very much to start by interviewing the families of the deceased."

"Now?" Manu questioned.

"The sooner the better, Mr. Ando. We can't let any leads go cold," Kasko said.

"But they grieve now," Manu said, furling his brow. "They not for the talking."

Dupree reached his large hand over the seat and rested it on Ando's shoulder. "We won't press them during this grieving time, but we must talk to them. It is for their good and the good of the island."

Manu turned briefly to look at Dupree and tried to explain. "But our people...they got the shut mouth, our people do."

Dupree shot a look over to Kasko. "I think he means they will be difficult to interview. They're not overly receptive to outsiders."

Manu agreed with a vigorous nod.

Kasko smiled from behind his shades. "Well, don't worry about that, Mr. Ando. They'll talk to me." He looked out of the passenger window at the passing brush. "Little do the people of these islands know how charming Miller Kasko can be."

2:48 PM

"Hey! What the hell do you think you're doing?"

Tyler stopped. He almost grabbed his weapon but thought better of it. He slowly turned to look behind him, raising his hands at the sight of the spear gun— now aimed right at his nose.

He relaxed a bit as he stared at the woman before him. She stood tall with diving gear at her feet, holding the gun, a finger pull away from killing him. But as dangerous as her next act might be, Tyler was intrigued by this woman. She captivated him at first sight, standing there in her menacing pose, dripping wet in the tiniest of black bikinis.

"Galeegi Police. My badge is in the boat. I'll get it for you," Tyler said.

"Move one muscle, and you're skewered. Got it?"

Tyler nodded and flashed his smile. "Just look at my boat, will you? You can see it's a police watercraft. I'm Patrolman Tyler Miles. I was just checking out other vessels in the area. My badge is on the console."

"Why were you on my boat? What are you doing back here?"

"Like I said, I'm with Galeegi Police. We had an incident here last night, and I was charged with checking suspicious boats in the waterway."

"So you feel like you can go aboard any boat you want whenever the hell you feel like it?"

"No, ma'am."

"Don't call me *ma'am*. Do I look like a fucking *ma'am* to you?" she asked, tossing wet strands of hair from her face with a quick, hostile turn of her head.

Tyler smiled sheepishly and looked the woman up and down again. She had rock hard abs, taut runner's legs, and long, sleek hair as black as her bikini. "No, I'm sorry if I offended you."

Tyler lowered his arms just a bit. "May I ask what you're doing way back here?"

"Diving. And if you were worth a damn as a cop, you'd know that by the diving buoy out beside my boat."

Tyler looked off the port side and grimaced at the sight of the red-and-white marker bobbing against the reeds. "I see that now. I must have missed it. I apologize." He paused. "May I put my arms down now?"

She lowered her weapon, and he in turn lowered his arms. He smiled at her in relief, then quickly became flirtatious. "You always dive the marsh with a spear gun?"

For the first time, she returned his smile. "It's always best to be prepared, is it not?" She pulled the dart from the gun's banded shaft. "A JBL Woody Sawed-Off Magnum. Good for stopping barracuda, shark, and sea monsters of all kind."

Tyler drew down the corners of his mouth. "Impressive. I'm just glad you don't have an itchy trigger finger."

"Normally I do. Must be the sea water," she said, rubbing her thumb over her finger.

"So, what are you looking for down there? Sharks' teeth? Civil War relics?"

"POPs," she said flatly.

Tyler looked clueless.

"Persistent organic pollutants," she explained. "Those that cause campylobacteriosis, encephalitis, e-coli, even typhoid. I'm a research biologist for the Environmental Protection Agency. We've been testing the Galeegi River and Sound for evidence of certain disease starters. Unfortunately, a lot of pollutants go into your waters from the industries up river. They feed down toward these marsh areas and very subtly destroy the ecosystems. We usually find first signs of it in the beds along banks like these—the habitats of fiddler crabs, turtles, and even some species of waterfowl."

"How did we check out today?" Tyler asked with genuine curiosity.

"I have more tests of the marsh's bottom layer to run, but so far so good."

Tyler just stood there staring at her awkwardly.

Chloe scrunched her brow at his hesitance and then bit her lip to keep from laughing. "Well? Is there anything else, Officer?"

"Oh, I'm not an officer. Not yet. In fact, this is my first week on the job here in Galeegi."

"Imagine that," she said with a grin.

Tyler cut his eyes at her and blushed, looking at his watch. "Well, I reckon I should get moving. More of the river to cover, you know."

"Yeah, okay. Good luck finding whatever it is you're looking for. And in the future don't always assume an empty boat is an abandoned one."

Tyler smiled as he headed for the Contender. "I'll remember that." He paused as he straddled the two boats. "And you keep that spear gun handy. We really did have something bad happen not too far down the river. It could be dangerous to be alone out here."

"I'm not worried...as long as the river is being protected by Galeegi's finest."

Tyler smiled broadly; she was definitely flirting with him now.

"You plan on being in Galeegi for long?"

"Couple of days at least. The Galeegi is a huge river."

Tyler began pushing his boat silently through the marshy reeds.

"Good. Maybe I'll see you around the island then."

"Maybe."

As Tyler's boat idled back toward the river, he fired

up the engines. He turned and saw the woman still watching his progress. "Hey," he called out. "I almost forgot. What's your name?"

"Hart! Chloe Hart!"

"Okay, Chloe Hart! I'll remember that!" He steered into the river's flow.

Chloe Hart. Damn right, I'll remember you.

5:43 PM

Hank Johnson waddled into Tate's office and shut the door behind him. Tate put down the report he was reading and offered his sergeant a seat with a brief wave of his hand. Johnson plopped into the chair and leaned back.

"Another helluva day, huh?" Johnson asked.

Tate quickly nodded. "What've you got for me?"

The big man scratched his thigh. "Went by to see John Cane a little while ago. He's resting at home, but by God, he's still shook up from what he saw out there on the *Witch Doktor*. You'd think a man who'd been around cut bait all his life could stomach a little cut Geechee too," he said with his sadistic smile. "That son of a bitch sure did turn them boys into grade A chum now, didn't he?"

Tate pinched the bridge of his nose. "Did he say anything else to you, Sarge? Did John give you any details on what might have gone down?"

"Nope. Nothing significant. Nothing that the other eyewitnesses haven't already accounted for."

"Then we've got to keep searching. We've got to find an explanation for all this."

"An explanation?" Johnson leaned towards Tate's

desk. He kept his eyes down and spun a piece of paper around the desktop. "We don't need to keep digging to explain what happened, Fletch. Hell, I can tell you exactly what happened if you want me to." He looked back up at the chief with assurance.

Tate simply raised both eyebrows, inviting the theory.

"Saturday night on the island. Them boys got a hold of the go-go juice like they sometimes do and went a little crazy. They had themselves a party on the island somewheres and ended up diddling the wrong feller's wife. All five of 'em probably jumped her. And then big daddy comes in from the field, finds out, gets pissed, gets his axe from the woodshed, finds their boat and has at 'em. It's as simple as that, Fletcher. It's the same old story."

Tate shook his head. "No, this is different. "

"It ain't no different, Fletcher. Me and you grew up on this island. You know all about them Africans across the sound. They've been dancing 'round the fire and howling at the moon for years. And when they get to drinking, they ain't no different than the coloreds in Rutherford. It's the same story, I'm telling you."

"What about the blood painting on the wall?"

Johnson laughed. "Pffft. Looks like something a kid in kindergarten would draw. Don't mean a thing."

Tate shook his head. "It was too cold-blooded, too calculated."

"You're overthinking, Chief. It was a drunken orgy gone bad, that's all." Johnson quit smiling and whispered, "And if it didn't go down like I said, then really, who gives a damn. It's just like with that murdering, shiftless Jaja. Who gives a damn if Mr. Argeaux or somebody whacked his ass? They did the world a favor if you ask me. It's just a shame justice had to wait so many years."

"Hank, we're police officers. We have to protect..."

"...our citizens," Johnson interrupted loudly. He slammed his fist down on Tate's desk for emphasis. "We protect Galeegi and her citizens, Fletcher. You don't want to get mixed up with Amoyeli. It's a different world over there. They don't think like us. They don't act like us. They're animals."

Tate forced a smile. He knew he would never be able to convince the man of anything else even if he took a thousand years to do so. Hank Johnson was so much like all those he grew up with on Galeegi—the separate, but far-from-equal crowd.

Tate rubbed his face and stifled a yawn. "I'm beat. I think I'll head home."

Johnson stood. "Yeah, you do that, Fletch. Head home. Get some rest. Think I'll do the same." He reached for the doorknob but turned back and said, "And seriously, don't worry so much about this, Chief." He turned and pulled the door behind him. "It's only Amoyeli."

9:17 PM

"Well, it looks like nobody's home...again," Miller Kasko said as he peeped inside the trailer window. "Either no one wants to talk to us, or somehow everyone's gone on vacation at the same time."

"Like I say, they not much for the talk," Manu said from the back of the huddled group. "They know you here. They go away. It not proper to talk so soon about the dead."

Kasko rolled his eyes and then turned to face Manu. "'Cause their spirits are still around. And they can hear their kinfolk talking about them. Is that it?"

"Yes, Mr. Kasko. It something like you say."

"So, Manu, when do you think the people will be ready to talk about it?" Sheriff Sheridan asked.

"Days now. Could be weeks. Some have the shut mouth forever."

"Forever?" Kasko followed. "Are you kidding me? I'm running a goddamn murder investigation, Mr. Ando. I can't wait until these people feel like talking. Either they talk to me now or I'm going to have to start forcing them to talk. And you can tell every one of them that for me."

Dupree turned to face Manu. "It's the FBI, Manu. Your people can't go against them. This is a serious murder investigation. There must be some way."

Manu's eyes drifted to the ground and then suddenly shot back up. "I take Mr. Kasko to see Hammie. He can help. He talk for the people."

"Hammie? Who is Hammie? Is he an official on the island?" Kasko asked.

"Hammie Swantou. He conjurer, Mr. Kasko. He hoodoo man. Everybody listen to him," Manu said. He took off toward the truck.

Kasko stole a glance at Sheridan and then Dupree; both smiled. The FBI man rubbed his chin and then threw a what-the-hell shrug. "The local wizard, huh? Well, why not? When in Oz...."

10:17 PM

Chloe Hart grabbed her gear bags out of the side

door of her van, slid it shut, and walked to her rented bungalow. The path leading to the house was made of crushed seashells and bordered by pesky sand spurs. Even though she wore flip-flops and her shoulders sagged under the weight of the heavy gear, she still managed to navigate the awkward path without stumbling.

She climbed the steps of the front porch, which like the rest of the house, sat off the ground on stilts. She approached the door, finagled the lock, and made her way into the light gray, wooden framed house.

She placed the bags on the small table in the kitchen and sat at the counter that separated the room from the den. Aptly named the Oyster Cloister, the old beach cottage was built in the late fifties, and it still possessed much of its original charm. It had painted, beaded board slats for a ceiling with hanging fans in every room. The hand-hewed oak floors were darkly stained, and the oak paneled walls were littered with beach wood sculptures and the signature prints of local artists Jim Harrison and Steven Jordan. A sturdy screened-in porch wrapped around the back of the house.

Despite being tired and needing a shower, Chloe pulled out her laptop and began writing up the day's findings. She was relieved, yet surprised, that the Galeegi marshes had shown little irritation from the toxic run-off up river. Tests in the northern section of the river showed signs of some of the most deadly organic pollutants: aldrin, chlordane, DDT, among others—those belonging to a group of twelve the EPA called the dirty dozen. But it didn't appear to be spreading south as quickly as was initially feared. She would need to take a few more samples and have them officially run through the Department of Health and Environmental Control's coastal testing lab in Charleston. But this assignment would be quick. Two or three more days tops.

Thirty minutes later, Chloe shut down the laptop. She went to the fridge and pulled the last of the Diet Coke cans from the now empty shelves. She collapsed on the old couch and fumbled with the remote until she found a local news station. She wanted to catch tomorrow's weather to be prepared. As the nightly news images played on, she found herself tuning the TV out and thinking more about the young cop on the boat. He reminded her of an old high school boyfriend—same height, same kind of hair, but with a better smile. *That boy had some white teeth*, she thought, laughing to herself.

He was charming in a goofy, youthful sort of way. And there was no doubt that he was younger than her, by at least five or six years.

Chloe looked down at the white band on her finger where the ring had once been. She thought about it for a second and then shook her head. *Too early to be playing that game again. Just focus on your work. Work is all you need right now.*

Chloe slid down on the couch and rested her head on a small throw pillow. The weatherman said that it was going to be another hot one tomorrow, another scorcher up and down the Carolina coast. But she missed it. She was asleep—dreaming. She was back in the water again, diving, then back on the boat, talking to a young, shirtless cop with broad tan shoulders and the most perfect white teeth she had ever seen.

Hammie Swantou drew heavily on the offered cigarette; the fiery orange ash poked a small hole in the Amoyeli darkness. The four lawmen gathered tightly around him, making the anxious situation that much more volatile. They stood out in front of his trailer between two large yucca plants and just to the right of his sleeping chickens.

"Mr. Swantou, so glad you're willing to speak with us tonight," Kasko said.

"Knew you was coming, Mistah Po-lice-man. Knew you was coming."

Kasko shot a knowing smile at the others. "Oh? And how did you know we were coming, Mr. Swantou? You had a dream about it, or did you conjure it up in some kind of vision?"

"No, sir," Hammie said pointing his long, yellow-nailed finger behind them. "Saw your headlights down the road and knew you was coming."

Kasko momentarily turned to look at the ribbon of road that led to Hammie's trailer; then he realized he had been had. He turned back to see the other men trying to suppress their laughter. He smiled wickedly at Hammie. "That's very good, Mr. Swantou. Very clever. Let's just hope we can solve this case soon so that I might be as jovial."

"You will not solve this soon like you say, Mr. Po-lice-man," Hammie said in a sudden, callus tone. "More blood come to Amoyeli. More blood come to Galeegi. Much more."

"What do you mean? If you really know something."

Hammie spit the cigarette to the ground and moved

away from the group. He closed his eyes. He put out his hands as if feeling vibrations coming from the ground. "He here. He here," Hammie whispered. "He here on Amoyeli now."

Kasko cut his eyes at Dupree who shared the look with Sheridan. "Who's here, Mr. Swantou? You wouldn't happen to have a name for us, would you?"

"He bring the storm. He bring the ram. He swallow the Igbo whole. He come." Hammie's voice trailed off into a mumble.

Kasko's intrigued look melted into one of disgust. "This is a goddamn waste of time." He looked directly at Manu. "Take us back to our boat, Mr. Ando. We tried this your way tonight. Tomorrow, I want to talk to somebody involved. Somebody who will talk straight. Not this hoodoo bullshit. And if they don't want to talk to me, then I'm throwing their asses under the jailhouse. Got it?"

Manu chose not to answer but certainly understood as he led the group back toward his truck.

Hammie removed his beret and ran his hand over his bald head as he watched them drive away. The men from the outside world would not understand. It had been that way since the earliest days of Amoyeli.

He eased down on the wooden porch steps of his trailer; his eyes searched the darkness of the night. Hammie knew well what they did not. He knew Xevioso had been watching and listening.

And he knew the morning light would reveal more destruction.

91

JUNE 6

Braya Conakee walked barefoot down Crossing Cut toward the west beach of Amoyeli. The island's school had been out for two weeks now, and this walk to find gathered friends on the isolated beach had become a daily ritual for the twelve-year-old.

The South Carolina sun touched the tops of the palmetto trees and evaporated the evening dew from the island floor. The summer heat and the heavy humidity caused Braya to sweat through her t-shirt and shorts, making her walk all the more uncomfortable.

As she neared the beach access road, Braya cut through the dunes to save a little walking time. She swung her arms up and down like a soldier as she marched across the sand hills.

After reaching the tallest of the dunes, Braya stopped for a moment, closing her eyes. A strong wind pushed in from the ocean and enveloped her, cooling her skin—a singular, pleasurable moment—one of the unique gifts of island life.

Braya opened her eyes and refocused on the surrounding beach, noticing something unusual. No more than thirty yards from where she stood, she spied something jutting out from a cluster of sea oats. At first she thought it was wind-blown trash or a broken tree limb carried from deep within the forest behind her. As she moved closer, she made out the particulars of a human leg—a shin, a kneecap, an ankle.

A person sleeping or lying down, taking in the beautiful morning, she thought.

Braya slowly approached the leg, the compact sand crunching and squeaking beneath her feet. As she eased past the appendage, she was shocked to see a mutilated body. She squinted in confusion.

She turned away from the horror and faced the ocean. Tears poured down her cheeks, and she screamed. Her voice echoed across the dunes, over the sandy shore, and out past the breaking waves.

10:12 AM

Manu Ando led a line of police investigators through the dunes of Amoyeli marked by young Braya's tracks to the grisly murder scene. Every day presented a repulsive new challenge for the island's constable. As he trudged closer to the latest crime scene, his emotions overwhelmed him, and he desperately searched within himself for the strength to maintain his composure. Death had never frightened the experienced and extremely devout man before, but Manu had never been through anything like this. And if Hammie Swantou was right about more blood coming to Amoyeli, then the carnage was not likely to stop anytime soon.

Miller Kasko, his blue blazer slung over his shoulder, walked directly behind Manu. He chewed on a sea oat stalk that he had picked along the way. He held up his hand when he saw the body. "All right, gentlemen, hold it right here. Keep a twenty-yard distance from the body until I say so." Kasko looked at Manu. "And you stay here." He then pointed to a crowd of islanders that had gathered beyond the dunes. "Don't let any of those people cross beyond this point."

Manu turned and looked at his neighbors, the ones

who came as news of the latest atrocity spread. Even the Amoyeli children were among them. They bent their heads in sorrow and stood quietly on the beach.

"Chief Tate, you and Lieutenant Dupree come with me," Kasko said. "The rest of you fan out. Look for prints, blood trails, pieces of clothing, anything that shows signs of the struggle or how our killer got in and out of this area."

Tyler adjusted the Costa's on his nose and turned with the other investigators as they spread out. As he searched the area, he found it hard to believe that he was helping investigate yet another attack. Earlier in the morning, he had taken the police boat out for a second round of river patrol before he was rerouted back here to Amoyeli. The moment felt agonizingly familiar to Tyler. He had trouble catching up, catching his breath even.

Tyler distinctly remembered his instructors telling him how police work for the most part was routine and mundane. One older instructor told him that a policeman's job was twenty percent adrenaline and eighty percent pushing papers and sipping coffee. But it had not been that way for him. His indoctrination was swift, a baptism of pain and sorrow, and it left him reeling and questioning his choices. He looked at his uncle and the others as they surrounded the latest victim.

Kneeling next to the body, Kasko slipped his hands into a pair of latex gloves and examined the body. The victim was an islander, middle-aged, slashed across the chest like the fishermen on the boat. Blood puddled around the man's torso. His right hand, in a saluting position, was missing the tips of three fingers and part of his thumb.

"Look at his forehead," Dupree said from behind Kasko. "Is that what I think it is?"

Fletcher Tate moved to Kasko's left to see. It was small and hard to make out, but there was a mark made in blood at the center of the man's forehead. "It's the same marking as the one on the *Witch Doktor*," Tate said.

Although most of the detail of the drawing was lost, it had the two flare marks leading away from the central circle.

"Our artist has been busy," Kasko said.

"What does it mean?" Tate asked.

Kasko shook his head. "I've got the best intelligence analysts in Washington running it through GangNet and our high-profile murder database, but so far we got nada."

Dupree squatted down as well, resting his arms on his knees.

"My guess is it has local significance—inherent to this island and these people. I think that's where we need to concentrate. Talk to these people. Find out what they think."

Kasko laughed sarcastically. "We tried that, remember? They got 'de shut mouth.'"

"Okay. People with expert knowledge of the island then," Dupree said. "I'll contact my office in Walterboro and see who they recommend. Somewhere, somebody knows what that symbol means."

"Sir? Excuse me. You can't be out here," Tyler said to a skinny, black man in the red beret, who walked up to the perimeter. "All locals must remain on the beach until the investigation is complete."

Hammie stood between two of the front dunes. He closed his eyes and put his hands out to his side, palms down.

"Sir?" Tyler asked.

He made a low mumbling sound—humming ancient and secretive words Tyler couldn't understand.

Hammie's eyelids popped open, and he batted them as if waking from a deep sleep. "Xevioso. He here. He here."

"What? What did you say?" Tyler waited for the man to respond, but he said nothing. "Sir, you must return to the...."

"He here. Xevioso. He swallow the Igbo whole. He bring the storm. The ram."

"I'm sorry, but I don't understand."

Hammie pointed his long finger at Tyler. "You. You stop him. You stop the storm."

Tyler smiled awkwardly and shook his head. "Sir, I really don't have any idea what you're talking about." He reached out and took hold of Hammie, turned him around, and ushered him toward the beach. "You're going to have to go."

Hammie stopped and turned, facing Tyler. He put his hand on Tyler's chest and focused his eyes on the patrolman. He flashed a rotten gum grin and whispered, "No...you stop the storm, Tyler. You must stop it. It come your way."

Tyler froze when he heard the stranger use his name. The hairs on his neck rose, and he felt dizzy. It was an eerie sensation—as if the old man had crawled inside his head and read his thoughts.

Hammie nodded, turned, and walked toward the crowd.

Tyler called out, "Wait! How did you know?"

Hammie Swantou kept his back to Tyler. "After the storm, Tyler. Look to what the tide leaves behind. You find your answer there. After the storm."

Tyler remained still, watching Hammie shuffle past the islanders and disappear down the beach.

11:45 AM

Chloe Hart stood on the pier at the Galeegi Marina—her hands on her hips and her long, black hair cascading down her back. She wore blue Soffee shorts and a grey University of Miami t-shirt over her bathing suit. She was dressed for another trip up the river, another day on the job. She cocked her head to the side as she talked to interim dock master, Amos Carlton, who stood with his arms crossed.

"I'm sorry, miss, but all the waterways are shut down right now," Amos said. "They ain't lettin' nobody go out there. I've had to turn around the shrimpers, the fishermen—everybody."

"But it is vital I check the Galeegi today. My work has to be completed within a certain timetable."

"I'm sorry. There's nothing I can do."

Chloe looked past the old dockhand to her Bayliner, secured in its slip. "So whose authority do I need to get out there?"

Amos scratched under his cap. "The order came from the Department of Natural Resources to shut us down. I imagine Galeegi Police made the request. But I wouldn't go out there if I were you. Bad things happenin' around our island lately." He tilted his head toward the crushed portion of the pier.

"What exactly is going on? I can't seem to get a straight answer from anybody."

Amos looked out at the waters lapping against the quiet boats. "Death. There's a killer out there, miss." Amos turned back to Chloe, excused himself with a brief nod, and ambled back toward the watchtower.

Chloe walked down to the foot of the dock and stared out at the inlet where the river met the ocean. It appeared calm and peaceful. But just as the waters churned violently beneath the surface, something more sinister churned within these islands. Chloe Hart was on the verge of being caught up in its powerful flow.

1:56 PM

A forensics team worked around the crime scene doing the necessary work before they bagged the body and shipped it to the mainland. Miller Kasko took refuge from the sun in the shade of a nearby palmetto. He was on the phone with his office in Washington, giving updates and soliciting advice. "No, sir," Kasko said, "nothing yet, but we're hoping to get more cooperation from them today."

He turned to Tate, Dupree, and Tyler as they walked up. "Yes, sir. I'm expecting the profile team in at any time now. I'll report as soon as we know anything." He ended the call and slipped his Blackberry into his pocket. "We're gonna bring in the FBI's medical examiner from Atlanta. He'll want to see the bodies. All of them."

"I'll contact the Colleton Coroner's office and let them know," Dupree said.

Tate indicated his nephew with his thumb and said, "Patrolman Miles here had another conversation with the root doctor."

Kasko looked at Tyler. "What did he say, Patrolman?"

"He said something about a ram and a storm. And he mentioned someone by name—Hea-vee-oso or something like that; said he was here on the island."

"Same jibberish as last night," Kasko said.

"He also mentioned me by name—my first name—said I was to stop the storm."

Kasko laughed. "Well, good luck with that, Patrolman." He paused. "Look, I don't know how he knew your name, but I wouldn't put too much stock in it. He's probably a local con man; has all these islanders eating out of his hand with his mind tricks. I've seen it before."

Tyler nodded but only to keep from looking like a fool. He was still on edge from his brief encounter with Hammie Swantou.

Kasko put his hands on his hips and kicked a little at the sand in front of him. "Okay. So the crazy shaman aside, what have we got so far?" he asked rhetorically. "Five fishermen from Amoyeli murdered and now this man. All in the same manner with the same weapon—an axe or blade of some kind. And Constable Ando said the latest victim was a small-time farmer here on the island. He didn't know of any other connection to the men on the boat."

"And in both cases the same symbolic drawing," Dupree reminded everyone.

Kasko nodded. "Anything else?"

"What about Jaja?" Tyler asked.

Kasko ignored the rookie and looked at Chief Tate.

"Just prior to the fishermen's deaths," Tate explained, "the new caretaker of the Amoyeli lighthouse was found dead of an apparent suicide, which is somewhat suspect. Colleton County has it as an on-going investigation."

"How was he killed?" Kasko asked.

"Revolver to the mouth," Tate said, demonstrating with a finger to his own mouth.

"No axe or blood drawing?"

"No. But Jaja was a native-born islander. He was also the lead suspect in the Katherine Argeaux murder forty-odd years ago."

"Oh, right," Dupree said, "I remember hearing about that. Charles Argeaux's daughter. The father is a wealthy resident over on Galeegi. His family is old money—slave owner money. They've had their hands in these little islands for over three centuries."

"I'll have my people pull together files on all this," Kasko said.

"We've managed to keep the news sequestered so far," Tate said. "But now with these latest developments, I don't know how Galeegi is going to handle it. And the timing of this really hurts. It's the wrong time of year for us to be shutting down the river and beaches. Thousands come here every summer." Tate paused and then added, "It's just a tidal wave of bad news all at once."

Kasko's Blackberry rang loudly. He looked at the caller ID and then answered, "This is Agent Kasko." He listened for a moment. "All right." He put his hand to his head. "*Jesus*, yeah, okay, we'll be right there." He looked back up at Tate. "Looks like your tidal wave is a full blown tsunami, Chief. They just found another body."

Charles Argeaux pulled his club car up under the giant oak that fronted the par-3, seventeenth green at the Cottonseed Golf and Fish Club. He had laced his 8-iron the one hundred forty yards from the tee box and faded his ball perfectly over the outstretched bough of the oak so that it landed soft on the green, taking a two-step bounce before hugging the cup.

He gingerly got out of the cart, grabbed his putter, and walked assuredly onto the green. He stood coolly under the hot sun in his ocean-blue Cutter and Buck knitted shirt and crisp white slacks. He smiled at his playing partners' dilemmas: a wayward, plugged shot in the front bunker; an out-of-bounds, replayed tee shot; and an over-clubbed rip that found an awkward lie. A tap-in birdie here would close out his playing partners and secure the ten thousand dollar bets.

Of course, it wasn't the money that mattered. That had lost its hold on him years ago. But winning, coming out on top, kept the old man's blood flowing. He would take their money eagerly, knowing that it would hurt them far more than if he had to give triple to them. Then he might just burn their money, right there in front of them. Argeaux smiled at the thought.

Argeaux's good mood evaporated as he saw the cart bounding down the path toward them. "I'll be right back, Steve," he said to the man playing out of the sand. Argeaux walked over to the cart and leaned into the driver's side. "What the hell are you doing here?"

The Latino man with the crew cut and hard appearance looked up from behind reflective shades. "You wished to be advised."

Argeaux glanced behind him. "Okay. What is it? Make it quick."

"The police found two more bodies on Amoyeli." He paused. "That makes seven now."

"I can fucking count, Major."

"What do you want to do?" the Major asked. Argeaux rapped his ring finger on top of the cart in thought. The Major cocked his head. "Sir?"

"Just give me a goddamn minute," Argeaux commanded. A bead of sweat formed on his temple and ran down his cheek. He leaned back inside the cart. "Can you ask for more time?"

The Major shifted in his seat. "I can ask, but you know what they will say."

Argeaux slapped his hand hard on the top of the cart. "Then explain it to them so they understand!"

Argeaux turned and stomped back to the green as the cart pulled away. His playing partners gathered around the hole with wads of cash in their hand. A rotund man in a Callaway golf shirt handed him his stash. "Yours again, Charles. Don't you ever get tired of taking our money?"

A cool, snake-like smile came to Argeaux's face as he picked through the bills. "Don't care about your money, Jim, but I never tire of whipping your asses."

5:49 PM

Tyler sat on the back of the Contender next to the engines. His hands were folded in his lap, and he had a lost look on his face. His uncle Fletcher volunteered to drive the boat back to Galeegi, and Tyler had time to reflect even more on the horrors of the day.

The last victim was an elderly woman, another islander. They found her in a ditch near her home with the same slash wounds as the others and the same strange marking, although this time, drawn in a blood splatter on her back and right shoulder. Another victim, another senseless killing.

She was a weaver who spun the sweetgrass baskets and sold them to the tourists who had ferried over from Galeegi. Tyler was sickened about what had happened, and he wondered about the diseased mind of this killer—so callus, so cold.

Kasko and Dupree stayed on Amoyeli and made the preparations for the incoming South Carolina Emergency Response Task Force and the National Guard. The task force would be the liaison between federal and local authorities. They could help with an evacuation if it came to that or bring in their dedicated K-9 search unit if need be. The National Guard's 202nd Armored Cavalry Company out of Beaufort would camp out on the island to support the task force and to keep a watch on the roads and houses. The island's inhabitants did not welcome the help; they were a private group of people, wary of any outside interference. But most realized it was in their best interest.

As the Contender cut across the sound, Tyler joined his uncle at the console. Tate turned and smiled at his nephew. "I know this has been hell for you, Tyler, and I'm sorry."

Tyler patted his uncle on the back. "It's been hell for everyone, Chief. I just hope we can catch him soon and put an end to this."

Tate returned his focus ahead to the sea. "We will. That much I promise." He waited a few moments and then added, "I want you to come to my house tonight. Marie will make you some of her world-famous she-crab soup."

Tyler smiled. He vividly remembered the summer he made a pig of himself downing five bowls of the creamy bisque in one sitting. "It is good stuff, but I think I'll pass. I need to clear my head tonight."

"Okay. Clear your head—just don't lose it. I'll need you back on river patrol early tomorrow."

"I'll be ready," Tyler said. He turned and looked behind him. Amoyeli grew smaller in the distance—trees morphing together, the beach shrinking into a thin, white line. Such a tiny barrier island to be saddled with such an enormous problem. *Why Amoyeli? Why should it happen to these islanders? Who would have that much hatred for such a benign people?* Tyler thought about it all the way back to the marina, but like the countless number who wondered why bad things happen in a good world, he came up with no real explanation for it.

Sometimes bad things just happen.

5:47 PM

SLED's Howard Dupree stood under a yaupon holly fanning the heat and sand gnats from his face. The heat was bad enough, but the island's biting gnats were an aggravating curse. Dupree alternated between checking his watch and swatting away the tiny, swarming devils.

The FBI believed that whoever had committed these crimes used Amoyeli's intricate trail system to move about undetected. So while Agent Kasko set up a base of operations nearby, Dupree handled the vital task of guarding the main trail to East Cove, the island's most populated and vulnerable area. From his vantage point, Dupree could see the roofs of several of the small island houses of East Cove and the rising slope of Wachasee Hill. The trail behind him was dark and quiet, and it led into the thick maritime forest.

Dupree looked up as several gulls suddenly flew overhead, making their desperate calls and breaking the island's silence. He watched them bank in unison toward the ocean beyond.

He turned slightly as he heard a different type of sound in the distance behind him. A group of the islanders were walking down the trail—chanting in harmony and clapping their hands to the same rhythmic beat. There was a musical tone to it all. One man sang out first in his baritone voice, and the others followed in a called response. Though Dupree could not make out the exact words, it sounded something like "coming out of the wilderness."

An island procession, he thought. A unique Gullah ritual, processions were often performed in times of spiritual and emotional need. And there was little doubt of that need lately.

The lawman moved from under the yaupon to the edge of the trailhead. As the islanders emerged, they stopped singing and walked silently. One by one they walked past Dupree. They were mostly elderly women, hardened and dark-faced—direct descendants of a forgotten past.

Dupree smiled saying, "Please don't stop singing on my account." But they remained quiet as they returned to their East Cove dwellings. Dupree watched them go with his hands on his hips, wondering about the future of these people and their island.

Moments later, another noise came from the forest behind him—this time the sound of twigs snapping and island brush palms moving back and forth. Someone else was coming down the same path—following. Dupree quickly stepped off the trailhead and crouched in the brush.

The SLED agent waited for a moment, a bit unsure. Then he called out, "Manu?"

The burly constable spun on his heels. He looked startled and blew out a quick breath. "Lord A'mighty. Thought somebody done snuck up on me."

"Out for a walk?" Dupree asked.

Manu pointed in the direction of those who had dispersed.

"No, sir. Keeping up with my peoples is all. Making sure no harm come to 'em."

Dupree moved in closer, nodding, accepting Manu's explanation. He looked back toward the houses. "This has been tough for them, I know."

"Yes," Manu confirmed. "They used to hard times, hard living. But they ain't never been through nothing like this."

"They won't have to worry much longer, Constable. We'll catch this killer. Get him out of your hair for good."

Manu nodded but then frowned and lowered his voice. "I hope so. But we got us a saying out here on the island." Manu looked at the forest behind him and then back to Dupree. "If the devil ain't gone by sundown, he dance on yo' grave all night."

The Lucky Shark was wall to wall with the summer tourist crowd. With the beaches and waterways on lockdown, everybody was there looking for a little action. Knowledge of what happened at the marina and on Amoyeli was well known; it was the source of much speculation in random conversations throughout the bar. But indifference and hidden prejudices reduced the severity of the murders to a temporary summer rainout.

Poppa worked the back bar, steadily tapping out micro brews and whipping up blue hurricanes and salt rimmed margaritas. He paused every so often to play the crusty old barkeep and to regale the young co-eds about his heroic days at sea, although truthfully he had never set foot on the deck of a Navy ship.

A beer-only bar, set up on the back deck, overlooked the marina. Tyler preferred drinking beer there. Less crowded. He ordered a Red Stripe and joined Robbie Cone at the railing. Each had changed out of their uniforms and blended right in with the shorts-and-sandals crowd.

"Always this packed?" Tyler asked.

"From May to September. In February, you might be the only one to come in here all night," the portly policeman said.

"He doesn't close in the off-season?"

Robbie held up two fingers. "He takes two days off in April to do a little charter fishing. Other than that, you'll find Poppa here. Always."

Tyler nodded and looked toward the marina. He leaned on the railing and stared out at the secured boats. He thought of Amoyeli again. A vision came to him of the old woman dead in the ditch, and then the farmer in the dunes, and the fishermen splayed out on the *Witch Doktor*. "Do you really think we'll catch this guy?"

Robbie took a sip of beer. "Yeah, we will. In cases like this, the perp gets too comfortable; that's when he gets careless. He'll mess up soon enough. Then we'll nab him. That's the way these things go. Usually."

Tyler turned back to Robbie. "I hope so. I don't mind telling you, I can't seem to get away from it." He tried to find the right words. "It's been difficult. I've had a hard time sleeping. This whole thing is haunting me."

"Don't let it eat you up, Tyler. If you do, you're no good to anyone."

Tyler kept his back to the crowd and turned up his bottle. *Maybe enough alcohol will have a numbing effect*, he thought

"Excuse me," a woman's voice said from behind. "Does anyone know where I might find a policeman?"

Tyler spun around and instantly smiled. Numbing problem solved. Chloe Hart stood in front of him, a drink in her hand and a wry smile on her face. She wore a stunning Nicole Miller blue-and-black striped jersey dress that hung perfectly on her tanned shoulders—the dress's hem extended close to mid-thigh.

"Actually, we're with Galeegi law enforcement," Tyler said, playing along. "How might we be of service?"

"Someone has stolen most of my drink," she said playfully. "And I'd like to either file a complaint or..."

"Uh, no, please allow me," Robbie said. He pulled away from the railing, took her cup, and did a quick inspection. "Vodka and grapefruit?"

Chloe smiled. "Absolut, please."

As he headed through the throng of people, Robbie looked back at Tyler and received an appreciative nod.

"So, I see you found our little watering hole," Tyler said.

"Yeah, well, doesn't seem to be too much else happening on this side of the island. But to tell you the truth, I was hoping to run into you again anyway."

Tyler flashed his smile again. "Oh?"

Chloe looked past Tyler to the open marina. "Yes. They have my boat held hostage over there, and I need to finish up my work in the Galeegi. The dock master told me I would have to go through the police to get permission. So I did."

"You checked with our station?"

"Yeah, spoke to some fat ass with roaming eyes," she said, at which Tyler could not help but grin. "He told me the only way I could get back out there was if I went under police supervision."

She paused, allowing her eyes to do her bidding. "I was hoping that might be you."

Tyler straightened up. "At your service. Actually, my next patrol on the river starts tomorrow at seven."

Chloe smiled. "Perfect. That will work out great." She tugged at his arm. "I can't thank you enough."

Tyler took another draw from the bottle and winked. "No need to thank me, Ms. Hart. All in the line of duty."

10:45 PM

Pavilion Avenue branched off from the Island Highway and the old plantation estates and led across the entire front beach of Galeegi Island. Many vacation homes and rentals dotted the family friendly area, home to the most popular of the island's pristine beaches. The avenue served the populace well, as the marina was accessible around the south end corner, and the pavilion stores and restaurants were available on the northern-most point.

In the middle of Pavilion Beach, as it was called, a corps of environmental engineers aligned several heavy quarry rocks to help stem erosive tides. The barrier held the trappings of cast seaweed and blown debris. The public generally avoided the area, but on this night, a solitary figure stood waiting atop the rocks.

Collin Rutherford parked his black Porsche Boxster Spyder in a beach accessible lot and ambled along the wooden deck until he was out on the darkened beach. Even with the scotch flowing heavily through his veins, Collin easily found the dividing jetty. He stood under the starry night as the wind picked up and tussled his hair. He reached inside his coat pocket and pulled out a pack of cigarettes. He lit one and took a hit. The smoke streamed out of his mouth and quickly caught the wind over his shoulder.

"You alone?" The voice came from somewhere in the blackness surrounding him.

Collin took another drag and located the shadowy figure. "What the hell do you want?"

The Major moved off the rocks and closed in on Collin. "Argeaux wants more time, and I think it would be in your best interest."

"Shut your trap, Major. There is no more time to give. What has been set in motion, remains in motion. Tell the old bastard that."

The Major took another step closer, pulling a .44 Magnum revolver from his waistband. Collin sneered. "That will do you no good," he said. "My death means nothing, and you and Argeaux damn well know it."

11:36 PM

Tyler and Chloe moved inside the Lucky Shark and sat at the bar. It was almost midnight, and the place was packed. Robbie had excused himself earlier in respect of the three's-a-crowd rule.

The noise level of the Shark was extreme, and Tyler and Chloe had difficulty hearing each other. They decided to leave.

Poppa squeezed himself past the draught pulls and brought Tyler his change.

"Here you go, babe," he said and left the bills on the bar.

Tyler slid a couple in the tip jar and stuffed the rest in his pocket. "Thanks, Poppa. It was a great time. I really needed this."

"Always open for you, my friend."

Chloe stood up saying, "Yes. And it was very nice meeting you."

Poppa shuffled her way and took her hand. "The pleasure, darlin', was all mine." He kissed her hand and cocked his head wistfully. "Oh, if I were only thirty years younger and a hundred pounds lighter!"

Chloe laughed. "Goodnight, Poppa."

Once outside, Tyler stood tall and waited until Chloe joined him. Both said nothing for a few moments.

"So, I will see you at the docks around seven?" Tyler asked.

"Yeah, I have a few things I'll need to bring along, but I promise I won't take up too much room."

"Bring whatever you need. It should be fine."

"What about those hot spots I need to check? Will we be heading up river again?"

"That I won't know until the chief issues morning orders, but I'll eventually get you to the areas you need."

Chloe pushed the wind-blown strands of hair back from her face. "Okay. Sounds great. I'll see you in the morning then."

Tyler nervously rocked in his stance a bit as he watched her walking out into the lot. *She's getting away. Come up with something.*

"Uh, Chloe? Can I give you a ride home?" *Way to go, idiot. That didn't sound desperate at all.*

She kept walking. "No, thanks. I've got my van." She held up her keys.

Tyler jammed his hand into his cargo shorts pockets in defeat. *So close.*

Chloe stopped and turned back towards him. "Of course, you could always follow me. Make sure I get there safely. Is that within the permissives of the Galeegi Police?"

Tyler's eyes widened as did his famous smile. "As I said, Ms. Hart—at your service."

JUNE 7

Chloe reached inside the bungalow, flipped on the light, and walked in, throwing her van keys on the table. Tyler followed.

"Not bad," Tyler said, looking around. "It sure beats the hell outta the tiny apartment that I'm squeezed into."

"The agency is usually not so generous. We must have come into some extra funding from somewhere. After Katrina, I had to stay in a tent for two weeks while we tested the runoff in the waters of Lake Pontchartrain."

Tyler moved into the connected den. "Must be interesting work."

"Not all the time. But we look out for the environment, and that's a good thing," she said with pride as she headed to the kitchen. "Want a beer? I picked up a six pack this afternoon."

Tyler sat on the couch. "Yeah. Thanks."

Chloe grabbed two Amstel Lights and joined him on the couch. They clicked bottles. "Thanks for seeing me home," she said.

Both remained quiet for a few moments until Tyler said, "So tell me, how does one end up a research biologist for the EPA? Something you always wanted to do?"

Chloe kicked off her sandals and drew her legs up under her. "Well, I was always a bit of a science nerd, and I grew up in Florida, so we were outside a lot—usually on the water. I guess I just gravitated to it naturally. Got my B.S. from Miami and then my Ph.D. in marine science from William and Mary. The EPA came calling after that." She took a sip. "What about you? Why police work?"

Tyler smiled and put his bottle on the small acrylic-topped coffee table fashioned from an old ship's steering wheel. "Good question. I guess it's because I always admired my uncle. He's a cop—the chief of police here in Galeegi. He's always been a big part of my life. My dad died when I was young, and Uncle Fletcher stepped right in. He was at my side when they buried my father. He put his arm around me, I'll never forget that. He stood tall and strong and encouraged me to do the same.

"For several years, my mom and I lived in Asheville, North Carolina, up in the Smokies—my Mom is still there in fact; she's remarried now. But, when it was just the two of us, we would come back to Galeegi every summer and stay with Fletcher and my aunt Marie. It became a ritual. Ever since, I've loved these islands, the beaches, the warm weather..."

"... and the girls." Chloe added coyly.

Tyler smiled. "That too."

They talked for another hour and downed another beer each. Their conversation was light and harmonious, feeling each other out. They talked about nature and wildlife, the importance of conservation, and the need to protect the coast. Although she was a few years older than him, they had much in common. Both enjoyed hunting and fishing, surfing and swimming.

Then Chloe leaned toward him and said, "It must be awful with what's been happening lately. Rumors are flying around here. A possible serial killer? With some kind of axe maybe?"

Tyler took the last swallow of beer. "It's as horrible as it sounds. But we'll get him. We'll nail him before long." He focused on the bottle as thoughts of the murders resurfaced in his mind. He forced the images away and leaned back on the couch looking at Chloe instead. She smiled, twisting strands of her black hair around her finger.

God, she is so beautiful.

Chloe sensed the connection between them growing deeper. She thought about falling in love, and how easy it was to fall out of it. She knew passion often comes quickly, and true love rarely follows. She also remembered her fiancé, David, and their broken engagement, about the timing in such matters—so many things.

Chloe stood and moved in front of Tyler, reaching out for his hand and sliding her fingers next to his. Tyler looked deep into her blue eyes—his pulse quickening.

"Are you sure, Chloe?" he asked, barely above a whisper.

Chloe nodded and took a step back. She crossed her arms and reached down to the sides of her dress. In one swift move, she pulled the dress over her head and let it fall to the floor beside her. The lighting in the den was soft and cast long, striated shadows over her nude body.

Tyler rose and embraced her. He ran his strong hands up and down her back and felt her smooth skin and the curves of her body. He sensed her warm, excited breaths on his neck. Her racing heartbeat matched his. She lightly touched his face, angling it towards her. They kissed gently at first, then more deeply as all barriers melted away.

Chloe took Tyler's hand again and led him into the

adjoining bedroom. She backed him up against the foot of the bed and stripped off his shirt. Her hands felt their way down to his waist and in seconds had his shorts down around his feet. Tyler kicked them to the side and lifted her to meet him. She gave in freely to his strength, wrapping her legs tightly around him.

They fell on the bed, interlocked, and bound together in perfect motion. They were both young and strong and beautiful. There were no limits now. No boundaries. On this warm, summer night, Chloe and Tyler crossed over the threshold of intimacy and became one.

2:37 AM

Xevioso stood still inside the closet and watched through a crack in the door, making sure the young lovers were asleep. Standing there watching them make love heightened his excitement, but now he must do what he had come there to do. He would summon the ram, the power, the storm.

He eased the door open, commanding every ounce of his power and concentration. He stepped out god-like and approached the bed with slow assuredness. He spun the Oshe in his hands, finding the right grip, the right balance. He took one more step, bringing him to the bed. The couple lay naked and spent on the ruffled comforter. The woman rested her head on the man's chest. He would dispatch her with the first blow, the god's head, and then follow with the finish across her lover's chest. It would be swift, glorious justice.

Xevioso, his eyes enflamed, raised his arms above his head: The moment of truth had arrived. He brought the Oshe crashing down onto the bed. Blood, pain, and terror erupted like a seething volcano. Within seconds the slaughter was over. Xevioso stood over the blood-soaked scene. The screams had been quick, and their breathing had stopped. Xevioso heard only death's eternal silence.

6:47 AM

Fletcher Tate rose from behind his desk and went out into the station's Control Central. Robbie Cone sat at his desk nursing a slight hangover.

"Robbie? Have you seen Tyler this morning?"

Robbie straightened. "No, not yet, Chief. Want me to try his cell?"

"No, I'll give him five more minutes. The FBI wants us to continue our river patrols, and I wanted to get him to the boat as soon as possible. I sure hope he didn't oversleep."

Robbie nodded and turned back to his desk. He thought about last night—Tyler talking to that beautiful woman—and grinned.

Tate returned to his office and took a look at a topographical map of the Galeegi Islands sprawled out on his desk. There were two other islands in the same vicinity and with enough shared history to be considered part of the chain: Amoyeli the barrier island to the south and the much smaller St. Agnes nestled against Galeegi's northern shore. He used a red felt-tip pen to mark the exact locations where each attack occurred. He traced a line between all three attacks and measured various points of entry to the island from each site. The most logical theory was that the killer was from Amoyeli, but Tate's instincts told him that may not necessarily be the case. There were numerous ways the attacker could have approached and escaped the island without detection. There were a myriad of inlets and drudged marsh trails that would allow the killer to come and go as he pleased.

Tate leaned back in his chair and tapped his pen on the desk. He thought about what Johnson had said to him, about how they were there to protect Galeegi only. *But what if this disease begins to spread? What if this madman comes to our shores?* Tate brought his chair forward and rubbed his chin. *What if he's already here?*

Tate's private line on his desk phone rang. The chief hesitated before grabbing the receiver and punching the line.

"Fletcher Tate," he said and then listened for a few moments.

"What? Are you sure?" Tate slowly rose from his desk. "Both of them? Jesus Christ!" He listened some more and then, "Yes. Yes, of course." He hung up the phone and stepped from behind his desk. "Robbie! Get in here!"

Wide-eyed, Robbie poked his head in the doorway. "Yeah, Chief?"

Tate grabbed his sidearm from his desk's pull drawer. "There've been two more murders. I've got to go."

"What? Two more?" He paused as Tate continued to gather his things. "Should I stay here? Wait for Tyler?"

"Wait for me for what?" Tyler said as he suddenly appeared behind Robbie.

Tate looked up at his nephew. "A couple was killed in their home on Amoyeli last night. Same M.O. as the others."

"Do you need me to come with you?" Tyler asked.

"No. Get to your patrol on the river." Tate said. "There are over a hundred cops and guardsmen searching the island now. If that bastard is running, he may be coming this way."

9:21 AM

Fletcher Tate hopped off the boat and onto the dock at Amoyeli. The shy, forgotten island had changed overnight. National Guard troops, heavy-handed and heavily armed, lined the shore as UH-60 Blackhawk helicopters flew overhead. For Tate, it felt like Vietnam all over again. Lasting images he could do without.

A military jeep waited for him at the end of the dock. A man in camouflage fatigues came up to greet him.

"Chief Tate? Lieutenant Brantly Fender, 202nd Transportation Company, S.C. Army National Guard, Beaufort. I'm here to escort you to the latest crime scene."

Tate acknowledged the guardsman and hopped into the jeep. Within ten minutes they arrived at East Cove, the most populated area on Amoyeli. Several unnamed roads cut a checkerboard pattern into a wide field— cornered by small homes and trailers throughout. Tate took note that each house had some form of blue painted on the door, boxing or windows. He recalled that many in the Gullah culture painted the blue colors on their homes, so the evil spirits, or *haints* as they were sometimes known, would be fooled into thinking it was the sky or perhaps even heaven—and evil spirits didn't want a thing to do with heaven. It was a superstitious custom that had been a part of these islands for years.

A large contingency of troops and policemen gathered in front of a simple block home in the far end of the field. In the center of the group and still wearing his white Oxford shirt and striped tie, Special Agent Kasko stood in command. He was unclean, unshaven, but he was still very much the man in charge.

"Chief Tate," Kasko said. "I'm afraid our killer has struck again."

"They told me on the phone there are two more victims."

"Yes, a young couple in their home. Another blood bath. I'd like to hear your opinion after you've taken a look."

A sudden thumping noise drew everyone's attention. A Huey transport helicopter broke through the morning clouds, circled the cove, and then landed in an open area next to the house. The vibrations of the propellers pounded in the lawmen's chests.

Kasko kept his focus trained on the copter's cargo door as it opened. A tall, black woman emerged. Aided by a guardsman, she came from under the forceful, rotating blades. She wore the traditional West African garb of *gelede* head wrap; *buba* shirt; *iro* wrap skirt—all in a matching leopard style print. She kept her hand atop the gelede until she was well clear of the stirred air. Kasko greeted her. "Dr. Chabari, I'm Special Agent Kasko of the FBI. We're glad you're here."

Dr. Yolanda Chabari looked at the gathered force and frowned. "I'm not so sure I can say the same, Agent Kasko," she returned in her heavy island accent.

"Yes, I understand. But we were hoping you might be able to help in our investigation. We could use someone with your expertise."

"Amoyeli was my home many years ago, Agent Kasko. I will do whatever is needed to bring peace and stability back to my island and my people."

Kasko cut his eyes toward the house. "We'd like you to take a look inside the house first. But I have to warn you, nothing's been touched since the bodies were discovered. The blood—the mess—it can be a bit overwhelming."

Chabari looked past the FBI agent and walked into the house. She passed directly to the back bedroom. Kasko and Tate followed. SLED's Howard Dupree, Sheriff Dan Sheridan, and several forensic analysts stood quietly inside.

The bodies had not been moved. The woman was turned over on her stomach, half off the bed—her chest pressed against the bloodstained far wall. She had her left arm stretched toward the ceiling as if she was trying to crawl away from the madness. The man remained on the flat of his back, his arms by his side. He would still appear to be asleep if not for the deep, open gash running across his chest.

Chabari gasped. Kasko moved in behind the doctor, quietly watching her reaction. "Dr. Chabari, are you all right?"

She nodded. "And these two murders make nine all together?" she asked in a weak voice.

"Yes, nine bodies so far." Kasko moved past her and pointed toward the wall behind the headboard. "This is where we need your help, Doctor. We were hoping that as head of the department of African Studies at the University of South Carolina and with your connection to Amoyeli, you may be able to help explain this."

It was the same image from before—drawn in blood—but this time on a much larger scale. Chabari took a deep breath and pulled herself together to evaluate the depiction—as hideous as it was. She removed glasses from a fold in her garment and got very close.

"We've asked others what it means, other islanders, but no one will say."

She nodded slowly. "And they never will, Agent Kasko."

10:45 AM

Tyler kept the police scanner on in the Contender, monitoring the back-and-forth messages of the island's task force. The main buzz was about the suspect's uncanny ability to avoid detection. He left no tracks, prints, or any other indicator of how he managed to get in and out unnoticed. The callers used words like *vanished*, *ghost*, and *phantom* throughout the rapid-fire conversations.

And the task force had spied nothing on the waterways—ocean and river watches all reporting in. Tyler could testify to that. He had made the circle from the marina to Poston's Landing twice already and saw nothing but police craft on patrol. It would have made for an unbearable assignment if not for his passenger keeping him company.

Chloe sat just beyond the Contender's console. She had her hair pulled back into a ponytail and wore a green ball cap with the Miami Hurricanes' "U" emblazoned in orange and white across the front. To her credit, she sat quietly throughout his patrol, only periodically glancing behind her. She had her gear packed at her feet, but she knew full well that at any moment her work for the EPA might have to be scrubbed. It was only due to Chief Tate's reluctant 'okay' that she was even allowed on the boat.

Tyler maintained a diligent watch. He had admonished Chloe about the potential dangers involved and hinted that perhaps she should not go. But she never hesitated in her decision—and for that, he was secretly glad. Her courage was one of her many qualities that he admired.

As they motored down the river, he looked at her from behind the wheel. She had her head slightly bent forward reading a journal. He admired the shape of her neck and the perfect lines of her profile. She had pulled her right leg up on the seat and casually rested her arm on her knee. She flexed her toes up and down as if keeping time to some unknown beat. Her toenails were painted the same fiery red as her fingers.

Tyler's attraction to her was growing stronger, and he had to discipline himself not to fall too fast. But with every second they shared, he found it more and more difficult. Tyler had known other beautiful women and had been with quite a few through the years. But she was different. He knew it. He could tell. This one was something special.

11:56 AM

Yolanda Chabari stood outside the house where the most recent murders had been committed. The midday sun burned through the heavy white clouds and sizzled at her plum-black skin. She spoke as the sweating policemen encircled her.

"Xevioso is the Vodun sky god, the god of thunder. He is a powerful loa, known for bringing swift justice to those who have committed certain wrongs or who have wronged his disciples. He often dispatches the evil-doers with the Oshe, the double-headed battle axe that was used in there."

"Wait a minute," Kasko said. "Did you say Vodun? As in voodoo?"

"Yes. It has many pronunciations and spellings, but most of the English-speaking world knows it as voodoo. But probably not like what you are thinking. Vodun is a polytheistic religion born in West Africa. It was, and at times still is, practiced throughout the coastal territory from Ghana to Nigeria. It has a distinct history, unlike the other animistic religions practiced in these countries. It has less to do with the occult practices one sees in Haiti or even southern Louisiana. When used in connection with the official beliefs, the word voodoo can refer to the many different spirits within the Vodun religion itself."

"But as I always understood it," Tate said. "The people of this island believed in hoodoo, a harmless, Christian-based faith that borrowed only a few elements from voodoo. They believe in simple conjuring and root magic. Not this."

"Yes. Amoyeli's religion, like our language, like our customs, is a harsh blend; a syncretism of several separate cultural traditions," Chabari answered. "The African roots of our ancestors were stolen many years ago and replaced with what our slave masters allowed. We held on to very little from our mother countries."

"Well, apparently, somebody held on to it just a little more strongly than most," Kasko said. "And you say that drawing in there is the mark of this Xevioso?"

"Yes. The drawing is what the Vodun priests call a

veve. This one is the symbol of the ram. The flares coming out of the top, as you described them, are the horns of the ram. The open mouth of the ram indicates that Xevioso is engaged in seeking justice—the power of Xevioso, the storm, the Oshe is depicted as coming out of the mouth. The people of Amoyeli may be far removed from the true Vodun religion, but they know well not to speak his name or interfere while he administers justice."

"Hammie Swantou, a root doctor here on the island, said something about Xevioso 'swallowing the Igbo whole.' What did he mean by that?" Kasko asked.

Chabari smiled her acknowledgement. "We are Igbo—all of us here on Amoyeli. We are descendants of the Igbo tribe in West Nigeria. Like our Sierra Leone brothers on nearby St. Helena Island, our ancestors led a common track here after being taken from our homes." She paused and pointed at the house. "He means that we will all be punished. All the Igbo will fall victim to his wrath."

Kasko took a quick look at Dupree. "Seems our Mr. Swantou knew more about this than I realized. Maybe we should have another talk with him."

Chabari moved in front of Kasko. "I know Hammie Swantou. I have known him for many years. He is a brave man. He only speaks to you because the others will not. He has been gifted the ability to conjure. However, he knows only of Xevioso's presence. I feel certain he has told you everything that he knows."

"His presence? But, Doctor, surely he nor you nor these people actually believe that an African god has come to Amoyeli to punish the wicked?" Kasko said. "That's just crazy talk."

Chabari bristled at the agent's comments. "Not crazy, Agent Kasko. A belief system is in place here—a conviction. Many believe the spirit works within others. This is not only a direct tenet of Vodun but of the Christian religion, as well."

"Yeah, well, not that I've been to Sunday school in a while, but I don't remember Jesus taking an axe to the chests of those who broke the Ten Commandments," Kasko said smugly.

"Perhaps not directly, but don't be naïve about Christians punishing and killing others in His name. And they too thought they were doing the right thing—with His guidance."

"So, it's your supposition, Doctor, that someone is punishing the islanders here in the name, if not the embodied spirit, of Xevioso?"

"Yes, Agent Kasko. That is exactly my belief."

"And what then is this great sin that was committed on Amoyeli? Why has this thunder god chosen now to punish these people?"

"I do not have an answer to that. But I will remain on this island until I do." Chabari leaned into Kasko's ear and whispered, "Believe me; I want this stopped as much as you—if not more so."

2:16 PM

Tyler leaned over the port side of the Contender and cupped a handful of the Galeegi's swirling black water, splashing it up on his face and chest. The ninety-eight-degree high and the sudden stillness of the marsh area drained him. He had pulled the boat onto a sandbar not too far from the estuary where he first met Chloe.

She had jumped out and began using an enzymatic test kit to sample sand and water. She carefully placed her findings into marked tubes and bags.

Tyler watched her with interest for a bit before he called out over the rail, "Are you hungry?"

Chloe stood up and looked back to the boat. "I'm okay. I brought some granola bars if you need something. They're in my backpack."

Tyler held up four of the wrappers. "Yeah, I know."

Chloe smiled. "Tell you what: When your shift ends and if everything goes smoothly today, I'll take you out to dinner tonight. How does that sound?"

"Sounds good. What do you have in mind?"

"Seafood, of course. Do you know a good place?"

"Seafood? Here at the beach? I dunno, Chloe. Sounds like a tough order to me."

Chloe smiled again. She adjusted her hat and bent down, getting back to work. Tyler leaned back in the captain's chair and propped his feet up on the console. He took out his binoculars and followed the horizon on the southwest side of the river back towards Amoyeli. It was a heavy marsh area filled with tall cattails and brown panicum sea grass. Several small cuts had been made through the marsh, which gave the islanders access to the river. Tyler rose to his feet as he caught sight of an old wooden rowboat making its way down one of the twisty waterways.

"Chloe, I need to check something out. Think you can suspend your investigation for a second?"

Chloe did not hesitate as she collected her work and immediately pulled herself back on board. "What's up?"

"Probably nothing. But I can see an unauthorized

boat making its way through the marsh. I'll need to check it out."

Chloe took her seat as Tyler fired the engines. After reaching the target area, he cut the engines again and drifted into the open inlet. He took out the reach pole and worked his way into the shallow, muddy waters. The creek had many short, twisting turns that caused Tyler to struggle with the navigation.

Chloe did not notice his plight as she sat mesmerized by the beauty of the marsh. She marveled at the varying Spartina grasses that sprang up so close to one another. Some reached enormous heights. A jagged oyster bed rose up out of the murky water and stood solid and white against the green and golden grasses. She counted seven different species of bird nesting in those grasses and many others in flight. She even spotted a coastal mink scurrying along the muddy banks looking for shellfish. None of this was unusual for these marshes, but it made Chloe happy to witness nonetheless.

Then as Tyler pushed around the next bend, something totally unexpected came into view.

3:07 PM

Special Agent Miller Kasko sat at an old wooden power line spool that substituted as a yard table behind the home of the murdered couple. With the overbearing heat reaching its daily peak, the table was strategically placed under a large, shade-producing live oak that served as a boundary line with the neighbors.

Two fellow FBI agents—Donald Lockwood, a heavyset older forensics investigator, and Mario Heyward, a young, black, surveillance officer—joined Kasko at the table. The men had dispatched their coats and ties; their sweat-stained shirts were rolled up to mid-arm.

"It was another clean hit," Lockwood said. "We've done every conceivable test, and we can't find a thing. No prints of any kind. Initial tests on the bodies included. We'll need to prep them and then send them over to the Colleton Medical Center. Sanders, our Medical Examiner from Atlanta, is there. He should be able tell us more."

"Well, how the hell does he do it, Lockwood? How does he go from place to place without being seen? How does he do so much damage and paint these blood tattoos without leaving a trace of DNA for us to pick up on? And if you say he's a ghost or a phantom, I'm gonna shove my fist down your throat."

"No, sir. But he is, well, elusive."

Kasko gave up, a disappointed look crossing his face. He turned to Heyward. "What about Swantou?"

Heyward shrugged. "Besides the one time he went outside to whack one of his chickens, he's remained holed up inside his trailer. He has no computer, television, radio, cell phone, or even a land line. He just sits in there and talks to his crazy ass self. Hardly seems like the type to do this kind of damage though."

"Yes, but talking crazy and executing chickens make him the closest thing to a suspect right now. Have your men stay on him, Heyward. He's the only one who called this Xevioso by name and knew that he would strike again. I sure as hell don't think someone can come up with that simply by looking at chicken guts."

"Yes, sir."

Fletcher Tate ambled up to the shady oak. "Agent Kasko, I'm going to head back to Galeegi. I've got other work to do, and I don't think I can be of any more help to you here."

"Keep a tight lid on your island, Chief. And maintain your river patrols for now."

Tate wearily saluted and turned to leave. He made it half way across the yard when his phone rang out. He continued walking as he looked at the caller I.D.

"Chief Tate. That you, Ty?"

"Yes, sir. I have a situation to report."

"What's happening?"

"Some of the islanders are trying to leave. Caught a boatload of 'em trying to row through the marsh."

"No one leaves Amoyeli. That's FBI orders. You'll need to turn them around."

"Yes, sir, but that may be a problem."

"Why? What do you mean?"

"Well...because we're in a bit of a standoff, sir. One is holding a shotgun right now—and it's aimed right at my head."

3:15 PM

Tyler stood in a power stance behind the wheel of the Contender. He had his Glock 22 in his right hand pointed at the shotgun-wielding islander. He held his cell phone in his left hand—his uncle Fletcher still on the line. Chloe hugged the bottom of the Contender at Tyler's request.

The wooden long boat was loaded down with eight islanders and personal belongings. There were four women, two children, and two men. They remained seated, unafraid of Tyler's weapon. They had more to lose by staying, and Tyler quickly realized this.

130

"Chief, I don't think I will be able to talk them into returning. They seem hell-bent on leaving."

"They can't leave, Ty. It'll just make it worse for them if the FBI thinks they're running. Better explain it to them somehow. Give me your location. I'll send a chopper. Be there in a few minutes."

"No. That won't be necessary. That may set them off. I'll handle this," Tyler said, ending the call. He slipped the phone into his pocket and then slowly holstered his weapon. He kept his hands in the air and walked to the front of the Contender—the barrel of the shotgun now inches away. "My name is Patrolman Miles. I'm with the Galeegi Police." He paused, taking in their worried, but determined, faces. "I understand why you want to leave. I know there have been some terrible things happening on your island. But it really is in your best interest for you to return. There are plenty of people there to protect you now. National Guard troops, sheriff's deputies, FBI."

The shotgun did not budge. Tyler turned briefly and saw Chloe's worried look. She stared up at him, shaking her head, helpless. Tyler knew he had to do something. He turned back to the islanders.

"You do not need to be afraid. I am Tyler. I have come to stop...the ram," he said. He felt foolish saying the words, but he knew he had to say them and say them with conviction. "I will stop the storm. I will stop Xevioso, but I need your help. We must not allow him to see our fear. We must work together—Galeegi and Amoyeli. We must work together to end the punishment. It is the only way. But first, you must show Xevioso you are not afraid. You must return to Amoyeli."

Chloe slowly rose from her position and looked to the

wooden boat. The islanders now glanced subtly at one another. The man holding the shotgun receded from the bow and lowered his weapon. He turned and briefly whispered to the others—hurried and unintelligible to Tyler and Chloe's ears. A woman seated in the middle grabbed the oars and rowed the boat away. They pulled back up the inlet and headed home.

Chloe joined Tyler in the bow. She put her hand on his back as they watched the boat disappear beyond a turn. She kissed Tyler on his cheek in relief and leaned onto his shoulder. "This situation really is getting out of hand, isn't it?"

"This needs to end soon. Or that whole island is gonna explode," Tyler said.

He broke away from Chloe's embrace and retrieved the reach pole. As he dug at the mud and black water pushing them back into the river, he had no idea how prophetically close his words would turn out to be.

7:25 PM

Tyler returned to his apartment, showered, changed into his favorite aqua green button down and khakis and drove over to Chloe's. He pulled his Ranger back into the driveway of the bungalow. He looked and felt refreshed, eager for their dinner date.

He hopped out of the truck and made it quickly up the steps with three giant strides. Two quick knocks later, Chloe appeared at the door. She was as radiant as ever. She had on another sporty, summer dress—black, mid-thigh hem. Her hair was again long and full, spilling over her shoulders and down her back. She smiled at Tyler. "Well, you certainly clean up nice."

"Amazing what a little soap and hot water can do," he said. "And may I say that's another great dress. Who knew a little trip down a winding, black river required such an extensive wardrobe?"

Chloe ran her hand behind his neck. "Like I told you before, Patrolman Miles, it's always best to be prepared." She kissed him warmly.

Minutes later, they were in Tyler's truck heading down Old Safari Road. "You never did say where you're taking me tonight," Chloe stated.

"Cotton-N-Gin. It's an upscale restaurant on the mainland—close to the Argeaux Bridge. I managed to sneak in a reservation for eight o'clock."

"Good seafood?"

Tyler nodded enthusiastically. "My uncle used to take me there on special occasions. They have the best shrimp and grits you've ever tasted in your life."

"I hope it's not too pricey. I mean we are just two public servants, after all."

"Don't worry. I've got it tonight, Chloe," Tyler said. He looked out the driver's window at the day's dying sunlight. "Overtime pay may be the only good thing to come out of this long, hellish week."

The Cotton-N-Gin Restaurant was constructed out of a defunct cotton gin that belonged to the Argeaux family generations before. It sat adjacent to an old depot where, for over a hundred years, trains hauled the island crop to the seaports of Charleston and Savannah.

As a five star restaurant, it served the island's well-to-do inhabitants and the occasional lucky visitor. The gin's original massive wooden beams ran exposed throughout the restaurant's main dining facility. Faux cotton bales hung from hooks tied to those beams as part of its realistic antebellum atmosphere. The restaurant walls sported murals of dark figures toiling in sunlit cotton fields. And management had cleverly constructed a cigar and brandy bar at the front of the restaurant under the old gin's enormous bale loft.

Tyler and Chloe sat at one of many small, round tables dotted around a roped-off power loom, many years gone since pruning out its last cottonseed. They neared the end of a bottle of Grgich Hills Chardonnay, ordered to complement their dinner of pan-seared tilapia, served in a sherry-based sauce and topped with lump crabmeat. Chloe edged the last of her saffron rice onto her fork. "Well, you were right about this restaurant. This was excellent."

"Yeah, good as advertised." Tyler paused as he drained his wine. "Of course, I might have said the same about a fish sandwich from McDonald's, I was so starved."

Chloe laughed. "I see we can add discriminating connoisseur of fine foods to your résumé as well, Mr. Miles."

"Don't poke fun, Ms. Hart. It's not every man who can claim to appreciate a king's and a pauper's menu."

Chloe smiled again, raising her glass towards him. His give-and-take wit had once again left her impressed. She took a quick sip before taking a more solemn tone. "Tyler, I'm really worried about those islanders. They were so desperate to get out."

"They're protected now, Chloe. There is one law enforcement officer or National Guardsman for every five of the islanders. I don't see how anything could happen to them at this point. Last thing I heard was most were staying at the emergency shelter on Amoyeli until it's over with."

"But, beyond catching the guy, how will they know when it is safe again? I can't imagine what it would be like living there, always having to look over your shoulder. And certainly the FBI can't keep them there forever. I mean, there have to be legal issues involved in this as well. You can't keep an entire group of people on an island if they want to leave, can you?"

Tyler sighed. "That's a good point. The truth is, I have no idea how this is going to play out. The particulars of the case are just so strange."

"What are the particulars? I mean, if you can share them with me."

As Tyler sat there debating how much to tell her, his eyes drifted to the bar area. A figure moved out of the smoke and darkness of the bar, stared in their direction, then moved back into the shadows. It was brief, but it made Tyler slightly uncomfortable.

He dismissed it with a slight frown and refocused on Chloe. She leaned forward in her chair now, looking intently at him with her blue eyes. It was a look of connection—a look of care and trust. "Well, after we got off the river today, I reported in at the station. My uncle told me that an expert on Amoyeli's culture had been brought in. He said she thought the killings were a part of a religious ritual from their African heritage."

"How so?"

"I don't know everything, but in Vodun, their ancestral religion, there is this deity whom they call Xevioso, a god of the sky. Whoever has been doing the killing has been doing so as this sky god, using his ancient weapon, leaving his symbol on every victim, in their own blood."

"Jesus."

Tyler agreed with a nod. "He supposedly is killing those on Amoyeli for some sin they committed."

Chloe raised an eyebrow. "What sin?"

"Another good question. No one seems to know. These are simple, peaceful people, Chloe. I can't imagine what they could have done so wrong."

Chloe thought about it for a minute. "And how many people have been killed on the island so far?"

"Nine," Tyler said as he held up nine fingers. He lowered them to drum along the table. "Ten if you count Jaja."

"Jaja?"

Tyler blew out a deep breath. It was hard enough for him to keep up with all that had happened much less try to recount it to someone else. "Right before the first incident at the marina, we were called in to help investigate the suicide of this islander, Jaja. He was the new caretaker at the lighthouse on Amoyeli. But the thing is, neither my uncle nor I are convinced it was a suicide. It may have been staged just to look that way."

"Do you think he was murdered by this Xevioso?"

"Don't know, but get this: Jaja was the chief suspect in the murder of Katherine Argeaux back in 1968. Katherine was the daughter of Charles Argeaux, the wealthy industrialist whose family virtually owns Galeegi."

Chloe hurriedly took the last sip of her wine, "Yes, I certainly know of Charles Argeaux. Despite his reputation as a hardass, he's actually a big time environmentalist. He serves on many of the clean water and clean marsh committees here in South Carolina. It was his influence that got the EPA into yearly testing of your local river. He's probably the reason why I'm here today."

"Small world, huh?" Tyler said with a grin.

She smiled back. "Actually it's a huge world with huge problems, and sometimes those problems shrink our world connections, and we end up with odd partnerships—like Argeaux and the EPA. It's not always easy making deals with the devil, so to speak, but that's the reality of it." She paused, frowning. "So, what happens next, Tyler? What do the police intend to do?"

Tyler was about to give his standard "don't know" answer when he noticed the man step out of the shadows again. He hovered just beyond the bar's entrance, obviously staring at them as before. "Excuse me for a second, Chloe."

Tyler hopped up and crossed the room at a steady pace toward the man who again receded into the darkness. Tyler entered the smoke-filled room. It was an old-world, full leather and mahogany style bar, lit with a soft golden light. As he scanned the interior, he noted three couples sitting at small tables. His target was alone, leaning against the plush-rimmed serving bar. The man had a drink in front of him and was lighting a cigarette. Tyler stood next to him and stared.

"Can I help you?" the man finally asked, blowing blue smoke at Tyler.

"Patrolman Tyler Miles, Galeegi Police."

The man made a rolling motion with his hand. "Whoop-de-fucking-doo. Can I help you, Patrolman?"

"No, I was wondering if I could help you. I noticed you were staring out into the restaurant. You seemed to be eyeing my table."

The man lifted his face in mock surprise and put his cigarette hand to his chest. "Is that a problem?"

Tyler shrugged. "No. Not if you can tell me why."

The man faked a smile as his eyes took in all of Tyler. "Well, perhaps I was captivated by your handsome face and rock-hard physique, Patrolman." He rubbed his free hand down the sleeve of Tyler's shirt. "After all, I'm sure this isn't the first time you've had an admirer."

Tyler shook his head. "No, just the first time I didn't care to admire back."

The man made a pouty face. "Aw, am I not your type, Patrolman?"

"My type? No, I doubt you're even my species. From now on, you'd better just stick to the bar. Got it?" Tyler turned and walked back into the restaurant.

The bartender in a gold vest and tie walked up to the man. "Another scotch, Mr. Rutherford?"

Collin Rutherford nodded. "Yeah. And keep 'em coming."

9:27 PM

Agent Kasko followed up the path of Wachasee Hill behind Manu Ando. The bow-legged constable's flashlight streamed ahead of them. The night sky colored the hill a dark blue and provided definition to the surrounding tree line. Once at the top, Kasko moved past the foundation of the old church and peered over the far side.

"This is it?" Kasko asked.

"Yes, this Wachasee Hill. East Cove beneath us, where most of my peoples live."

"Not much of a hill though, is it?"

Manu shrugged. "Amoyeli is an island, Mistah Kasko. Maybe you want yo' men to spy on my peoples from a palm tree instead."

Kasko frowned. "Not spying Mr. Ando, observing. Keeping track. We have some rather sophisticated instruments we can use up here. With the infrared capability, we can make sure no one comes or goes from East Cove without us knowing. At any rate, it beats the hell outta surveying with the naked eye."

Manu said nothing, unimpressed with the FBI's techno-capabilities. Kasko turned back to observe the church and connected graveyard. "I imagine this place is somewhat hallowed ground."

Manu grinned. "Yes. This where the first church was built after slavery times. Many of our peoples still choose to be buried here."

He shined the light on one of the headstones and tapped his chest. "My momma." He continued to scan. "My uncle—he here somewhere."

Kasko walked closer to the graves and knelt down in front of a newer-looking headstone, which was set off from the others. He ran his finger across the inscription as Manu held the light on it. "It just says: Roger. Died 1982. How about this one? Know him?"

Manu paused for a long time—to the point where Kasko turned back to look at him. "Yes, Mistah Kasko. Roger was caretaker of the Amoyeli Lighthouse for many years."

"Caretaker of the lighthouse? Wasn't the man who killed himself the other day the caretaker also?"

Again Manu did a slow nod, carefully choosing his words. "Yes. Jaja Nayu." He pointed at the headstone. "This was Jaja's grandfather."

10:01 PM

It was a cloudless, star-filled night on Galeegi. A slight ocean breeze came in to squeeze out the night's warm, humid air. Tyler and Chloe arrived back at the bungalow. They walked hand in hand slowly up the steps. The dark palms framing the porch swayed slightly in the wind.

"Everything okay?" Chloe asked. "You seem a little quiet."

"No, I'm fine. My mind is just spinning, I guess. Everything we talked about. Sometimes it's just hard to put it behind me."

Chloe stopped him on the front deck of the cottage and turned him to face her. She ran her fingernails up and down his back. She then rocked up on her toes and placed her mouth to within an inch of his. "Maybe this will help." She pressed her lips against his—her tongue finding its way. Tyler held her close. The pressures of the world instantly melted away.

They broke from the long kiss. Chloe glanced beyond his shoulder and suddenly pulled back. "Tyler! The front door! Look!"

Tyler wheeled around and saw the slight gap between the door and the frame. "Did you forget to lock it?"

"No. I remember locking it. I always lock it."

Tyler knelt next to the door and ran his finger along the frame.

He felt a heavy indention near the lock catch. "It's been jimmied," he whispered.

A thumping noise came from within. Tyler and Chloe looked at each other. He put his finger to his lips and then ushered her quickly back down the steps. Tyler opened the passenger door of his truck and helped her slide in. He leaned over her and retrieved his Glock from the locked middle console. He handed Chloe his cell phone. "Hit two on the speed dial. That's the station. Tell them what's going on."

"Wait. What are you going to do?"

"I'm going to check it out. Stay here. Keep the door locked." He handed her the truck keys. "But if something goes down, get the hell outta here." He carefully closed the door and headed back to the cottage.

Tyler held the Glock with both hands as he ascended the stairs. He went to the door and pushed it open. The inside was dark—lit only by a light over the kitchen sink. He moved into the room, taking slow, methodical steps. It was difficult to see, but he made out strewn materials all over the den floor. He heard the thumping noise again—this time coming from Chloe's bedroom.

Tyler backed up against the den wall and moved stealthily toward the bedroom. His heart pounded. He tried to focus and stay true to his training, but it was just as his instructors had warned him—the intensity of Academy scenarios failed in comparison to this real-life situation.

As he inched closer, he heard someone in the bedroom rifling through drawers. He took another step, and the old oak floorboards of the bungalow squeaked beneath him.

The noise coming from the bedroom stopped. The house became completely still. Tyler sucked in a breath, blood pulsating in his ears. He made up his mind to make the first move and rush the room. As he took the initial lunge, a thunderous blast, followed instantly by a flash of white light, knocked him away from the wall. Bits of sheetrock and wood rained down on him, and he felt an immediate searing pain in his left shoulder. Tyler stumbled, almost dropping to the floor. He felt a burning sensation, like a streak of fire racing down his back.

A blurry mass ran towards him in the darkness. Tyler pivoted and fired the Glock in the blur's direction. The runner slammed into Tyler, knocking him onto his injured back. Tyler shook off the stun of the fall and raised his chest to fire again, but the intruder was out the front door.

Tyler struggled to his feet as his shoulder wound leaked blood. He was stumbling to the front door when he heard another blast outside the house.

Chloe!

Tyler scrambled onto the front deck. He took short breaths as he held his weapon at chest level, scanning the darkness. He made it to the steps and looked down at his Ford Ranger. The intruder was gone, but the damage was done. A gaping hole remained where the passenger side window had once been. Tyler's shoulders slumped at the mere thought of what he might find, but he kept his gun raised and approached with caution. Tyler peered into the hole. He saw Chloe lying face down on the middle console, shards of glass over her back.

"Chloe?" Tyler saw her head turn slightly. He reached in, pulled the lock and opened the door. "Chloe, are you okay?"

"Yeah. I think so," she responded in a shaky voice. She sat up, careful not to let the glass cut her. "He saw me sitting here. I ducked when he pointed the gun at me."

Tyler leaned in and helped to pull her out. "Are you hurt?"

Chloe stood next to the Ranger brushing the small glass pieces from her dress. "Just some cuts, but I'm okay." She noticed the blood seeping through Tyler's shirt. "Tyler, you're bleeding! Are you okay?"

"He got my shoulder, but I'll live." He changed the subject. "Did you get a good look at him?"

"Too dark. It happened so fast. What was he doing in there? What could he possibly want?"

"I don't know," Tyler said, glancing at the cottage, "At least, not yet."

JUNE 8

Tyler sat on a cold examination table at Colleton Medical Center. He was shirtless, and his left shoulder was wrapped in white bandages. Aunt Marie, in jeans and a burgundy College of Charleston t-shirt, sat on a stool at the end of the table.

"You need anything, Ty? Coke or something?" Marie asked.

"No, thanks." He winced as he rolled his wounded shoulder. "Might could use something a little stronger later."

Marie attempted a smile. She got up and moved in front of him. "Ty, are you sure about all this?"

"About what?"

"You know, about being a cop. About doing this kind of work."

Tyler slowly blinked his tired eyes. "You worried about me, Marie?"

"Of course I worry about you, Ty." She ran her fingers through his hair. "I love you, Bud. You know that. And it's not that I don't think you can't do this. It's just this world is getting so crazy. I mean this past week has been something out of a nightmare. It's nothing like what we're used to on our sleepy little island."

"Think I should quit?"

She hesitated and then said, "You're so darn smart, Ty. I'd hate to see somebody with your potential gunned down by some punk robbing a beach house. That's all."

"What about Uncle Fletcher? How come you don't worry so much about him?"

Marie's eyes instantly watered, and she bit down on her thumbnail. "I do," she whispered. "It's just..."

Tyler squint his eyes, a bit puzzled. "It's just what?"

Marie shook her head. "I don't know. It's so hard to read him lately."

"What do you mean?"

A tear ran down her cheek.

Tyler reached out and held Marie by her wrist. "Marie, I'm sorry. I didn't mean..."

Someone knocked on the examination room door. Marie turned away as the door swung open. Tate and Chloe entered.

"Well, there's the walking target himself," Tate said with a wink. "How're you feeling, Ty?"

Tyler glanced back at Marie and then smiled at his uncle. "Bullet just grazed off my shoulder. The doctor gave me some good painkillers, said I'll be fine. What did you guys find out? Anything stolen?"

Tate looked at Chloe as if giving her permission to tell. "Nothing stolen. But my laptop, my records, my equipment have all been destroyed."

"From your work on the Galeegi?" Tyler asked.

Chloe nodded. "Apparently someone had a problem with me checking the water quality of the river."

"You lost all your samples?"

"All except those I sent away from my first day on the river."

Tyler turned to his uncle. "What do you think, Chief? Sounds like an industrial backed job to me. Maybe we should check all the polluters up river. See who has the most to lose."

Tate frowned. "It's a federal case, Tyler. The EPA is sending a representative down sometime tomorrow to meet with Chloe, and I've already contacted the Bureau. They'll check any prints they find against the AFIS database. At any rate, we have our hands full with what's happening on Amoyeli. We'll help in any way we can, but ultimately it's another problem for the Feds."

Tate paused and looked at Marie. "I'm gonna take my wife home now. Try to get a little sleep. Chloe said she'd get you back to your place."

Tyler glanced at Chloe quickly and nodded, then turned to Marie. "Thanks for being here."

Marie managed a smile, leaned in, and kissed him on his forehead. "We will always be here for you."

"Take a few days off, Ty," Tate said. "Rest up. If I need you, I'll call. Okay?"

"Yes, sir," Tyler said. He acknowledged them with a slight wave as they walked out.

As soon as the door closed, Chloe moved next to the table and pressed herself up against Tyler, forcing his legs apart. She leaned her forehead against his. "Are you sure you're all right?"

"I'll be okay, Chloe. What about you?"

"Confused—scared—but I'll be okay, too." She leaned back, looking at him with a sudden realization. "But I really don't want to stay at the bungalow tonight. Can I stay over at your place?"

Tyler smiled and gave her a kiss. "How many times do I have to say it, Ms. Hart? As always, at your service."

7:47 AM

Sheriff Dan Sheridan and two National Guardsmen,

Billy Hicks and Lorenzo Rodriguez, were out on morning foot patrol, making house-to-house safety checks on Amoyeli. Hicks and Rodriguez were twenty-year veterans of the Guard, both having done police tours in Iraq and both having specialized in this type of neighborhood patrol.

Most of Amoyeli's shacks and trailers were vacated as their occupants had moved to the island's shelter. The few holdouts seemed untrusting of the protective forces and only glared at them from behind closed windows or doors.

Sheridan held up a crudely drawn map in one hand for the guardsmen to see and pointed with the other. "There's a little shack at the end of this road, gentlemen. We'll check it and then circle through the backyard, hit the beach area and come back up through Crossing Cut. That'll cover all the houses we need to verify this morning."

"Sounds like a plan," Hicks said.

"Whatever gets us through the patrol the quickest, I'm all for it," Rodriguez added, already soaked in sweat.

They walked down the twisty dirt road as thousands of cicadas sounded the alarm of another hot, blistering day to come. They arrived at the tiny clapboard shanty with its sunken and rotted roof.

"You go first today," Hicks said to Rodriguez. The short, stocky guardsman nodded and cautiously approached. He knocked on the door. "National Guard. House check," he yelled out. He rubbed his neck, feeling the penetrating sun despite the surrounding mossy oaks. He knocked a second time. Again, no reply. He rattled the locked door. "Perhaps they've gone to the shelter," he said, turning back to the others.

Sheridan held up his clipboard and ran his finger down the names. "They were not signed in at the shelter as of last night. O-no-ga and Nik-e-chi Ok-o-ro or something like that. An elderly couple if I remember correctly. I had this route yesterday."

"Maybe they're still asleep," Hicks said.

"Or hiding," Rodriguez added.

Sheridan squinted at the house as if he had the power to see through it. "I'll check around back. See if I can get a look inside." He walked around to the side and disappeared behind the house.

Hicks stared up and down at the old place and then out into the yard. "Wonder what they'll be serving us for lunch today?"

Rodriguez chuckled. "Probably shit-on-a-stick like yesterday. I mean we had better chow in the desert."

"Hicks! Rodriquez!" Sheridan yelled. Both men reached for their pistols and took off behind the house. They quickly met Sheridan around back. The sheriff was backing up, grabbing at his call-mike pinned to his shirt. "This is one-ten! We got a situation down here." Sheridan yelled into the mike.

Hicks and Rodriquez saw it too and came to a dead stop. On the wall of the back of the house was Xevioso's symbol. Freshly painted in blood, the detailed artwork dripped down the faded clapboards.

9:21 AM

Tyler stood alone in his tiny kitchen—his eye on the dripping coffeemaker. He wore only his boxers; his hair the definition of bedhead. He rolled his bandaged shoulder every few minutes, wincing with each twist of muscle and pull of adhesive on skin. The pain was excruciating, but he had popped additional Percocet and would soon feel its pharmaceutical magic.

Tyler rolled over in his mind all that had happened: the suspicious suicide involving the lead suspect in one of the most controversial cases in Galeegi's history, the serial killer with a god complex on the loose, the break-in and his shoulder wound, the mind-reading root doctor, dangerous river patrols, a tyrannical sergeant, defiant islanders, and the list kept on growing. And it was all definitely bad—wave after wave of negativity. All negative except one.

"Good morning." Chloe stood in the doorway wearing only his police academy sweatshirt.

Tyler flashed a smile.

She spread her arms out indicating the borrowed garment. "Hope you don't mind."

"Not at all. That old sweatshirt never looked better." He pointed at the coffee maker. "Would you like a cup?"

Chloe nodded as she tiptoed closer. "Caffeine is no substitute for sleep, but today it'll have to do."

As Tyler poured the coffee for her, she touched his back lightly. "How's the shoulder?"

"Like intense sunburn—as if I laid out on the sun itself."

Chloe smiled as she cradled her cup in both hands. "You were very brave last night."

Tyler chuckled. "Brave or foolish. There's a fine line between the two."

Chloe paused, drinking in the warmth of the coffee and the moment. She used her left index finger to push strands of her hair back behind her left ear. "So, what's your game plan today?"

"Fletcher wants me to lay low. I guess that's what I'll do," he said. "Feel like I need to be doing something though. I should be out on river patrol at least."

"I imagine they have it covered. Your uncle said last night you haven't had a day off since you started. You need time to relax."

Tyler nodded. "What about you? You're still meeting with the EPA, right?"

"Yeah, I'm meeting with our national water projects director at one o'clock. See what our next move will be."

"How long do you think it will take?"

Chloe shrugged her small shoulders. "No idea. I hope not too long."

"Maybe we can get back together this afternoon. I want to show you another one of my favorite places here on Galeegi. I think you'll love it."

"Sounds intriguing." She glanced over at the built-in clock over the kitchen's stove. "I guess I should run back to the cottage in a little while to get a change of clothes." She paused and then said, "Shouldn't take too long."

Tyler grinned. "So, we have a little time then."

Chloe put her cup on the counter and smiled. "What do you have in mind?"

Tyler reached out and lifted the sweatshirt over her head. Within seconds they were rolling on the kitchen floor—his injured shoulder taking a pounding on the linoleum.

Pain never felt so good.

10:12 AM

"Two more?! Two more deaths?!" Miller Kasko screamed incredulously—his face red, veins bulging.

150

He slapped a handful of papers down on the long conference table in the emergency shelter. "How the hell did we lose two more people?" He looked into the faces of those gathered around him: Dr. Yolanda Chabari, Howard Dupree, Manu Ando, Dan Sheridan, and a number of guardsmen and investigators. They offered only puzzled looks or blank stares. "We have over a hundred guard and police on 24-hour patrol. I mean, my God, people; somebody had to have seen or heard something." He pointed to the projected image of the Oshe on a screen behind him. "Look at that thing. It's like Paul Bunyan's axe for crying out loud. You can't just hide that in your back pocket."

He paced in front of the table like a frustrated coach at halftime. His hands were on his hips, and he periodically stopped to rub his eyes. "We have an obligation to protect these people—to help them. We cannot let this continue." He paused as his anger swelled. He turned and pounded the table. "Damn it! We've got to do something!"

"Agent Kasko," a voice shot up from midway down the table. A woman in a military uniform rose. "Captain Amy Harper, South Carolina Guard and Emergency Task Force."

"Yes, Captain," Kasko said as he calmed himself by pushing the papers around on the table.

"I think we may need to consider evacuating these people. We have the resources to move all indigenous peoples to shelters within the county and within a matter of hours."

Kasko looked up at the officer. "To what means and for how long, Captain?"

"Sir?"

Kasko exhaled in frustration. "Well, I know this is a small

island, and I know you and your troops can move them. But how much time away from this island will be enough?" He paused. "And we should also consider the real possibility we may be evacuating our killer along with them. To this point, nothing has happened beyond Amoyeli's shores."

"Move the people, you remove the target and your chance to get him, is that what you're saying?" Chabari asked.

"Not at all," Kasko retorted. "But it's not some outsider committing these crimes. He knows these people and their ways. And he knows his way around this island. Quite frankly, Doctor, I wouldn't put it past anyone outside this conference room, would you?"

Chabari looked around briefly. "No. But I wouldn't put it past anyone *inside* this conference room either, Agent Kasko. The only thing that's changed since the last time I was on Amoyeli is that you and your task force are now here."

Kasko nodded. "I stand corrected, Doctor. You're right. No one is above suspicion."

"Which leads us back to square one," Dupree said. "This island is small, but it's hard to protect. The infrastructure is limited. There are no permanent surveillance cameras, satellite images have been useless, there's no security on the houses. There are also large, natural areas good for hiding and striking. Not to mention a people dangerously unaware of the ways of the world. It's a serial killer's dream come true."

"A serpent in the garden of Eden," Sheridan added.

Kasko scratched the back of his head. "I've got my full investigative crew out at the latest crime scene as we speak," he said, "but if the past few days are any indication, they may not find much. So, in lieu of physical evidence, I'm asking that we look at this from a motivational standpoint. Dr. Chabari believes that this person is acting as the Vodun sky god, Xevioso. She believes that our killer is punishing the people of the island for some sin they committed."

Kasko pushed a button on the projector and a picture of the latest veve from the old couple's house appeared on screen. "As you can clearly see, our killer is quite the artist now. He's taking his time with his blood drawing. The details are quite clear. He's mocking us. Xevioso walks this island without any fear that he will be caught. That kind of arrogance and disdain will be his downfall."

Kasko passed out papers to each team member. "Now, I've asked Dr. Chabari to provide as much information as she can on this sky god to you. I want you all to study this and start formulating a theory as to why he is making these attacks. No theory will be dismissed. No potential tie-in suspect will be ignored."

Kasko waited until everyone at the table focused on him. "I've been here only a couple of days, but this son of a bitch has already made a fool of me several times. I will not allow his so-called 'punishment' to go on any longer. This Xevioso will be stopped, and he will be brought to justice—our justice."

With the meeting over, Captain Harper and Todd Buckridge, another member of the joint task force, walked out of the shelter together. Several of the islanders stirred about the area.

"Can you believe this?" Harper asked. "We got a madman chopping up people out here, and the FBI has us learning about goddamn African mythology."

Buckridge laughed. "Yeah, next thing you know, we'll be sticking pins in voodoo dolls to wake the zombie army so that we can all do the ghost dance with Baron Samedi."

They laughed as they headed back to their camp.

From the shadows, Xevioso watched. He knew the police were desperate. He knew they just wished he would go away. Xevioso smiled. *By the time law enforcement figures everything out, the Legba will be open, and I'll be gone.*

1:08 PM

Chloe walked into The Lucky Shark and scanned the near empty establishment. Poppa was behind the bar washing beer mugs and did not notice her, but a hand shot up in a booth in the back and waved her over. Chloe slid in on the opposite side.

"Is this your idea of a good place to talk?" the man scowled. "Smells like a frat house on Sunday morning." He cocked his eyebrow disapprovingly.

Chloe looked at him with irritation. "It's convenient, David. What more do you want?"

David Mayfield was a good-looking man in his late forties; he had brownish-blonde hair with streaks of gray in his faded goatee. He wore a suit jacket but was tie-less and his shirt was unbuttoned at the top with a hint of the same color chest hair showing. He winced and started again. "You're right. Sorry. It's good to see you, Chloe. How are you?"

"I'm fine, David," she said quickly. "What's the word on the Galeegi project?"

"What? You can't say 'it's good to see you too'?" He paused, searching her eyes. "I'm just trying to be genuine, Chloe. That's what you wanted, right?"

"A little too late for that," she answered flatly. "Now, what about the project?"

David laughed incredulously. "Come on, kid. I'm offering an olive branch here. That is, if you haven't noticed."

"I don't give a damn about apologies or olive branches or anything like that, David. I'm speaking strictly on a professional level. You're the projects director, and I need to know about my work on the Galeegi."

David held his offended pose for a moment and then relaxed his shoulders. He took a quick drink from the water glass in front of him. "Okay, okay. Well, as you might imagine the project is suspended indefinitely." He scrunched up his brow. "By the way, why didn't you let someone know that there was some kind of murder spree happening down here? We would have pulled you home sooner."

Chloe stammered and shook her head in a frustrating attempt to explain and not explain at the same time. "Uh, it all happened so fast. I wasn't really aware of much until yesterday. But what about the project, David?"

"It's dead for now," David said. "The FBI and the island's police will be looking into the break-in. Industrial espionage probably. It's always the first sign of a sinking ship. My guess is Waldorf Enterprises. They're woefully mismanaged, and they're not too far upriver. We caught them doing a chemical dump in North Carolina seven years ago. They've paid through the ass ever since."

"So, I'm out of Galeegi?"

"I've already reassigned you. You'll report back to the Federal Triangle tomorrow, and then you can join

Adrianna in Montana in a few days. She's doing stress-or identification tests in some of the ranchers' field streams out there." David stopped momentarily reading her disappointment. "I thought you'd like that assignment. You said you always wanted to work Section Eight—to see Montana."

"But what about Galeegi?"

"Are you kidding me? Are being shot at, having some asshole break into your house, and a serial killer running around not enough for you? We'll get to Galeegi, but it's not that pressing." He studied her some more and then added, "Look, if it's that important to you, I'll let you come back for the next cycle after everything settles, okay?"

Chloe was about to protest but stopped. She nodded and forced a contrite smile. "Okay."

David reached into his jacket. "Here's your plane ticket. You'll fly out of Charleston tomorrow. Axel will send someone from the Atlanta office to pick up the boat later, so don't worry about that. All you have to do is pack and turn in the rental key."

David shifted out of the booth and stood over Chloe. "I had hoped that maybe you'd want to reschedule your flight and come back to DC with me. But I guess that ship has already sailed as it were."

Chloe stared straight ahead without answering.

"Well, then, I'll see you back in the office."

He headed for the door. She smelled the familiar heavy cologne and felt the familiar pains. Nothing was different. Nothing had changed.

Chloe looked up as Poppa walked over and slid an ice-cold draught onto the table in front of her. He looked to the door and back to Chloe.

"You can do a whole lot better, babe." Poppa shuffled back toward the bar.

Chloe ran her finger around the glass's rim as Poppa's parting shot hung in the air. "I already have," she whispered.

1:55 PM

Tyler, dressed in khaki shorts and a solid black Polo golf shirt, walked down past the multi-million dollar homes on Tradd Street in Charleston. He intermittently checked the house numbers against the sticky note he held in his hand. He stopped in front of a beautiful, yellow-sided carriage house. A giant, swarthy oak tree stood pinned between the sidewalk and the brick wall that surrounded the house. The tree's bulbous arms stretched over the fence and cast plenty of shade for the blue hydrangeas that popped out in front of the double-decker porch.

Tyler peeped in between the spaces of the fence's ornate, iron-forged gate. He knew he had the right house but was unsure if he had the nerve to go through with it. There was no lock on the gate, so he lifted the handle and followed the brick pavers in.

Tyler walked leisurely up the steps admiring the expert craftsmanship of the smooth, wooden porch rail. He loved coming to Charleston for side trips when he spent summers at Galeegi. There was something special about being on the storied peninsula for Tyler—the architecture, the history. It fired his imagination. But today, Civil War cannons and Revolutionary War forts were not even on his mind.

Tyler rapped on the solid door with the antique brass

knocker. He waited, and then hearing nothing, peered into the entranceway's rectangular side glass window.

"Can I help you?" a booming voice came from behind him.

Startled, Tyler turned and saw a robust, older man in a denim work shirt entering the side yard from a back gate. He had long, gray hair down to his shoulders. From the sweat on his brow and the dirt smears on his face, Tyler figured he had been out back doing some kind of yard work.

"Hello, sir. My name is Tyler Miles. I'm looking for Leonard O'Dell."

"You've found him. I'm Leonard O'Dell. To what business can I attribute this unexpected visit, Mr. Miles?"

Tyler walked back down the porch steps and greeted the man who was standing on a perfectly manicured St. Augustine grass lawn. "You're Leonard O'Dell? The lawyer?"

O'Dell nodded again but held up his hand. "I'm retired now. Are you in need of legal advice, young man?"

Tyler reached out and shook his hand. "Uh, no, sir. I'd just like to speak to you if I may."

O'Dell smiled, although a bit hesitantly. "What about? I'm not in any trouble, am I?" he asked.

Tyler fired back one of his own charming smiles. "No, sir. I'd like to talk with you about one of your old court cases. I'm with the Galeegi Police Department."

"Galeegi? I haven't been to Galeegi in years." He said, warming up. O'Dell grasped Tyler by the arm and ushered him towards the porch. "A beautiful place, Galeegi. Pretty beaches and some of the state's best oysters come from down your way—in my not so humble opinion."

"Yes, sir."

O'Dell led him to the pair of rocking chairs at the end of the porch. Tyler waited for him to sit and then did the same. "So what can a crusty, old lawyer do for the good people of Galeegi?"

Tyler leaned forward. "I'd like to discuss a case you were a part of in 1968."

"Jaja Nayu?"

Tyler nodded. "I know you were his defense attorney, and I know the case never made it to trial, but I'd like to ask you a few questions about it, if you don't mind."

O'Dell cleared his throat. "What's your interest in this, Mr. Miles?"

"Jaja Nayu returned to Amoyeli last Friday to take over as caretaker of the island's lighthouse. The next morning he was found dead of a gunshot wound to the head."

O'Dell looked puzzled. "Self-inflicted?"

"It's been ruled a probable suicide. But circumstances are suspect."

O'Dell ran his fingers along the arm of the rocker. He stood. "Come inside with me, Mr. Miles," he said. "I think we could both use a drink."

2:12 PM

Charles Argeaux walked into the spacious study of his eighteen thousand square foot mansion. He sat at his antique crescent-shaped desk, which had been in the Argeaux family since the first sprig of cotton shot through the fertile Galeegi soil three hundred years before. His ancestors became kings of the kingly crop through shrewd business dealings, fortunate timing, and the backs of over a thousand enslaved Africans.

Eventually they branched out into other lucrative agriculture enterprises, and at one time or another had additional farms of indigo, corn, and soybean. Their wealth multiplied with each passing generation, and the modern era saw industrial and phosphate mining operations added to the Argeaux enterprises. During Argeaux's lifetime, the family had controlling interest in construction, real estate, medical supplies, and the Internet. But his accumulated wealth was of little value to him now.

Argeaux read the Major's latest report of the events on Amoyeli: Two more killed this morning—eleven total—eleven punished. He knew his time was coming. He reached across the desk and grabbed at his bourbon and ice and drained it dry. He then stood in anger, turned, and threw the tumbler against a life-size portrait of himself behind his desk. The glass, like his world that he had meticulously controlled throughout his life, shattered into tiny pieces.

2:25 PM

"How do you like your whiskey, Mr. Miles? Soured? Rocky? Or straight from the teat?"

Tyler swung around on one of O'Dell's bar stools and said, "Sir, I really have no idea."

O'Dell laughed. "Forgive an old lawyer. A young man like yourself, you may have another favorite." He looked through his cabinet. "Let's see. I have gin, some rum." He pulled out an oddly shaped bottle, pulled the cork, and sniffed. "Brandy?"

"Beer?" Tyler asked.

O'Dell snapped his fingers and then walked over to a

small refrigerator and found a Molson Golden among dozens of other brands. A full wine rack was built into the wall next to the cooler. The rack was the centerpiece of O'Dell's "drinking room." He opened the beer, slid it across the bar to Tyler, and sat next to him on the black leather stool. He wiped the sweat from his brow. "I have yet to learn from my fellow Charlestonians the rule of never working in the flower garden until just before sunset. One of the many ways you can still tell I'm a damn Yankee."

Tyler smiled, looking around. "A carriage house on Tradd? I think you're fitting in quite nicely."

O'Dell laughed again. "I have found, after fifty years of living here, I should stop trying to force a carpetbag down everyone's throat and simply let my inner-Southerner shine through."

"Different story during the Nayu case, I imagine," Tyler said.

"A pariah—a goddamn pariah, I was back then," O'Dell said with a smile. "Of course, at the time, I wouldn't have it any other way." He added, "It was a contentious time, no doubt."

"What can you tell me about the case, Mr. O'Dell? And before you ask, I really have no idea what I'm hoping to find here. It just seemed like a good idea to start with you."

"As my lovely wife, Barbara, has now departed this world, I feel unencumbered by time constraints or foolish questions. So, ask away."

"Okay. Why did you feel Jaja Nayu was innocent?"

"Did I? I am a lawyer, Mr. Miles. It was my job to defend Mr. Nayu—at all cost."

"So you think he killed Katherine Argeaux?"

O'Dell raised a finger. "I did not say that, Counselor. Evidence was spotty at best. They found Mr. Nayu on the property. That is all."

"Fingerprints? The girl's blood on him? Semen?"

O'Dell shook his head. "They found her in the river. Other than the gash in her head and the bindings, she had nothing on her. And this was 1968. There was no DNA. We had no CSI Galeegi," he said with a slight laugh.

Tyler thought about it for a moment. "What was it like defending him? I know there had to be enormous pressure."

"We were the villains of the piece. Everybody wanted this island nigger hanging from the nearest moss-covered oak tree." He thought about it some more. "It was the times, young man. Civil rights, segregation—the world, this world in particular, just wasn't ready for it."

"Who would have had it out for him? I know Charles Argeaux had the capability and the motive. Anybody else?"

"Jesus, God, yes, I would have to say everyone in Galeegi. Everyone below the Mason-Dixon Line really," O'Dell said before he downed his whiskey.

"But Charles Argeaux certainly, right? I mean she was his little girl."

O'Dell furled his bushy gray eyebrows at Tyler's tone. "I suppose."

Tyler finished his beer and set the bottle on the bar. "Mr. O'Dell, is there anything else you can tell me about this case?"

O'Dell swiveled his whiskey glass and eyed the young man closely. "Sounds like you know all there is to know."

Tyler focused his eyes and lifted his chin to be more direct. "All except how a radical, Yankee lawyer transplant from New York got involved in a case like this. How did that happen exactly?"

"I imagine my reputation," O'Dell said, grinning.

"You represented an Amoyeli islander, Mr. O'Dell," Tyler interrupted. "A black kid who was in the care of his dirt poor grandfather. There was no money to retain a super lawyer such as you. Was this all done pro bono?"

O'Dell just grinned.

Tyler continued, "I guess I could tell you that I know after the trial was dismissed you were able to move to a house South of Broad and purchase optimum office space near the downtown area of the Four Corners of Law, but I'm sure you could tell me that it was due to loans, new clients, future prospects."

O'Dell, still smiling, rapped his fingers along the bar, "Care for another Molson?"

Tyler stood. "No, sir. I think I'm finished. I thank you for your time."

O'Dell followed Tyler as he walked back onto the front porch and down the steps. He stopped at the bottom, turned, and said, "I didn't mean any disrespect, Mr. O'Dell. I only asked because I feel that your former client was murdered, and quite frankly, I can't explain it. In fact, I can't explain anything I've been through the past week. But I do want to see justice done."

O'Dell had his hands in his trouser pockets. He took another long look at Tyler. "I received an unmarked envelope with one hundred fifty thousand dollars in cash and a typewritten plea to take the case. After Jaja was set free, I received another one hundred fifty thousand. I don't know who sent it or why."

"Argeaux has made a lot of enemies over the years."

O'Dell nodded. "Men like that usually do. I suppose it could have been someone who wanted to watch his daughter's killer walk. But I'll tell you something, Mr. Miles, that I've never told anybody else. When that judge dismissed the case and set that young Negro free, the only reaction I saw on Charles Argeaux's face was relief."

3:45 PM

Yolanda Chabari sat among a group of Amoyeli women outside the shelter. With the island on lockdown there was little for them to do except talk.

Dr. Chabari remembered a few of their faces from the brief time she had spent on the island. Her history with Amoyeli was a direct connection. She knew the exact spot where her childhood home once stood. But her family had moved from the island when she was five in search of a better life. Her father worked on a shrimp boat out of Beaufort until he died six years later. Her mother cleaned houses for several of the white folks who lived on Beaufort's Petigru Drive. Chabari went to the Beaufort public schools, and under her mother's watchful eye, she excelled. Scholarships followed, and she found herself at Bethune-Cookman majoring in African Studies. Through a fellowship, she continued her studies in Nigeria in the city of Abuja for two years. Upon her return to the states, Chabari began her teaching career, and after stays at Howard and then Spelman colleges, she accepted an offer to become the head of the African Studies Department at the University of South Carolina in Columbia.

She never forgot her early days on Amoyeli, and the

recent events pained her greatly. Her dialogue with the women of the island was rapid and frantic. But this was intentional. She wanted their confidence.

"How much longer must we stay here?" one of the women asked in her thick, island dialect. "I must go home—tend to my house, my animals."

"I know, I know." Chabari said. "Hopefully soon. But there is no set time—no hour, no day."

"Xevioso will not stop," an older woman said. "He will punish all the Igbo. This will not end."

"What have we done? What has happened?" Chabari asked as she looked into the eyes of each woman. "Why does the ram strike Amoyeli?"

"We have forgotten our way. Not a one respects the old ways," the elderly woman insisted, shaking an authoritative finger.

"We have done nothing to deserve his anger," another added defiantly. "Jesus will protect me. Jesus will protect us." Many shook their heads in agreement. "Xevioso is but one loa. Jesus Christ is Lord of 'em all."

"Xevioso is the ancient god," another insisted. "He has no place on Amoyeli. He has no claim to punish the Igbo."

The older woman grabbed the last woman's arm. "You do not say such blasphemy. Xevioso hear everything. He come for you and yo' family."

As the women continued to fuss, Chabari leaned back against the shelter wall and closed her eyes. It was typical island talk—old world versus new—and it had been that way since the beginning. How much to hold onto and how much to give in. Even after being taken from their homes, as they sailed to the unknown world in the belly of those ghastly slave ships, her people debated how much of their life to preserve. After the slave ships landed in Barbados, the cargo was seasoned in the ways of the white man's world. Priests forbade the slaves to practice their religion, and they were baptized into the Christian faith. Even as many still secretly practiced their native beliefs, their new masters villainized their religion. Vodun became evil, black art—the voodoo of the white man's nightmares—cannibalism, human sacrifices, zombies, *botonos*.

Chabari opened her eyes and leaned forward. "Botono!" The women stopped talking and looked at Chabari. She met their quizzical stares momentarily. "Excuse me, sisters."

Chabari stood and went back inside the emergency shelter. She bypassed the large sleeping area where cots had been placed head to toe. She went into the back conference room where the FBI had set up headquarters. Kasko sat on the conference table still in strategy conversation with Dupree.

"Agent Kasko," Chabari interrupted. "I need one of your helicopters, and I need it now."

6:57 PM

Chloe followed the zigzag path through the palmettos and cabbage palms. She found the triangular washout area and then traced the footprints along the bank of the creek. After she rounded the bend, she climbed the mountainous dune, crossed to its pinnacle, and there at the top, she saw him.

Tyler was waiting for her on the seaward side of the dune on a beautiful stretch of sandy white beach. He held a bottle of pinot noir in one hand and two wine glasses in the other. He stood still, flashing his million-dollar smile. Chloe sauntered across the beach to greet him.

"I see you can follow directions," he said.

She smiled sweetly. "Well, I can read a text. After all, I am a Ph.D."

Tyler laughed. "How'd your meeting go?"

"Okay, I guess." She quickly turned and indicated the beach with a lift of her chin. "Beautiful. I can see why you like it out here."

Tyler agreed, also looking around. "The best part is its privacy. Not too many beachgoers come down this far because of the undertow." He pointed behind him. "The Galeegi's final push into the Atlantic. It will scoop you up and suck you under. But for the in-the-know crowd, it's the best part of the beach to take long walks, look for sharks' teeth, or share a bottle of wine." He rattled the bottle in his hand. "Shall we?" He offered her his arm.

Tyler led Chloe to a picnic blanket a few more yards down the beach. They sat as he popped the cork. "We still have a little wait yet, but when the sun hits the ocean it will all be worth it." He poured the wine and leaned over to give her a kiss. "To us," he toasted.

Chloe forced a quick smile and took a sip. She wasn't ready to tell him just yet. "So, did you find Leonard O'Dell?"

"Yeah. He's quite a character actually. Much more accessible than all the gossip would lead you to believe. I can't say I found out any more about Jaja, but I did find out that someone beyond O'Dell and Jaja's family wanted to see him free. Someone with deep pockets."

"The plot thickens."

"Just what we needed, right?" He looked directly into Chloe's eyes. "So, tell me about the Galeegi. When are they going to let you back in the river?"

Chloe sighed. "It's, uh, been suspended indefinitely. With all that's happening on Amoyeli and with the break-in, they didn't feel like it was safe anymore."

"So, what's next for you then?" he asked tentatively.

Chloe tried to smile. "I'm out. I have to head back to DC tomorrow. I've been reassigned to another project."

Tyler allowed it to sink in. "Tomorrow?"

"It was supposed to be a routine test on the Galeegi. I would have had to leave in the next three or four days anyway."

"Right." Tyler took a long look at her. "I never really considered it—your leaving—I guess I should have."

"It is the nature of my job," Chloe said. "There's so much travel involved in my work, with all the research and testing I have to do. The world it not as clean and healthy as it should be, thanks to man's ignorance and greed. My work is important to me. It's my life. I keep a bag packed at my door at all times." They sat in silence for a minute.

"You know, Chloe, this doesn't have to be the end," Tyler rationalized. "We can always keep up with one another—calls, emails—and I can visit when I build up some vacation time."

Chloe laughed out of desperation, her eyes watering over. "You've only been working for one week, Tyler."

Tyler attempted his best smile. "Come on, I'll just put in a lot of overtime."

Tyler set his glass down and slid over next to her. He draped his long arm around her shoulder and held her close. He looked into her sad eyes. There was so much he wanted to say to her. He wanted to tell her that she was the one—that they belonged together—that she should quit her job and never leave his side. But he knew that wasn't going to happen. He knew she was going to do what she had to do; what she was supposed to do.

Tyler looked out to the ocean and the outgoing afternoon tide. He watched the waves as they crashed against the beach—stretching their bands in as far as they could go—striving to hold on to the shoreline for as long as possible.

10:47 PM

Dr. Chabari walked down the darkened hallway of the South Caroliniana Library on the Horseshoe of the University of South Carolina campus. She trailed Thomas Washington, the building's night watchman. He stopped in front of Archives Room 303, the manuscripts division, and unlocked the door.

"Thank you, Mr. Washington," Chabari said as she slipped into the room.

"No problem, Professor. I'll be at the front desk if you need anything else."

"I'll stop by on my way out," she said as she closed the door behind her. Chabari turned and flipped on the overhead light. Room 303 was not a large room in comparison to the other archive rooms, and it contained few important historical documents. But 303 held numerous donated family collections, and one was of special interest to Chabari.

The collection was alphabetized by surname, and Chabari located her target rather easily. After donning gloves, she pulled the three-hundred-year-old manifest from the hermetically sealed locker. She brought it to the reading table and gently laid it down. The reading light sensor came on, and Chabari began her careful study of the leather-bound text.

She ran her finger down the names. The ink was faded and the handwriting was in a hard-to-read cursive, but she could make out the overseer's listings for each new shipment of slaves that had been sent from Barbados. The Argeaux plantation was so vast that the slave brokers often made volume trades at Galeegi before continuing to the slave market in Charleston.

Each page of the manifest was dated at the top, and she flipped through the pages trying to find the exact one. The one she had remembered seeing previously. When Chabari accepted the teaching position at South Carolina, she had made use of its extensive archives to do a search of her connection to Amoyeli.

Using the Argeaux records, she had found what she believed to be her family line. The names were somewhat different from what she was told by family members, but that might have been due to any number of reasons, mostly the indifference of the slave traders themselves.

It was during this initial search that she came across an oddity in one of the entries. The trader or the recorder had put a double-crossed star next to an entry and attached the word "botono" beside it. Part of the Vodun hierarchy, botono was an ancient name for a sorcerer or sorceress who had the power to call on the gods to seek out punishment for some injustice or sin. However, more often than not, the botono used that power for a far more nefarious purpose.

Chabari moved delicately but swiftly though the

browned-edged papers. After several minutes, she finally found the page with the recorder's star and the word botono. She then ran her index finger across the faint manifest entry. The recorder had listed the slave's weight (130lbs.), height (5'2"), amount paid in sterling to trader (43), estimated selling price in sterling (96), and sex (female). But as her fingertip rested on the name next to the star, her hopes for a quick connection vanished. There was nothing there. Either the name had not been recorded or it had faded away with time. Chabari closed her eyes and then the book.

So very close.

JUNE 9

6:09 AM

Tyler opened his eyes and batted them clear. He pushed himself up onto one arm and scanned the shoreline. The morning sky was a deep purple and the tidal breakers pushed the Atlantic far up the beach. He rose to his feet and dusted the sand from his naked body. He stood tall and held out his arms, allowing the ocean breeze to buffer his skin. He rolled his shoulder and felt residual pains from his gunshot wound. He still couldn't believe he'd been shot. He then looked down at Chloe. She was still asleep, partially wrapped in the picnic blanket. Her black hair helped to cover her exposed shoulders and upper back.

He smiled as he thought about last night. They spent their last night together on the beach, splashing around knee-deep in the dark ocean waters and making love throughout the night. But as the sun rose on the horizon, the reality that she was leaving today hit him again. A new wave of depression swept over him.

Tyler dropped to his knees, reached into a pocket of his shorts, removed his cell phone, and checked for messages. There were none. Either it was a quiet night on the islands or his Uncle Fletcher was keeping him in the dark. Either way, he felt obligated to go by the station later to make sure. He leaned over Chloe and gently nudged her.

She turned, squinted up at him with sleepy eyes, and smiled. "Nothing like waking to the sight of a naked man."

Tyler laughed. "I don't know whether to be insulted or not."

Chloe sat up within the blanket and reached out, touching his face. "Don't be. I can't think of anyone I'd rather wake up next to."

Tyler's smile was filled with conflicting emotion. "I thought I'd wake you—give you a chance to get dressed before the beachcombers arrive."

Chloe turned to look behind her. "Oh, I don't know." She dropped the blanket from around her. "Let's risk it for a little bit longer."

8:32 AM

Miller Kasko, with two other FBI agents trailing, passed through the dimly lit foyer of the Colleton County Museum, located in the Old City Jail in Walterboro. The neo-gothic structure stood out from the other small city buildings with its gold painted tones and castle-like turret.

They walked to the back of the building and entered a storage room. Sitting at a long table were Dr. Chabari and an older African-American man. They were looking at crumbling manuscripts and other faded documents.

"Dr. Chabari, still at work I see," Kasko said.

Chabari looked up, more than a little tired. "My eyes will fail long before my will, Agent Kasko." She pointed to the man across from her. "This is Mr. Lionel Jackson, curator of this museum."

Jackson nodded at the three men.

Kasko tilted his head at the agents behind him. "Donovan and Williams. They're FBI linguistic analysts, Dr. Chabari. They are highly trained in all kinds of writing and language forms; they may be able to help research through all this and find whatever it is you're looking for."

173

"Good. At this point I am not sure what it is I am looking for myself."

"Neither am I," Kasko said, pulling up a chair. "In your call last night, you said that you found a manifest of slaves who ended up on Amoyeli Island. And that there was one slave who was of special interest, right?"

Chabari pulled her reading glasses down her nose and peered at the FBI agent. "That is correct. One was identified as botono. In the hierarchy of the Vodun religion, the botono is a priest, a powerful caster of evil spells; one who calls upon the gods to punish others."

"Like Xevioso."

"Yes. It would be in the realm of the botono to call Xevioso to punish others when a sin had been committed by an individual, a family, or an entire tribe. This service was rarely needed and was frowned upon by many in the Vodun religion."

"So you think that there may be someone on the island acting as this botono—a descendant of the original—the one on the slave manifest."

"Perhaps," Chabari said, choosing her words carefully. "The art of sorcery is a genealogical trade. It is passed down from one generation to the next. This is a covenant that was established well in the history of Vodun. In many instances, the dark art has passed through multiple generations."

Kasko leaned over. "So explain to me why we are here now? In this museum?"

Chabari looked to Jackson and then back to Kasko. "The archives at the University include only the records of the early plantations in this area. They include those of the Argeaux family who brought most of the Africans to Galeegi, and who after the slaves had been freed,

174

abandoned them on Amoyeli Island. There was no slave name on the manifest in Columbia. It is my hope that this museum has other records of traders, overseers, or perhaps even some slave diaries that will give us clues regarding the botono. This museum is more intimate; it has an extensive collection from the people of this area, including those of Galeegi."

"But, Doctor, names can change through the years, especially slave names. We might not find a connection to a living individual on the island."

"I did not say it would be easy, Agent Kasko. Or even possible."

Kasko slumped in his chair and rubbed his face in his hands. "Another wild goose chase then, another search for the proverbial needle in the proverbial haystack."

"Perhaps, Agent Kasko, but consider this: What other leads have you uncovered in your investigation thus far?" Chabari held her stare momentarily, then pushed the glasses back up her nose and continued her research.

Kasko stood and turned to Donovan and Williams. "Well, what are you boys waiting on? Get to it."

9:04 AM

Tyler held Chloe by the hand and led her into the Galeegi Police Station. Control Central was unusually crowded. Most were law enforcement officials from neighboring cities who had volunteered to help. They were there under good pretenses, but they used the station's computers and phones, and they drained the coffee maker dry. Tyler also noted a few men stirring about the room with press credentials around their necks. Knowledge of Galeegi's problems had spread beyond the islands.

Tate's office door was open. Tyler and Chloe bypassed the crowd and walked straight in. Tate sat at his desk; he was talking to Sergeant Johnson, who was looking uncomfortable seated on the small couch. When Tate noticed them enter, he stood.

"Oh, hey Ty, Chloe." He moved crossed the room and shut the door behind them, before returning to his desk.

"Quite the crowd out there," Tyler said.

"Yeah, and it's only going to get worse," Tate replied. "Have either of you seen the paper this morning?"

Tyler and Chloe both shook their heads. Tate grabbed *The Post and Courier* off his desk and held it up: Serial Killer Terrorizes Amoyeli Island. Tate turned the newspaper back to his view. "It goes on to say how many have died and how we, the police and the FBI, are baffled, but it states very few details."

Johnson snorted. "Yeah, well, it gives the good people of the Lowcountry something new to talk about, now don't it?"

Tyler ignored the comment. "Anything on the break-in yet?"

"Not yet," Tate said. "Some forensic people from the FBI came, collected the casings, and pulled fragments out of the wall. And, of course, they interviewed Ms. Chloe yesterday and have you scheduled for later. But I think everyone is more tuned to Amoyeli right now. At least that's my impression."

"It's a lot for our little world to handle," Tyler said. He hesitated and then asked, "Do you think they'll need Chloe anymore? She has to fly back to DC today."

Tate glanced up at her. "No, I think they got everything they need from the interview. They can always contact her up there if they need something later." Tate smiled

176

at her. "I'm sorry this happened, Chloe. Please believe me when I say break-ins and shootings are a far cry from what we're used to down here. I hope you're not totally turned off of our island."

"Of course not," she said. "I hope to return in a few months to finish my work in the Galeegi." She rubbed gently on Tyler's back. "Actually, there's a lot I find about your island that's quite charming."

"Chloe, do you mind giving us a second? There are some police matters I need to discuss with Ty."

Chloe turned to Tyler without hesitation. "I'll be outside."

As the door closed behind her, Sergeant Johnson got up off the couch and stood behind Tyler.

"What's up, Chief?" Tyler asked.

"Ty, where did you go yesterday afternoon?"

"To Charleston; you gave me the day off, remember?"

"What did you do there?" Johnson demanded—his breath hot on Tyler's neck.

Tyler turned to look briefly at Johnson but refocused on his uncle. "What's this all about?"

"It has been brought to my attention that you went to visit Leonard O'Dell," Tate said.

"I did. Is that a problem?"

"Why would you go see that asshole?" Johnson pressed. "That old man's brain has gotta be nothing but cream cheese and shit by now."

Tyler stayed focused on his uncle. "I thought he might be able to offer some insight into Jaja's case."

"There ain't no case, kid. The son of a bitch shot himself—sucked his gun dry. End of story," Johnson said, his voice rising.

Tate held up his hand. "Easy, Hank." He smiled at

his nephew. "Did he say anything to you? Anything that might help us?"

"Not really. He talked about the trial. What it was like back in the day," Tyler paused. "How'd you know I went to see him?"

"It's like we tried to tell you, kid. Argeaux has his hands into everything around here. He knows all. Sees all," Johnson offered unsolicited.

"What? So, Argeaux had one of his goons follow me?"

"No, actually, I followed you," the sergeant said smugly.

Tyler turned to face Johnson—fire in his eyes. "You followed me? For how long?"

Johnson laughed and rolled back his shoulders in an arrogant way. "Well, let's just say I know when you get home you're gonna need to wash all that sand out of the crack of your ass."

Tyler snapped and immediately exploded into Johnson, clutching his throat. He pushed him back until they both plowed into the couch. Tate jumped from behind his desk and tried to pull Tyler off the sergeant.

"Get off me, goddamnit!" Johnson spit out. "Get the hell off!"

Tyler kept a chokehold around Johnson's meaty neck.

"Tyler! Let go! Let go of him, Tyler!" Tate yelled as he tried to pry his nephew away.

The door of the office flew open, and three policemen who heard the commotion rushed in and managed to pull Tyler back.

Tate jumped in front of him. "Calm down, Tyler! Now calm down!" Tyler's face remained tight as he stood restrained, breathing like a mad bull.

Johnson rolled from the couch to the floor. His face was swollen and red. He struggled to his feet, getting his breathing under control. "Punk...ass...just who the hell do you think you are?" he managed to spit out.

Tyler jerked his right arm away from the cops holding him back and pointed at Johnson. "You just stay away from me. Stay away from me and Chloe or the next time, so help me God, I'll fucking kill you!" Tyler shot a hard glance at Tate and then stormed out.

Johnson leaned menacingly toward the door and said, his voice still cracking from a lack of oxygen, "Oh, yeah? I'd like to see you try."

Tate held up his hand and pointed Sergeant Johnson back to the couch like a battered boxer being ordered to his corner. The chief composed himself and turned to the other cops. "Forgive us, gentlemen. We've been working around the clock for several days now. We're a little on the tense side."

The policemen murmured that they understood and hastily left, pulling the door closed behind them. Tate turned back to Johnson.

"Why *did* you follow Tyler, Hank? I didn't give you any order to do that."

Johnson sat on the couch still rubbing his neck. "With all due respect, Fletch, this is bigger than you. Much bigger."

"You are a member of the Galeegi Police Department. You work for Galeegi, not Charles Argeaux."

Sergeant Johnson narrowed his eyes and grinned savagely. "Yeah, Chief, that's right. Keep on telling yourself that."

Tyler burst through the station doors and headed out into the lot. Chloe, who was waiting outside, saw his fury and immediately went to him. "Tyler? Is everything okay?"

He stopped, placing his hands on his hips. "No. Everything is not okay."

"What happened in there? What did he say?"

Tyler looked to the station and then back to her. "This whole thing is crazy, Chloe. I don't understand it. I don't even know who to trust anymore."

"What's going on, Ty? You're scaring me."

"Yeah, well, after that, I'm starting to get a little scared myself."

11:55 AM

Howard Dupree walked toward to the VIP tent at the Guard camp and gently rustled the front flap. "Agent Kasko?" He listened for sounds of movement, then continued, "The Adjutant General has landed. He's here to talk to you."

Kasko stumbled out of the tent, stuffing his shirt into his pants and then raking the hair out of his eyes with a small, black comb. "Nothing like getting an hour of sleep to start your day."

Dupree smiled as he fell in behind Kasko. They walked across the compound and cut through island scrubs into the landing pad area.

Major General Robert J. Sparks stood on the sand talking to the commander of the Beaufort 202nd. Sparks was six feet, three inches tall and well over two hundred thirty pounds. At sixty-four years old, the major general had a Karl Malden nose on his aged and heavily wrinkled face. His eyes were still bright and clear, and he allowed them to linger on the FBI man as he stuck out his large hand. "Special Agent Kasko? I'm Major General Sparks."

"General Sparks," Kasko responded. "Glad to have you

here, sir. But may I ask why the commander of the South Carolina National Guard has decided to pay us a visit today?"

"They won't let me go to Afghanistan or to any of the other hot spots where they have my people deployed around the world, so I thought I'd pay my coastal troops a little visit; see them in action," Sparks said with a politician's smile.

"You can't kid a kidder, General," Kasko said quickly. "Really, sir, why are you here?"

Sparks threw out his arm in the direction of the camp. "Let's go over to the camp, Agent Kasko and have us a little talk; maybe drink out of the same canteen if you know what I mean."

Moments later Kasko and Sparks sat alone in the mess hall tent—each with a bottle of water in front of them. "General, I don't mean to sound like a genuine pain in the ass, but we've got a lot to do. This investigation is on full go, and I don't have any time to waste playing toy soldier."

Sparks, slightly offended, smiled a yellowed-toothed smile. "Okay. I'll cut right to the chase then. I'm getting word up in Columbia that you're misusing my people in your investigation of this matter."

Kasko drew in his brow. "Sir?"

"As I understand it, you have some islander down here who thinks he's an African god or some horseshit like that, murdering people."

"That's right. He's killed eleven people, General. Eleven. Whether he thinks himself an African god or the Queen of England, it's my job to stop him. Your troops have been instrumental in patrolling and protecting this island. Is there some problem with that?"

"Well, uh, no, not exactly." The general swallowed some water. "The fact is, Agent Kasko, the people I have to answer to see this investigation as a waste of time and resources."

"A waste?" Kasko turned his head in disbelief. "Come on, Sparks, you're the goddamn adjutant general. Who is it you have to answer to anyway?"

"Oh, I'm a general all right. But I'm an elected general. I have my constituents to think of."

"Constituents?" Kasko paused, mulling over the general's words. "Wait a minute. Does this have something to do with Charles Argeaux?

Sparks relented. "Argeaux is a big supporter, Agent Kasko. He's a mover and shaker of the politics in South Carolina."

"So what? Does the son of a bitch not want a killer stopped in his own backyard? I mean, Jesus, do you know how ridiculous this sounds, General?"

Sparks frowned. "Look, Kasko, I'll admit it doesn't make a whole lot of sense to me either. But I'm a soldier—old school. I don't question my superiors. My emergency task force is for natural disasters—hurricanes, earthquakes— not detective work."

Kasko shook his head again. "So, what is it that you're saying, General Sparks?"

"You have seventy-two hours with these coastal units. After that we're gone, and Amoyeli is on its own again."

"And if we haven't arrested the perpetrator by that time?"

"I'm sorry, Agent Kasko. It's seventy-two hours, and then we bug out."

Sparks finished his water and stood. "At any rate, good luck to you. I sincerely hope you find your man." The general placed his hat on his head and walked out of the mess tent.

Kasko sat at the table at a loss for words, spinning the empty water bottle around on the table. *Is there anyone on these loony islands who wants this killer stopped?*

12:34 PM

Tyler drove the Ford Ranger up Highway 17 toward Charleston. Chloe sat beside him. A taped piece of cardboard covered the hole in the passenger's window. Her flight left Charleston at three o'clock, and Tyler wanted to have her there early to bypass all of the check-in headaches. He was so focused on what had transpired at the station that in the long drive he had not said much at all to Chloe. And now their minutes together ticked away.

"Tyler, I hate rushing out on you like this, especially after what just happened," Chloe said.

Tyler looked over at her from behind his sunglasses. "No, Chloe, I'm the one who should be apologizing. You're getting ready to fly out of here, and I'm letting this case and the people I work with distract me."

"You have a right to be upset. I can't believe that they had us followed."

"It's the *they* part that bothers me the most. I mean does everyone in Galeegi answer to Argeaux?" He turned towards her slightly. "Think about it, Chloe. What would Argeaux care if I went to O'Dell anyway? I mean, I don't know if this ties him in to Jaja's death, but it certainly makes it seem that way."

"You think Argeaux had Jaja killed?"

"It was my uncle's suspicion from the very beginning,

and it would make sense. When Jaja returned, the only person who would care to see him dead is the man who thought Jaja killed his daughter."

Chloe scrunched up her brow. "But didn't you also tell me on the beach that O'Dell said Argeaux showed relief after Jaja was set free?"

Tyler nodded slowly. "Damn. Yeah, that's right. A strange reaction if you really thought Jaja killed your daughter. So this doesn't make any sense after all, does it?"

Chloe's cell phone suddenly rang out, and she checked the caller ID. "Oh, it's the coastal testing lab. Hello?" She listened briefly. "Yeah, hi, CJ. No, it really doesn't matter now. The project's been bumped. We've run into several snags the past few days."

As the caller continued, Chloe's face darkened with concern. "Wait a minute, wait a minute. Are you sure, CJ?"

Chloe dug through her carry-on bag. She kept the phone pinched between her shoulder and ear. "No, my write-up was on my laptop, and it's been disabled, but I still have my original notes." She pulled out her Palm Pilot and quickly found the entry. "Yeah, I got it now. Marker 1A—below Poston's Landing." She continued listening and shaking her head in disbelief. "Are you certain, CJ? I mean you have got to be absolutely certain on this." She listened for a minute more. "Right. Send me the latest SEDD info and then put a lid on it until I can get back to you. Thanks." She ended the call and slid her cell into her carry-on.

"Is everything all right?" Tyler asked.

"We need to go back, Tyler. We need to go back to Galeegi."

"Galeegi? But what about your flight?"

"Screw the flight. You have got to get me back on that river."

3:36 PM

Yolanda Chabari was asleep. She had escaped for a few moments to Lionel Jackson's private office and made excellent use of his leather-backed chair. She had pulled off her shoes and propped her feet up on his desk. She had pulled her gelede from the top of her head and used it as a makeshift mask to cover her eyes. A rap on the door awoke her.

The door swung open, and Agent Donovan stuck his head in. "Excuse me, Dr. Chabari, but we think you may want to have a look at this."

Chabari got up and quickly followed the FBI linguist back to the storage room. Jackson and Williams had an ancient looking manuscript under the lighted magnifier.

"What have you found, gentlemen?"

"A captain's log, Doctor," Jackson said. "Darrow. A slave ship captain."

"Darrow?" she asked.

Williams turned to face her. "Wells Darrow. He was an employee of the Royal Bond Trading Company. He ran the triangular route—African slaves to Barbados, cotton and sugar to England. He made the circuit twice a year for twenty-two years straight before retiring to Charleston."

"How did his manuscript end up here in Walterboro?"

"Descendants," Jackson said. "Sometimes these families bring in their whole collections. 'Better here than the attic.' That's our motto."

Chabari nodded as she moved closer. "What connection have you made?"

"We cross-referenced the museum's entire catalogue with Amoyeli and all source material dealing with slave trading. We found few references, but we got lucky scanning this account. I think this may be the one you're looking for," Williams said as he offered his seat to Chabari.

Chabari slid in and pulled out her reading glasses. She then focused on the words in front of her:

May 16th in the year 1723 of Our Lord God —

The Night Jasmine has received safe passage into the African port of Badagary.

Chabari paused after reading Darrow's opening line, contemplating the name the Night Jasmine—such a pleasant sounding name for a ship doing such an unpleasant task. She dismissed the irony and continued:

The spring storms were difficult as expected. Doctor Haynesworth saw to Boatsman Laurie, but God's will knows no man's plea and has called him home. Young Laurie was put to sea on May 15th, a day before our arrival. May God, in his infinite wisdom, have mercy on his soul.

Rations and supplies paid through Company monies. Fine silks traded with Badagary. Slave shipment to be recorded by first mate Turkvant. Trade to Barbados.

Request made by Badagary trader. Additional slaves offered. Fon. Botono. She is to find God in the chains of the slave. I have agreed to take the black witch from the trader under condition of safe passage. I shall not hesitate to throw her and her family into sea if it is God's will.

Chabari looked up. "So, this botono was Fon."

"Fon?" Donovan asked.

"A tribe in Benin, next to Nigeria. The botono was not

of the Igbo tribe. Not of my people." Chabari leaned back in her chair and processed it all. She then turned back to Williams. "But how do we know this is the same botono? The one who came to Amoyeli?"

Williams leaned over Chabari and carefully turned the diary to another marked passage. "I actually found this entry first." The professor adjusted her glasses and read:

October 2nd, in the year 1723 of Our Lord God —

Turkvant reports clear skies for voyage to Carolina. One hundred and sixty-four slaves in holding. Divert to Galeegi before slave market in Charleston. Eighty-Seven to Argeaux plantation. We shall trade for cotton and oil for voyage to England.

Chabari looked to Williams after finishing the short entry. He read her mind and pointed to the bottom of the page. A small notation had been made. There was a double crossed star—the same as the one in the Argeaux plantation record book. And beside it was written a singular name: Nayu.

6:06 PM

Tyler was at the controls of the Bayliner cutting a quick path up the Galeegi. Getting Chloe's boat was the easy part. He had convinced Amos Carlton that he was continuing his patrols for the police and that they needed an extra boat. He figured the lie wouldn't do any more damage to his employment than what had already transpired back at the station. He felt bad about exploding as he had, especially in front of his uncle, but Johnson had it coming to him. Now Tyler had more pressing things on his mind.

Chloe's contact at the lab had processed all of her first day samples, running them through the various toxicology tests. All the areas had come back negative. Except one. Below the bridge at Poston's Landing, one of her water samples, in addition to unexplained traces of chlorine, showed a mind-blowing, dangerously high amount of plutonium oxide. There was no possible reason to have such a reading anywhere in the Galeegi.

There were no nuclear power related industries or nuclear by-products using plants anywhere up the river. And according to those samples sent in, the area just above Poston's Landing showed zero levels of the radioactive material. There was something there in the river. Something that shouldn't be. And Chloe was going to find out what it was.

She had discussed the most sensible approach with Tyler: call the EPA, call the police, simply let the authorities know. But the break-in and the act of being followed had them paranoid enough to believe that they needed more proof, more facts in hand before they went to anyone. The Bayliner was equipped with the latest technological advances in sonar research. A quick scan and grab picture of what was lying near Poston's Landing would be enough to call in the cavalry.

Going upriver, Poston's Landing was just past the huge Argeaux Bridge but still below Rutherford on the mainland. There was not much to the landing—just a bumpy, trashy, overused boat ramp next to the concrete bridge. Most visitors to Galeegi would bypass it without ever knowing it was there.

Chloe emerged from the small galley below. She had changed out of her traveling clothes and back into a working swimsuit and shorts. She also had her hair pulled back again into a ponytail and sticking out the back of her green Canes cap. She looked determined as she moved to the bow. All that she and Tyler had been through over the past couple of days had brought them even closer together. They both knew their relationship was building strength. As they continued to whip the Bayliner up the coils of the black snake, they needed that strength now more than ever.

6:14 PM

"Nayu?" Kasko asked. "That's the name of the man who killed himself in the lighthouse, right? Jaja Nayu, I believe it was?"

Chabari nodded. She stood in the back room of the shelter flanked by the two FBI linguists—all having just returned to Amoyeli via helicopter. "Yes, but before we proceed, I must warn you of a myriad of possible coincidences involved here."

"I don't believe in them, Doctor. And as you pointed out to me this morning, I have nothing else to go on right now." Kasko snapped his fingers at another FBI agent behind him. "Get me the file on the Nayu man." The agent, along with the two linguists, disappeared in search of the file.

Chabari sank down wearily into a chair. "I am, of course, familiar with Jaja as are most on Amoyeli. But I must tell you that I never knew he was of Fon descent as pointed out in the Darrow's logbook. But again, I am still not convinced he is a descendant of this same Nayu."

Kasko nodded as he swung a chair around next to Chabari. "Right. Let's assume that he is. Explain to me what 'Fon' means."

"The Fon are a different tribe from the Igbo. Most came from Benin, in the country next to my homeland. The Fon practiced Vodun as well. But during the slave trading days, many of them captured Igbo and sold them to the white traders. There was much back and forth in skirmishes between the two tribes."

"How would a Fon botono end up with Igbo slaves?" Kasko asked as a fellow agent slipped the Nayu file under his hands.

Chabari shook her head and frowned. "It is a guess, but I would theorize that the botono in question was of a particularly bad seed. That she had perhaps cast a hex on the wrong Fon tribal members, those powerful enough to have her and her family sold into slavery. A rare act, but not unprecedented."

Kasko nodded again, taking in her words. His eyes drifted to the file in front of him. "What do you know of Jaja? Beyond his involvement in the Argeaux murder?"

"Very little. I did not know him at all in the childhood years I was on Amoyeli. But by all accounts, he was a quiet, shy young man. He lived with his grandfather in the lighthouse. He liked to fish and cook. That is all I know."

Kasko listened while simultaneously reading from the file. "What of his parents? Why was he living with his grandfather?"

Chabari shook her head again. "I don't know. Dead perhaps. Sounds like a good place to start for the FBI."

Kasko looked up. "If he is indeed the descendant of this Fon botono, would his death be enough to bring Xevioso to the island? Could his death be the sin that was committed by the Igbo?"

Chabari rubbed her hands together and closed one eye in thought. "It would make sense. But it does raise another question. If Jaja's death was the Igbo sin, who called Xevioso to the island? According to Vodun belief, only a high priest such as a botono can call the gods into this world."

Kasko let her words sink in. "So you think there are more people involved than just the guy with the axe?"

"Just another theory, Agent Kasko. But, yes, I do believe we are only scratching the surface with who and what are involved in this matter."

6:34 PM

Tyler slowed the Bayliner once he passed the opening to the estuary where he first met Chloe. It was only a bend or two more up the river to Poston's Landing.

"Do you remember where exactly?" Tyler asked.

Chloe searched both sides of the river. She noted the high bank area on the right side with several Leyland cypress tree roots exposed through the bank's slope. "Could be anywhere in this part. Is the sonar up and running?"

Tyler checked the gauge on the C-Max 2 side scan sonar system. It was working, bouncing a grainy yellow picture back to the attached monitor. The river was darkly stained and some areas reached twenty-five feet in depth. But at 780 kHz, the CM2 was more than powerful enough to read the bottom.

Tyler slipped the engine into neutral and allowed the boat to drift as he checked the scanner.

"Are we getting video?" Chloe questioned from the bow.

"Yeah. But just hazy pics of mud and sticks so far."

Chloe nodded and then moved to the back. She stood behind Tyler and shielded her eyes. She spoke slowly. "Keep a close watch. I have no idea what could be causing such a heavy reading in such a small target area."

They methodically made their way around the first bend. With the downward flow of the river, Tyler punched the engine every now and then to give them a little boost. Over the next several minutes the sonar recorded tree logs of varying size, a drowned trolling motor, and an object shaped like a tombstone, but nothing that appeared to be the source of the plutonium oxide.

They rounded the next turn of the river. This stretch of the Galeegi was tighter, and soon Poston's Landing and the accompanying bridge came into view.

"There's the landing," Tyler said. "Were you this close in?"

Chloe looked around. Nothing was jogging her memory. "Maybe. If we reach the landing and haven't found anything, then we'll need to double back."

A high-pitched squawk suddenly registered from the sonar. A large shadow raced across the viewfinder. "Jesus, what is that?" Tyler asked. He cranked the engine and repositioned the boat back over the spot.

Chloe moved a bit closer to the monitor and adjusted the brightness. They both stared down at it as they backed over the target. "It's huge whatever it is," Chloe said.

As they passed over, the image encompassed the entire monitor. It looked like a giant rectangle. "What is that?" Tyler repeated.

"Pull up again, Tyler. But slowly," Chloe ordered. The image registered again. The rectangle was filling up most of the screen. "There! At the top, hold it here, Tyler." Chloe worked on the controls some more. "Do you see it?" she asked—a hint of a smile developing.

"See what? I don't see anything."

Chloe tapped the monitor with her index finger. "There along the side. Recognize it?"

Tyler lifted his sunglasses and squinted. "I'll be. Extended side mirrors. We're sitting on top of a truck, a whole damn cargo truck."

7:05 PM

Hammie Swantou sat in a threadbare lawn chair in the sandy area in front of his trailer. A rusty charcoal grill stood next to him—a singular flame from bits and pieces of burning driftwood rising from its center. Hammie had a bowl in his lap, and he was stirring a fusion of sulphur powder and Mayapple root. He took a wooden dowel and coated its end with a thick base; then he slowly pushed the end of the rod into the fire. The fire grew and changed in color from orange to green to white. He held the flame just inches from his face as it danced and sang to him. Hammie heard its words. It was quite clear.

"So, it is tonight. Tonight he comes," Hammie whispered to himself.

7:15 PM

Charles Argeaux was his old self again as he entertained diners at the Cotton Seed Golf and Fish Club. He laughed and made light of everyone and everything around him.

They sat at his usual table, the one in the center of the dining hall underneath the exquisite antique crystal and ormolu chandelier. The chandelier had been a gift to the club from Argeaux's grandfather who had made the sizable donation after renovating the family plantation home during the turn of the 20th century. It was ostentatious, which fit in nicely with the club.

Seated at the table to Argeaux's right was the young and

voluptuous Hanna Argeaux, his fifth wife. His additional table guests included golf and business partners and their wives or girlfriends. He had entertained them with several bottles of hard-to-come-by wines and stories of his success. He made mention of his favorite yarns: the corporations he had crushed, the small wars he accidentally started in small jungle countries, and his favorite: The story of how close the club's golf course came to being the site of the Ryder Cup in 1991 "before losing out to the bastards just up the shore at Kiawah Island."

It was going the Argeaux way until Robert, the maitre d', appeared at his table. "Your private line, sir."

Argeaux froze momentarily, contemplating whether or not to take the call. He looked to his guests and finally threw his dinner napkin on the table. He entered the smoking lounge, and finding no one there, sat at the table next to the marble fireplace. He picked up the black phone and punched the line. "This better be good," he said.

Argeaux listened for a moment, rose quickly from his chair, and yelled into the phone, "What?! They can't!" He breathed hard, and his jaw muscles tightened. He listened some more until his face became ruddy with anger. "Goddamnit, Major! They can't!" After a few more seconds, he whispered in an angry tone, "What the hell do I pay you for anyway? Take care of it now." He slammed down the receiver. Argeaux leaned against the fireplace and closed his eyes. His time was running out.

How did I ever let it come to this?

7:21 PM

The sun faded into the horizon, but there was no breeze, and the accompanying humidity was stifling. Tyler wiped

194

the sweat from his brow as he worked the throttle and kept the boat in position. The scanner recorded every angle of their find. The vehicle had settled perfectly on the bottom, so the top of the truck was clear. The thought that he was just a few feet away from something so dangerous weighed heavily on Tyler, but he could not help his fascination.

Chloe returned to the bow and carefully retrieved more sampling tubes she had cast over the side—her thoughts were all over the place. *Who could do such a thing? Was this done on purpose? How much hazardous material is down there?*

She was well aware of the volatile nature of plutonium oxide. The chemical compound had long been on terrorist watchdog lists. It was the active dispersal ingredient for the "dirty bombs" or the "poor man's nuke," which officials worried would be used on major cities. It took only five kilos of the compound along with a large quantity of C-4 and some blasting caps to do major damage. *But even if the truck was completely loaded with the stuff, why here? What possible advantage could there be to having a dirty bomb in this part of the river?* She almost laughed at the thought of Poston's Landing as a terrorist's target. *If it had been some kind of accident, why wasn't it reported? And who would be bringing plutonium oxide to the islands in the first place?*

Chloe capped the sample tubes and marked them with a Sharpie pen. Between the new samples and the documented evidence, the authorities would surely take action. She'd get the media involved if she needed to do so. But this much was clear: Somebody didn't want her to find this. Somebody had broken into the bungalow and destroyed her data. And somebody would rather kill than have this sunken cargo discovered. That thought was fresh in Chloe's mind when she heard the crack of a rifle and the bullet's report as it popped into the console, shattering fiberglass and metal.

"Get down!" Tyler yelled.

Chloe dropped the sample tubes and dove for the sunken area on the front deck. In a split second, Tyler threw the engine in gear, causing the boat to launch forward at an awkward angle. Chloe and the samples smashed up against the port gunnels. Another rifle shot sounded out, and a round whizzed overhead. Tyler managed to right the boat, and Chloe rolled up against the base of the console as they sped down the river.

The boat vibrated hard against the Galeegi as Tyler made the hairpin turns at top speed. Chloe drew a shaky hand to her face as she felt blood pouring out of her nose. The roar of the engine was so loud and the vibrations so great that she did not bother to call out to Tyler; she just hugged up against the console's base.

Tyler crouched at the wheel, intermittently looking ahead at where he was going and behind at the boat that was following. After the first shot, Tyler took a quick glance in its direction and saw the pointed bow of a powerboat speeding from under the bridge toward them. The driver had a sniper rifle laid out on top of his wraparound windshield. Tyler imagined the rifle's crosshairs squaring on the back of his neck.

Crack! Another shot and another miss.

The gunman's boat was much sleeker and faster than the Bayliner, and Tyler knew it. He was out of options, and the other boat was coming up fast. He prayed that one of the river patrols was beyond the next turn.

The Major held the throttle down on the Baja 245 Performance, a powerful white jet eating up the black water. He cursed his wayward shots, but he knew within seconds he would catch his prey, and he vowed that he would not miss again.

As he rounded the next turn, the Galeegi straightened out in front of him. The Major knew he could catch Tyler on this stretch. He leaned into the rifle and took a quick glance into the telescopic sight of the M21 assault rifle. The hard thumps and cast spray angered him, but his target was in range. He held his breath, pulled the trigger, and felt the smooth release.

The Bayliner fishtailed and then spun out toward the bank. It lifted hard and high into the air and then crashed down atop a marshy bank. With the prop out of the water, the Bayliner's 350 MerCruiser engine ran hot until it died in a quick puff of white smoke.

The Major powered down the Baja and coasted toward the Bayliner. He stood vigilant, keeping the rifle zeroed in for any possible movement. He eased his boat closer and searched for signs of life. But he saw none. It was quiet—a dead calm.

The tip of the Major's boat touched against the propeller of the Bayliner. The Major crawled over the console onto the bow with its steep hull. He carefully approached the narrow bow, keeping the rifle trained on the other boat and dragging a tie-rope, which he had wrapped around his wrist.

He pointed his weapon toward the aft cabin of the Bayliner. He saw no one in the bridge or engine areas, but the Major noted blood streaming from just beyond the shattered console. He eased onto the deck of the Bayliner, and after attaching the rope to a cleat, walked to the bow.

The girl lay there face down—her body in an unnatural position. A line of blood trickled out from under her head.

The Major smiled. He didn't think that he had gotten off such a lucky shot. But just as quickly, his smile was gone. *Where's the driver? Where's the guy?*

He turned to look behind the boat. Perhaps he had fallen off into the river. It had all happened so quickly. The Major moved next to the engine and scanned the Galeegi. The quick turns of the river's flow bounced against the banks, but he saw no movement—no floating body—no sign.

"Looking for me?"

The Major turned toward the marshy bank. Tyler stood knee deep in the brown grass and mud. His Glock was secured in the firing position. The Major swung his sniper rifle around, but he was too late. Tyler squeezed off a round, popping the man square in the forehead. His body lurched backward as the round split open the back of his skull. The Major and his rifle splashed into the Galeegi.

Tyler held his position, his arms still outstretched, the sting of the fired weapon in his hands. He swallowed hard at the thought of what he had done. He knew he had to do it, but as he was warned at the Academy, the jolt of taking someone's life is the hardest part of being a cop.

Chloe rose and stood on the foredeck. Her hand kept pressure on her bloody nose. Once Tyler saw her, he finally lowered his arms. Their eyes locked, both at a loss for words.

Tyler climbed out of the mud and onto the boat. He held Chloe tight. They were both shaking.

The Major's body was swept into the flow of the river. The brackish waters held it captive for only a moment until the silt and swirling flow pulled it under and into the belly of the black snake.

9:47 PM

Fletcher Tate sat in his recliner in the den of his home. Marie was curled up on the couch next to him doing a crossword puzzle. The ESPN baseball game of the week flashed across the big screen TV, but Tate's thoughts weren't on the game. He felt a sickening gnaw in the middle of his gut with all that had happened, and he feared more was to come. The situation was spinning out of control, and he felt helpless to stop it.

"Oh my, God!" Marie shouted as she pointed to the den's pull-glass doors.

Tate was quick to his feet, hurrying to turn on the back-deck lights. Tyler and Chloe stood outside the door. They were wet, muddy, eyes wide, still shaken. Tate slid open the glass doors and ushered them inside. "Tyler? Chloe? Are you okay? Get in here."

As Tate led them into the kitchen, Marie brought them blankets she kept in a basket near the couch. "What happened to you two?" Marie asked. "Are y'all okay?"

Tyler nodded briefly as they all sat down together at the table.

Tate leaned in. "What's going on, Ty?"

Tyler waited a moment more before he finally spoke. "Uncle Fletcher, we came to you because, quite frankly, you're the only person on these islands I trust. I think we have uncovered another twist to this little game somebody's been playing with us," he said angrily. "And this might be the most dangerous part of it yet."

Tate leaned back and looked over at Marie, who shared

his look of concern. Tate clasped his hands together, "Okay, I'm listening."

Over the next hour Tyler informed his uncle of everything they had been through, beginning with their ride to the airport. At one point, Marie made coffee for everyone. She also brought antiseptic and cotton swabs to the table to doctor Chloe's nose. Tyler calmly recalled everything in detail—even when recounting being hunted down on the river.

"It was Chloe's idea," Tyler explained. "When I yelled to her we were out of options, she came up with our trick of crashing the boat and then using herself as bait to lure the hit man in."

Tate looked briefly to Chloe. She had not said much. She was still in a state of shock.

"Did you recognize the man you shot?" Tate asked Tyler.

Tyler shook his head. "I saw someone talking to the sarge a few days ago outside the Lucky Shark. It may have been the same man."

Tate got up from the table and paced the kitchen. He had his back to them and rubbed his chin. "Do you have the images of the cargo truck?"

"We salvaged what we could from the Bayliner and took the man's boat back to the marina. I think the recording equipment and the tapes are okay." Tyler looked to Chloe, and she nodded.

Tate swung back around with a sense of urgency in his voice. "How much plutonium could possibly be down there?"

"It was a twenty-eight foot box truck, a freightliner. The container might be completely filled with the stuff. But as Chloe explained it to me, the water would act as containment. If the truck is filled with C-4 and if it were to be detonated, the explosion would be impressive, but probably not do a whole lot of obvious damage."

"What about the plutonium? It would be spread throughout the river."

"Dispersed," Chloe finally said. "There would be radioactive damage done to parts of the marsh and river, but unless there are a hundred or so of these truck bombs in the river, I don't see how it could be much of a threat to Galeegi or Amoyeli."

Suddenly, Chloe furled her brow in thought. "Unless..."

Everyone looked to her as she paused.

"Unless they added some kind of bio attaching agent, like a PCB." She paused again before adding softly, "CJ did say the sample had traces of chlorine as well."

"A PCB?" Tate asked.

"A polychlorinated biphenyl. It's one of the organic pollutants the EPA has on its priority list. It has a low water-solubility rate and is very deadly in and of itself. But if they somehow combined it with the plutonium then you have an extremely toxic cocktail on your hands."

"How so?" Tyler asked.

"The PCB could carry the plutonium through the river without dispersal, without breaking down. Theoretically, it could destroy everything that it touched. Killing the river and the marshlands. If it reached the aquifer, everything would become contaminated, including the islands. It's a dirty bomb but with the lasting ecological effects of a major nuclear explosion."

"What happens when it reaches the ocean?" Marie asked.

Chloe shook her head in frustration. "There's no way to know, but it could conceivably do damage up and down the Carolina coast. Some PCBs have crossed miles of ocean."

"If this is some type of bomb, then we have to stop it." Tate turned and said. "If there's even a chance we can get to it and unarm it before they decide to detonate it, then we need to try."

Tyler nodded. "Agreed, but how?"

Tate was reaching for his phone. "I'll call Kasko. The FBI can bring in their anti-terrorist squad. And I'll alert our Emergency Response Task Force."

Tyler grabbed his arm. "I don't think that's a good idea. Any official contact with the authorities will certainly get his attention."

"Whose attention?" He paused as he stared at his nephew. "Argeaux?"

"Who else, Fletcher? Who else has the money, the resources, not to mention the balls, to pull off something like this?"

"But why in God's name would Argeaux want to destroy Galeegi? This is his home for God's sake. He practically owns the whole island."

Tyler leaned over and put his hands to his face, then looked up at his uncle. "I don't know. But he did have us followed. He's got ties everywhere, including someone at our station. He's up to something."

Tate rubbed his eyes. He felt the weight of the island on his shoulders. He sighed. "Okay. I do know this one guy—Phil Nahigian. We were in 'Nam together. He was a tech for the Marines on one of their Explosive Ordnance Disposal squads. Plus he's an excellent diver. He's retired now—lives over on Edisto Island. I'll give him a call."

Tyler nodded. "Yes. Good. Let's try him."

Tate looked to his wife. "Marie, will you go get my black planner in the bedside table? It has all of my old contacts." She moved quickly to the back bedroom. Tate looked at both Tyler and Chloe. "Anything else you guys need to tell me while you're here?"

"That's it," Chloe began, "except that we're sorry we had to involve you in all this." She then attempted a smile and added facetiously, "I sure hope we didn't ruin your night."

Tate laughed briefly. "No, Chloe, it wasn't you two that ruined my night. Although I can't imagine how this night could get much worse."

11:39 PM

Mario Heyward stood and stretched his legs for what seemed like the millionth time. He was approximately two hundred yards away from the front of Swantou's trailer, his surveillance position for the past few days. Despite the relatively pleasant scenery on Amoyeli, the task of keeping an eye on the local root doctor had its issues. The heat and the gnats were relentless, and he was past boredom from this assignment.

Hammie Swantou was a strange little man who kept to himself, mumbling incoherently, and occasionally performing innocent hoodoo rituals. He seldom went out, and he had no visitors. Kasko believed that Swantou had some knowledge of the murders. But the more Heyward observed the man, the more he believed that was highly unlikely.

Heyward's walkie-talkie beeped. "Heyward, you on?"

He reached down and grabbed the two-way radio. "I'm here, Arnie. What's up?"

"Same ol', same ol'. Just bored. How's the front side of the trailer looking?"

Heyward laughed. "Probably like the backside—quiet as a whorehouse on Sunday."

"Aw, man, that's a terrible analogy. Where I'm from, Sunday at the whorehouse was one of the busiest times of the week. Went to church Sunday morning to find the peace of God, and in the afternoon, you went to the ranch to find a piece of ass."

Heyward laughed again. "Different strokes, partner. My neighborhood was much quieter. Fact is you had to travel a hundred miles to find anything resembling a whorehouse." Heyward paused. "By the way, did you hear what Kasko said? He thinks we may lose the Guard soon. This island is going to get a whole lot bigger without them."

"Yeah. We need our African boogeyman to strike soon, or we may lose our shot at him."

Heyward smiled. "Be careful what you wish for, Arnie. I don't think we're done with our man just yet."

Heyward waited for his partner's response, but there was none.

He grabbed his walkie-talkie a little tighter. "I said—don't think we're done just yet with this perp. What do you think? Over."

Silence.

"Arnie?" He waited. "Arnie, come in please."

Silence.

Heyward looked at the radio and checked the dials. "Agent Fogle, come in please." He turned the dials up and down again. "Arnie? Arnie, come in." Heyward threw the radio on his surveillance pack. "Damn it." Heyward looked to the trailer. Through the curtain-less window, he saw Swantou sitting at a small table—a votive candle in front of him. The root doctor seemed to be chanting and breathing in the smoke.

It would have been proper procedure for Heyward to call headquarters and report anything out of the ordinary, but Heyward hoped it was just a bad connection. Despite all of the high-tech gadgets the FBI had at its disposal, sometimes even they had to deal with minor snafus.

After failing to get reception on his cell phone, Heyward decided to circle around back. It was pitch black, and he approached cautiously. The last thing he wanted to do was to let Swantou know the FBI was camped out around his trailer. He rammed his way through the hanging limbs and underbrush that comprised Swantou's backyard. He finally made it to the spot where he thought his partner had established position.

"Arnie?" he called in a harsh whisper. "Arnie, it's me, Mario. Where are you?"

Heyward stumbled through the brush some more. He turned on his Maglite and came to an open area. Through the faint light, Heyward finally spotted him. Arnie was lying on the ground.

"Arnie? Arnie, are you okay?"

Heyward's light ran up the body of the other agent. As the beam reached Arnie's chest, Heyward saw that his shirt was soaked in blood. He shined the light on Arnie's severed head which was in the sand at the end of stretched entrails.

"*Jesus!*" Mario Heyward yelled and dropped the flashlight. He backed up—breathing rapidly, uncontrolled. He heard something behind him and reached for his gun. He turned around.

Midnight—a few ticks away. Hammie Swantou watched from behind the flicker of his candle as the doorknob on his trailer twisted and turned. It finally sprung the lock, and the door swung open. A heavy shadow was thrown against the wall.

Xevioso entered the small trailer with the bloody Oshe in his hands. Swantou rose.

"So, I am to be the last, Xevioso. You have now come for Swantou."

"You are the twelfth Igbo, the twelfth lock. Once you are gone, the Legba will be open. The gate will swing wide. Your death will bring the end to Amoyeli," Xevioso said as he drug sweat and blood splatters across his face. "The Igbo will be swallowed whole. It will finally be done. Justice will be done."

JUNE 10

5:28 AM

Yolanda Chabari sat up in her cot inside the emergency shelter on Amoyeli. She saw a few bodies moving about in the darkness, but most of the islanders were still asleep. She got out of her makeshift bed, went outside to where the water tanks had been set up, and poured a cup. She sipped the cool drink and scanned the dark edges of the waking island. Amoyeli had changed since she was a child.

It has lost its innocence, its simplicity.

Dr. Chabari stretched her arms and yawned after spending another long night in the pursuit of information on Jaja Nayu. Her focus now was on the islanders themselves and what they knew about him. But they gave her nothing she did not already know. He was shy, kept to himself, lived as a child with his grandfather in the lighthouse. She asked about Jaja and Katherine Argeaux, but no one responded. *They are too careful, too hesitant. They are holding back for some reason.*

She decided to go see Hammie Swantou. If anyone on the island knew of a botono connection to Jaja Nayu, it was Swantou. He would be brave enough. He would tell her everything.

7:15 AM

Collin Rutherford crawled into the dark and damp Hounfour. Very little light filtered through the cracks in the floor above him and the stench of death filled the room. He was terrified, but he had no other choice than to be there.

He held his flashlight tight in his right hand as he stood and walked across the creaky teakwood floor. He began a Vodun ritual by sliding his free hand up and down the *poteau-mitan*, a smooth wooden pole in front of the altar. He circled the pole and quietly chanted the words of a Houngan priest, asking that Xevioso continue to mete out justice.

Collin slipped his hand into his front pants pocket and retrieved a small silver box that looked like a Gatsby-era cigarette case. He set it down on the altar next to the candles. He felt a slight chill as he noted that all twelve of the black candles were now extinguished.

He placed the flashlight on the altar at an angle, opened up the case, and removed a finger-length vial. He held the glass tube in the beam of light and eyed its contents. *This should be enough. His time here is nearly complete.*

After placing the vial in a slot at the foot of the altar, Collin pocketed the case and reached for a bulky, rectangular container behind the candles. As he had done four times prior, he opened the container, removed a cloth covering and pulled out the bloodstained Oshe. The axe was heavy—well over twenty pounds—but he managed to lay it down with reverence on the altar. He ran a finger of his right hand up and down the black, twisted handle carved from African ebony.

Collin pulled his embroidered white handkerchief from his back pocket and slipped a corner of it into his mouth, allowing his saliva to saturate the end. Then he used his handkerchief to wipe the wide steel blade clean. It reeked of dried blood and flesh. He thought about the violence it had wrought and gagged.

Collin made sure the Oshe was absolutely clean before he retched. With his nausea pushing at his throat, he quickly rewrapped the axe in its covering and placed it back inside its container.

Collin left the altar room and crawled under the low-lying stone supports until he reached another dark room. The crawl space was tight and suffocating, but he managed to make it into the outer room. He stood up stumbled around, confused, before finding the stairway that led out of the darkness. He was light-headed and had tremors in his legs and hands. He placed one hand on the wall to balance himself as he climbed out.

He emerged into a hallway, turned, and locked down the trap door to the stairs. He scrambled through the old building trying to find his way out. His conscience tormented him relentlessly. He could not shake the gruesome vision of the bloody axe from his mind.

Collin opened the door to the outside, felt the sun on his face and swallowed fresh air. He ran down a narrow, overgrown path until he came to the back edge of the island. He almost made it to his sculling boat before his conscience overcame him again. He fell to his knees and balanced himself with one hand on the side of the scull. He vomited violently into the water hoping to empty himself of the misery he felt. Collin pulled the handkerchief from his back pocket and wiped his face. He stopped suddenly and stared in horror at the stained cloth. He balled up the handkerchief and threw it into the back of the boat.

Collin climbed into the scull and sat down in the middle seat. He drew out the oars and backed away from the island. He hated that place. He kept his head down, only periodically glancing behind him as he rowed through the twisting inlet.

It was not yet eight o'clock, and the tide was dead low. He knew he had to wait hours for the incoming tide so he could row through the marsh to safety, but Collin Rutherford knew exactly what he would do when he got home. He would hide in his room, crawl into another bottle of scotch, and pray to his own God to have mercy on his pathetic soul.

10:35 AM

Agents Kasko, Donovan, and Williams returned to Walterboro to visit Colleton County's Office of Vital Records. They sought any connection to Jaja, but so far the hour-and-a-half search turned up nothing. Kasko moved impatiently from behind Donovan, who was sitting at one of the office computers, to behind Williams, who was thumbing through a file cabinet. "Anything yet?" Kasko asked.

"No, and I don't think we'll find much. It doesn't look like they have any records around here that pre-date the 1970s," Williams said.

Kasko looked over at Donovan, who anticipated the lead agent's next question. "FBI files start with the trial. I can tell you everything about the man after the fact, including the kind of sandwich he had on the bus trip home eight days ago. But before the trial, he's a ghost, a specter. He just doesn't exist."

"He existed, Donovan. Just keep looking," Kasko barked.

The director of the office, a wide-bodied woman with a bouffant flip of red hair, waddled in from a back room and dropped a large cardboard box on the office counter. "Birth certificates from Amoyeli," she said, "These are all who were delivered at Colleton Medical. Those born on the island are not included."

"How so?" Kasko asked.

"These islanders don't exactly do things the normal way, Agent Kasko. The sun is their alarm clock, and the sea is their boss, if you know what I mean. Eventually, some go off to schools, get jobs, interact with normal society. We typically get their vital information second hand. But others never fill out a form; never get a number. Apparently, Jaja Nayu was one of those few."

"Maybe not here in this office," Kasko said, "but this man was charged in a court of law, worked in Atlanta, had a Social Security number. There has to be a family record on him somewhere."

Kasko's cell phone rang. "Special Agent Kasko," he answered then listened for a few moments as he fidgeted. "Okay," he said quietly. "I'll head back now." He slipped his Blackberry into his coat pocket. "Donovan, you and Williams stay here. Keep looking. I've got to fly back to the island."

"Another hit?" Williams asked.

"Yeah."

"Another islander?" Donovan asked.

Kasko nodded, turned to the records director, and said, "Ma'am, if this keeps up, you won't have to worry about searching for Amoyeli birth certificates anymore." He started for the door then added, "There won't be a single one of 'em left."

11:22 AM

Chief Tate held the Contender in place over the designated spot on the Galeegi River. Chloe sat in the

211

stern next to the idling engine watching the yellow rope as it slowly pulled through the swirling, black waters. The heat of the summer day was rising quickly, but neither one of them seemed to notice. The line slacked and bubbles rose from the water. Chloe pulled in the rope as a head broke through to the surface. "He's coming up," she said.

Chloe leaned over the side, grabbed a heavy metal clipper from the diver's hand, and tossed the tool onto the deck. The diver swam to the stern ladder and shed his tank and weight belt. Chloe worked quickly as she helped pull the equipment into the boat.

The man climbed up onto the ladder. He blew out a hard breath, stretched out his body, tumbled up and over the stern, and landed in the boat in a seated position.

"Freed the chain from the cargo door," he said. "You're right, Miss, that truck down there is loaded with the stuff. And they do have it wired." He tossed his mask to the side and pulled down the front zipper of his wetsuit.

Retired Master Gunnery Sergeant Phil Nahigian took a couple more deep breaths. In his mid-sixties, Nahigian still had a young man's body with only his gray crew cut and weathered face to indicate his age, but the current of the river and the tension of the dive had been a lot for the retired Marine.

"It's sitting in twenty feet of water. One of the barrels has been damaged—probably the source of your leak."

"Can you disarm it, Phil?" Tate asked from the captain's chair.

He took another deep breath, and then replied, "Must be thirty or more fifty-five gallon drums down there—double stacked. Probably wired with an acoustic remote, which can be a pain in the ass to disable. If you cut the wrong wire, it goes off. And this one is especially troublesome. Looks like the acoustic actuator and the detonator are wired to the back of the cargo bay. Damn near impossible to get to."

"Acoustic actuator?" Chloe asked

"Yeah. An offshore deck unit sends binary tone bursts through the water to the actuator, which then signals the detonator. The devil and the C-4 do the rest," Nahigian said.

"So where is this deck unit?" Chloe followed.

"Could be hidden anywhere within a three mile radius. And the deck unit can be activated by its own remote—a cell phone or laptop. Whoever drowned the truck could be on the other side of Rutherford when he decides to blow this baby."

"Can you jam the signal? Prevent it from going off?" Tate asked.

"Jammers are unreliable. Sometimes the frequency blockers themselves set it off."

"How much C-4 is down there?" Chloe asked.

Nahigian leaned forward and grinned, showing a gap between his two front teeth. "Enough to blow off your lollipop, I'm afraid."

Chloe rolled her eyes.

"We may be beyond the point of no return, Phil," Tate said. "I hate to ask, but..."

"You hate to ask? Yesterday I was pulling ugly mullet out of my seine like some old beach bum and today you want me to pull a dirty bomb out of the ass of a cargo truck submerged in twenty feet of water? And you hate to ask? C'mon, Fletch, you know I live for this shit."

Kasko's helicopter landed amongst a heavy dust cloud in a clearing several hundred yards away from Swantou's trailer. A large contingency of Guard and police had gathered in the yard. One of the FBI men broke through their lines and headed to the chopper. Kasko jumped down from the copilot's seat and headed straight to Agent Lockwood.

"Did you get the word about Agents Heyward and Fogle?" Lockwood asked as he pointed his thumb back at the trailer.

"They told me on the flight in," Kasko answered as he quickly surveyed the murder scene. "What about the recording devices?"

Lockwood shook his head. "They were destroyed. Visual and sound. Whoever did this knew we were in hiding and wired."

"Our man must be getting inside help."

Lockwood shrugged his shoulders. "There are a lot of the islanders at that shelter close to our base of operations."

Kasko stood still and said nothing as emergency personnel carried the bodies of the agents past him. The black body bags glistened in the sun. He refocused on Lockwood. "What about Swantou?"

"Dr. Chabari found him. Cut up pretty bad. I think she came out this morning to meet with him."

"Any residual evidence?"

"We're still at it, but nothing significant," Lockwood said. "Sorry."

"Where's Chabari?"

Lockwood pointed to the front of the trailer where she sat on the bottom wooden step giving information to

Howard Dupree. Kasko walked over and broke into their conversation. "I understand you found Swantou, Doctor."

Chabari nodded. "Another bloody mess, Agent Kasko. Another one of our people murdered." She looked back at Swantou's trailer and then to Kasko. "He was a good man; a man of the people; a holy man. I thought you were going to keep an eye on him. Protect him."

"We lost two men, Dr. Chabari, two professionals who were assigned to watch him. They were good men also." He raised his chin. "But this won't happen again. I swear we won't allow another islander to be harmed."

Chabari held up her hand. "Do not make promises you cannot keep, Agent Kasko. Your power here has been proven limited. Besides, as I was telling Lieutenant Dupree, I believe Xevioso is about to change his approach to Amoyeli."

Kasko looked at his fellow lawman. "Inside," Dupree said. "There's a new message for us."

Dupree, Chabari, and Kasko went inside the trailer. Swantou's hacked body was on the floor. Kasko noted the small table where Swantou had been sitting. It was covered with candles and wooden idols. A tattered, opened Bible lay in the center.

A member of the FBI Evidence Response Team was inside taking pictures of everything.

"Give us a few minutes," Kasko told the other agent, who quickly left.

Dupree pointed to the low ceiling on which another symbol was painted in the victim's blood.

"Another veve?" Kasko asked.

"Yes. See the three pointed lines and the twelve hooks within the pattern?" Chabari asked. "This is the Legba, the Vodun gate."

"Gate to what?"

"It has many meanings. It indicates new beginnings for the believer as well as the passageway to the spirit world," Chabari explained, "but it may also portend the endings of things." She bent down and took another look into the glazed eyes of Hammie Swantou. "And perhaps most disturbing, Agent Kasko, the Legba has in the past been used as an indicator of upcoming deaths, those on a massive scale."

1:37 PM

Charles Argeaux stood beneath one of numerous ancient live oaks at the back of his estate. The massive live oaks had age and beauty that were as much a part of the Argeaux home as the elaborate friezes and marble flooring. The tree under which he stood was the largest and the oldest, the one Katherine had claimed as hers alone. Its muscular, twisted limbs stretched out and up and back down as if reaching for both the sky and the ground at the same time. Katherine's tree was at the headway of the path that led through the ornamental gardens down to the docks.

Argeaux held his cell phone as he repeatedly hit the speed dial for the Major. Each time a recording noted the number was not available. "C'mon, c'mon, answer. Answer the call, damn it!" Argeaux screamed repeatedly.

Major Lorenzo Zandt was one of Argeaux's non-payroll employees who reported only when asked and was never afraid of dirty work. The former battalion commander in *las Fuerzas Especiales*, the Mexican Special Forces, had recently worked as a gun-for-hire for several mercenary groups and cartels around the world and had been called upon by Argeaux numerous times in recent years. He prided himself as an expert in many manners of death and destruction.

Finally, Argeaux quieted down and slipped the phone into his pants pocket. He had not heard from the Major since the previous day, and the Major reported to him daily without fail. *Something's gone wrong.*

Argeaux also assumed that the final lock on Amoyeli was opened by now; it was his time. He knew he must follow through or face the alternative. He trembled at the thought. Whatever choice he made, Charles Argeaux would lose, and he knew it. *But maybe, just maybe.*

Argeaux walked from the shadows of the oaks up to the terrace. He smelled the freshly mowed lawn, each blade cut to a near perfect quarter inch. It reminded him of all the cocktail parties, anniversaries, and birthdays celebrated in his enormous backyard. He stopped and looked around. He envisioned Katherine as a young girl, playing hide and seek amongst the oaks. For a moment he felt pangs of remorse. But only for a moment. He steeled himself and continued to the terrace.

Argeaux's two-thousand-square-foot terrace had been featured in dozens of regional magazines through the years. The veranda was a perfect blend of Old South practicalities and New South amenities.

He climbed the stone staircase to the lower tier, which housed the blue Italian-tile lounging pool and an outdoor kitchen with amply stocked cabinets and stainless steel appliances. A lap pool and spa were on the top tier. Crystal clear water from the pool was pumped over the side, creating a waterfall that splashed onto the edge of the bottom pool and cast a spray that cooled loungers from the brutal, summer heat.

Thirty-year-old Hanna Argeaux reclined in a chaise lounge under the falls. Wearing only thong bikini bottoms, the well-toned and well-tanned woman stretched up from head to toe on the plush, cushioned chair as she noted her husband's approach.

"Care to join me for a swim?"

"No!" he said as he walked past her and climbed the stairs to the second tier.

"Come on," she said seductively. "I'll make it worth your while."

"I said no, and put some clothes on. This ain't a goddamn nudist colony."

Argeaux crossed the ivy-draped top tier, entered his study through exterior French doors, went straight to his desk, and fetched a key hidden under the pull drawer. He went to his wall safe, spun open the combination lock, reached in, and removed a gray metal box, which he placed on his desk and used the key to open.

Argeaux reached inside and delicately removed a velvet-lined drawstring pouch. He opened the pouch and looked inside at his family's most treasured possession: a Victorian era, diamond necklace—eighteen-karat yellow-gold with a fine, silver flower-and-leaf motif. It was cushion shaped, and old single cut, with five-karat diamonds in various settings—a priceless work of art. He pulled out the necklace, draped it between his fingers and held it up to the sunlight. He marveled at its beauty and prayed it would be enough. He slipped the necklace into his front pocket as he stood up. He grabbed his light blue sports jacket from the back of his chair and hurried out the door.

Tyler's job was easy in a way. Just sit and wait. But ultimately it might be the most difficult. He was on Galeegi Island near the Argeaux Bridge. If his uncle's friend, the disposal tech, accidentally detonated the truck bomb, it was Tyler's responsibility to warn the islanders, maybe even lead the evacuation if need be. He stood next to his truck and trained his binoculars on Poston's Landing, only a half-mile upriver.

The latest text message from his uncle said they needed more sophisticated equipment to remove the detonator and were on hold until it arrived. Tyler nervously glanced at his watch. For the moment, the river was quiet. Only the constant bridge traffic and river's flow offered movement. But something to his right, about three hundred yards away, caught Tyler's eye. A sculling boat, about the same length as the row boat he encountered fleeing Amoyeli, made its way through a marshy inlet on the east side of Galeegi. Tyler focused his Steiner police binoculars on the occupant, who was struggling to paddle the boat through the heavy reeds. The man appeared to be dirty and exhausted. Tyler was sure that he had seen him at some point. *The man from the restaurant*, he realized.

Tyler moved from behind his truck and onto the gradient that led down to the river. He focused ahead of the boat as he knew the east side of the island was nearly uninhabited with only one huge plantation house on its high bank. When Tyler studied the Katherine Argeaux case, he remembered reading about the Rutherfords, whose lands were directly across the Island Highway from the Argeaux estate. The Rutherfords were also well off, often competing with the Argeaux family for wealth and status. The man in the boat appeared to be headed to the Rutherford mansion.

Tyler ran to his truck, got in, and slammed it into gear. He raced to the interior of Galeegi and pulled off just out of view of the Rutherford's front gate. It made little sense to follow or even care what the odd man was doing, but in a week of strange occurrences and well-played hunches, Tyler wasn't about to back away now.

Tyler walked to the gate, which was shut and required a code. He scanned the area and saw no other security apparatus. He used his long arms to scale the eight-foot stucco wall next to the wrought iron gate.

Once on the other side, he followed the paved drive through a series of turns that showcased the Rutherfords' extensive landscaping. The driveway was cleverly designed with many turns through the estate's woods. But the road was poorly maintained, and the decorative bushes and flowerbeds suffered from inattention. Tyler soon approached the Rutherford house, a three-story colonial with imposing columns straight out of the antebellum era. A canal cut just in front of the mansion with a connector bridge linking the drive to the large parking area out front and a five-car garage.

Tyler was about to cross when he heard something in the canal. He hid in the bushes on the bank and watched as the disheveled man sculled under the bridge and tied up to a ladder on a bulkhead near the garage. He climbed the ladder out of the canal and headed for the house's extended portico.

Tyler waited a few minutes, crossed the bridge and slipped over to the secured boat. He lay down on his stomach and looked down into the wooden craft for anything that might be out of the ordinary. Instantly, he saw the bloody handkerchief near the stern. He looked back to the mansion to see if anyone was watching and then cautiously climbed down the ladder and into the old boat. He picked up the bloody handkerchief, held it up to the sunlight, and examined it. He then carefully folded it and put it in his pocket.

Tyler started back up the ladder, and as he neared the top rung, he heard a car coming up the driveway. He peered from ground level as a dark blue Cadillac Escalade crossed the bridge and stopped at the front walk. The driver opened the door and stepped out. Tyler had seen the man several times before in photographs, so he had no doubt.

I'll be damned—Charles Argeaux.

2:37 PM

Emil Rutherford sat in a burgundy leather Queen Anne chair in the family library with a glass of sherry on the side table next to her. She had stretched her legs out on the chair's ottoman and crossed her ankles, trying not to doze off. Behind her, her maid stood on a stepstool dusting the left side of an enormous bookcase that straddled the fireplace.

"Now, you be careful, Ira," Emil said with a sleepy, two-glass drawl. "We don't want you falling from up there."

"Yes, ma'am."

"Goodness knows. You're almost as old as me. You'll break a hip," Emil said with a slight laugh.

"I'll be careful, Miss Emil, 'bout done up here anyhow."

Emil Rutherford sipped her sherry. "I should get Collin to help you. 'Course ain't no tellin' where he is now anyway."

Emil looked up and saw Charles Argeaux standing in the doorway with his hands clasped in front of him like a penitent schoolboy summoned by the headmistress.

"Well, I'll be," Emil said. "Charles Argeaux, what in the world are you doing here?"

Argeaux stepped forward. "You know why I have come."

Emil cleared her throat as she thought about it. "Well, no, I have no idea, Charles."

"I've done all that you've asked."

"All that I've asked? You've done nothing of the sort," Emil said.

"You cannot ask any more of me."

Emil furled up her brow. "Why Charles, I've asked nothing of you, and I expect nothing of you. Although, frankly, maybe I should. You and your family have robbed my family blind for years. You've taken advantage of our good nature. You, personally, broke all of our business agreements and ruined my husband—drove him to alcohol and to the grave. And now you have the audacity...."

Argeaux took another step forward and pulled the necklace from his pocket. "Here," he said and laid the necklace on the wing-back chair across from her, then backed away. "Take this as my concession. It's yours—all yours. Now please, please stop this madness and leave me be."

Emil's eyes narrowed, and she turned to put her glass down. "Charles Argeaux, I don't know what kind of trick you're playing."

When she looked back up, he was gone.

Emil forced herself out of her chair and hobbled over to the necklace. She lifted it and rubbed her fingers over the precious stones. She held the diamonds up to the light and whispered, "A day to be remembered: Charles Argeaux on his knees in my home." She smiled. "Burton Rutherford would have loved it."

4:15 PM

Chloe was bent over, sweat rolling down her face, straining her back as she helped Nahigian assemble the Mobile Abrasive Cutting Equipment, also known as MACE. A rectangular formation of iron tubes and pressure gaskets, Nahigian planned to use the high-powered water suspension jet to cut through the back of the cab of the truck into the cargo area, find the detonator, and disarm it.

Nahigian had already spent several hours cajoling and bribing members of his former unit to smuggle the equipment to the landing. Now, as he hurried to piece it together in the hot sun in the back of a cramped boat with a bomb in the back of a truck twenty feet below, the old Marine began to wear down.

"How much longer, Phil?" Tate asked.

Nahigian slammed down the wrench. "Am I not moving fast enough for you, Fletch? Maybe I'll just go back to the beach with my net and floppy hat, and you and the biologist here can do it your own damn selves."

Tate glanced over at Chloe, but said nothing.

"Are you sure about the entry? About going through the cab?" Chloe asked.

Nahigian wiped his brow. "It's our only option. The wires are set at mid-barrel, and since the detonator is not near the cargo doors, they probably put it and the actuator in the back of the container. Maybe they loaded the whole kit and caboodle that way."

"But you're not a hundred percent certain?"

Nahigian laughed through his exhaustion. "The only thing certain when dealing with bombs is that the people who try to dispose of them are bug-nuts crazy. Other than that, sweetheart, you don't know jack."

After ten more minutes of intricate work, Nahigian gave a final turn of his wrench and stood up. "All right, that's it. We're on go. Normally we'd work MACE with a remote control and cameras, but not in this situation. We'll manually place it the cab and go from there." He looked at Chloe. "I'll work the jet by hand, but I'll need you in the drink with me to watch the hoses, capiche?"

Chloe nodded.

"What do you need me to do?" Tate asked.

"Stay right where you are, Fletch, and be ready to haul ass. We shouldn't have to move, but you never know. If that thing down there goes off, you won't have to worry about moving the boat. The river will do it for you."

5:07 PM

Amoyeli was quiet. The crime scene at Swantou's trailer had been cleared, but a sense of foreboding engulfed the island. Xevioso's latest message, the sign of the Legba, hung over everyone's head like the Oshe itself. *Was the sky god finished administering justice? Were there more deaths to come? Would it be on a massive scale as Dr. Chabari indicated?* It was very conflicting and unsettling. All the islanders could do was sit and wait and worry.

Miller Kasko, on the other hand, returned to the shelter and reviewed Jaja's file. He was convinced that the islander's death was the missing key to unlock the case. Jaja's role in the murder of Katherine Argeaux remained unclear. But Kasko was convinced that Jaja was the descendant of the botono slave, and if Chabari was correct about the botono's ability to summon Xevioso, then discovering Jaja's background was to be his primary focus.

Kasko asked one of the guardsmen to drive him the ten minute ride to the lighthouse so that he could take another look around. He had borrowed Sheriff Sheridan's key to open the padlock on the station's door. Once inside he walked through the small mudroom and into the kitchen and flipped the light switch. The power was off, as he had been warned it might be. He pulled his pen light from his pocket and continued to the back.

Kasko eased into the small bedroom and sat on the old iron-framed bed. He looked around the room carefully and noted cracks in the walls, separations in the window frames, paint splatters, and corroded door hinges. He got up, walked over to the chest of drawers, and searched them. He shined his pen light through the openings in the floorboards but found nothing.

Kasko opened the slider door to the stairs and began the climb to the lantern room. He passed by the darkened service room, figuring he would search it on the way back down. He then ascended the final few steps to the top and took in the panoramic view, noting a few black clouds forming in the distance over the ocean. He scanned the island with its beautiful white beaches and the varying levels of blue to the ocean's sloping shelf. The case had so consumed him that he hadn't been able to appreciate Amoyeli as the island paradise it was. He remembered how the sheriff had described the killer as "a serpent in the Garden of Eden," and he wondered about his own role in the biblical scenario. *Am I the one being deceived, or am I just part of the deception? Or perhaps I'm one of the angels sent to guard the gate.* He laughed aloud at the thought.

Kasko turned toward the stairs and took one last look around. He noticed an odd marking on one of the wooden rafters. Intrigued, he put one foot on the sill and raised himself up, balancing against a panel of the heavy glass window and the rafter. He held onto the beam and swung his body around to get a better view of the marking. As he inched closer, he saw a crossing line between two other slanted lines that formed a point. It was crude, but it looked like the letter "A." He ran a finger past the letter along the beam and felt more indentations. *Whole words perhaps?*

So engrossed in his find, Kasko was completely unaware that someone had entered the lighthouse, climbed the one hundred eighty-nine steps, and was now standing in the lantern room directly beneath him.

5:46 PM

A slight wind blew down the tree-lined avenue leading to the Argeaux mansion. A summer storm brewed off the coast, and the islands would soon be taking the brunt of it. Charles Argeaux, a glass of bourbon in his hand, stood and watched the incoming clouds from the Palladian window in his front living room.

His contact at the police station had confirmed that the twelfth victim had been found and another message scrawled in blood had been left at the scene. *The Legba,* Argeaux thought. He was fully aware of the significance. The prophecy of which he had been warned was about to come true. The locks had been opened, and now he must finish the job.

But how could he even think to do what was demanded of him? How could he destroy the lifeblood of the islands he loved so much? How could he possibly sacrifice any more than he had already? *Perhaps the bribe will buy me some time.*

At that moment, his beautiful wife Hanna sashayed into the room. She wore a loose-fitting white robe and was fresh from her afternoon swim. Around her neck was the family's cherished diamond necklace.

"Where did you get that?" Argeaux snapped.

Hanna smiled. "As if you didn't know. It's beautiful, darling. I just love it."

Argeaux set his glass on top of the Steinway grand piano then walked over to her. He lifted the heavy, centered pendant from between her breasts. "Where did you get this?"

Hanna's smile faded. "One of the gardeners brought it to me; he said it had been delivered out front. Is this not an early anniversary gift?"

Argeaux's face flushed with anger, and he ripped the piece from her neck.

"Charles!" she screamed.

He looked at necklace in his hand and then to his startled wife. "Get out of here. Leave me alone."

"Charles? What's going on?"

"I said, get the hell outta here!" He grabbed Hanna by the back of her robe and slung her toward the door. Her bare feet slipped on the hardwood floor, and she fell against the wall. She quickly stood and ran crying from the room.

Charles calmly walked back to the piano, snatched his drink, and drained it as the summer storm's first flash of lightning popped outside the picture window.

5:59 PM

Chloe Hart was unaware that a storm had blown in as she minded the pressure hoses ten feet under the Galeegi River. She felt a sensory overload as she tried to maintain the MACE lines. Three Super Bright Yoke Lights were tied to a rope line from the Contender down to the submerged truck. The swift current twisted the lights, causing their beams to swirl in the watery darkness like an x-ray tableau of the slithering black snake.

She could hear the hum of the Contender's engines and the MACE pump rattling against the boat's deck. Below her was the drumming of the water jet as Nahigian worked the nozzle against the interior wall of the truck cab. She looked down and saw a light in the cab that Nahigian set up so he could see what he was doing. She prayed it wouldn't take much longer.

If there was a way to sweat under water, Phil Nahigian would have poured buckets. He bit down hard on the mouthpiece of his regulator as he held on to the powerful MACE. His hands cramped, and his muscles burned as the jet pounded loose the rivets that held the wall metal in place. He maintained a constant forty-five-degree angle knowing that with the wrong slant, the pressure might shoot past the cargo wall and rupture one of the barrels or sever a wire and detonate the bomb.

Nahigian finally managed to free enough sheet metal to bend it open and look inside. He saw a blinking red light on the rectangular-shaped acoustic actuator. The actuator was secured firmly against the larger detonator, and both were attached to a pack of C-4 taped halfway down one of the barrels on the back wall nearby. Normally, he would use the MACE jet like a pigstick disrupter that bomb-disposal personnel use to separate components of an improvised explosive device, thus rendering it harmless. But he saw that the actuator and the detonator were protected in a tightly bound pressure casing, making it impossible to erupt.

Nahigian swam out of the cab, grabbed the rope, and slowly ascended with the tubes and hoses in tow. He gave Chloe the thumbs up when he reached her, and they surfaced together. It was raining hard. Tate moved to the stern and helped wrangle in the equipment. Within a minute, both divers were safely in the boat. Nahigian leaned over, took a deep breath of fresh air, and flipped the pump switch.

"We're in," Nahigian said. "It's a delicate set up—pressure casings and bad angles. I might be able to do it by hand. Snip a couple of wires, and we should be free."

"Good work, Phil," Tate said.

"Don't thank me just yet," Nahigian said as he grabbed his bag and pulled out wire clippers. "It's risky down there. Good thing there's enough of last night's ale still swimming around my system to settle my nerves, huh?" He smiled and winked at Chloe.

"All you have to do is cut a wire? That's it?" Chloe asked.

"One little vasectomy, and the whole thing goes limp," Nahigian said with another elfish grin.

Chloe rolled her eyes.

"But we need to act quickly," Nahigian continued. "With the container open, all kind of shit is flowing into the truck."

"Are you ready to go back now?" she asked.

The aging Marine shrugged. "Yeah, hell, why not?"

Tate and Chloe helped him get his tank back on and Nahigian returned to the stern.

"What do you want us to do?" Tate asked.

Nahigian grabbed his dive knife and quickly severed the tie rope. "Just get out of here," he said as he splashed backward into the river. He popped his head out of the water and yelled, "Oh, yeah, one other thing, Fletch. When this is over, you're gonna have to buy me a cold one." He laughed like a madman before jamming his regulator into his mouth and submerging.

6:07 PM

Rain pounded the glass panes of the lantern room in the Amoyeli Lighthouse. Storm clouds hid the fading sun, and the top of the tower was cloaked in blackness. Kasko had pulled himself up on the thick rafter and was stretched out as he tried to read the carved message. The lighthouse's new arrival paced directly below.

"Can you make out any more?" Yolanda Chabari called out to him.

Kasko ran his pen light over the next marking. "Yeah... first two letters are definitely 'E' and 'B.' Then it looks like a 'G' and then an 'O'...followed by an 'R,' an 'A'...and then an 'M'...maybe...and the last one looks like an 'I.'"

"Any more?" Chabari asked.

"No, I think that's it," Kasko said as he rolled to the side then swung down to the floor, landing on his feet. "So how many is that? Five or six?"

"Six," Chabari answered. "Six names."

"Names?" Kasko asked.

"Ewansiha, Jaja, Nourbese, Irawagbon, Abiamu, and Imarogbe. Shine your light on this paper, and I will write them down."

"Good thing you came along when you did, Dr. Chabari.

I would have never figured that out." He paused and then added, "Of course, you damn near gave me a heart attack when you came in earlier."

"I am sorry, Agent Kasko, I did not mean to surprise you, but I too felt strongly that this place may hold clues about Jaja's past."

"I recognize Jaja, but who are the others?"

"They also lived here. They are Benin names, Fon names."

"Jaja's family?"

Chabari nodded. "His grandfather, the first caretaker, and the others."

"I thought Jaja's grandfather was Roger or something like that?"

"That was his English name, his inherited slave name. Look at the first one on the list: Imarogbe. It is a male Benin name. It would make sense that Imarogbe is Roger's African name. The next one is probably that of his wife, Abiamu. We know they had at least two daughters—one, Norine, who died when she was three months old. These next two are female."

Kasko focused on the list. "So, what you're saying is that Irawagbon could be the mother of Jaja."

"Yes, it would seem so."

"Then who is Ewansiha?"

Chabari paused. "I do not know. But it is considered a Fon male name. The name follows Jaja. Could have been a brother."

"I'll give these names to Donovan and Williams. They can run them through our computer databases. Maybe they'll find a match in government files."

"And I'll ask the islanders if they recognize any of them," Chabari said.

Kasko and Chabari then began the long descent down

the stairs as thunder shook the old lighthouse to its foundation.

6:33 PM

Argeaux patted the bottom of the twenty-three-year-old Evan Williams bottle, and the last golden drop of bourbon bled onto the ice. His glass was full. He took four gulps and felt the fire dull his senses, chill his fears. He turned toward his desk, determined to settle the matter. He had returned to his study and mentally prepared himself for what was expected of him, what he had been commanded to do. He had no more options, no more time. Xevioso would come if he failed her now. And then the unthinkable. She had rejected his glittering bribe, and deep down, he knew she would. She never wanted his fortune, only his soul, which he had sworn to her more than sixty years before.

Argeaux sat down at the desk and downed three more slugs of courage. He reached into his briefcase, pulled out his laptop, and placed it on the top of the desk. He flipped open the top, hit the power button, entered his password, and waited for the blue screen to materialize.

Phil Nahigian carried the severed tie-rope into the cab and repositioned the attached lights to get the best possible view of the cargo hold. The lights illuminated the swift-flowing water, giving it an earthy golden aura as silt and leaves and other debris swept past him en route to the sea. He pushed aside a layer of muck that had been captured in the cab and braced his knees against the seat. He stuck his hand-held light into the hole in the cab and managed to slip a shoulder and his head into the cargo bay. The actuator and attached detonator were now almost within reach.

He dug out the wire clippers from his dive belt and leaned back in through the hole. Removing just the actuator was not an option because it was hot-wired to the detonator. The whole igniter system would have to be removed. He traced the wires around the pressure casings until he was confident he knew what each one was. The explosive device consisted of the AA 100 Acoustic Actuator signal receiver, an Atlas 7D emulsion detonator, and some unmarked type of wide-bodied cast booster. All he needed to do was cut the yellow wire first to disengage the frequency receiver, then snip the red to unhook the detonator from the C-4 pack and the barrels.

The black wire was the Atlas system's hidden negative switch and would be left alone until after the detonator was secured.

But what if the bastard who constructed the bomb had reversed the hookup of the wires? Nahigian stopped momentarily, and then decided it was best not to consider the possibility.

Argeaux ran quickly through the start-up sequence. Major Zandt had taught him how. He raised the remote frequency icon, which appeared on his screen as a rotating beacon symbol. The screen asked for the arm code—six empty slots awaited his command. Argeaux quickly typed in the numbers and encoded the arming signal. Two and a half miles away, the EdgeTech deck unit attached to the underside of the bridge at Poston's Landing went hot and sent a sixteen-bit tone burst through the Galeegi River to its waiting target.

Shit! Phil Nahigian's eyes opened wide. He backed off and froze. The red light on the actuator stopped blinking and maintained a permanent glow—the arming system had been activated. Nahigian glanced at his dive watch. He was out of time.

Argeaux looked at the six new empty slots on the screen awaiting the fire command. He closed his eyes and drew his tumbler across his pained forehead. He brought his glass to his lips and took another swallow. *Why couldn't this be arsenic or hemlock or even venom from the black moccasin itself?* He opened his eyes and stared at the flashing screen. *You damn well know why. It has to be this way.*

Nahigian leaned forward and stretched his right arm toward the yellow wire. But it was just out of reach. *C'mon, c'mon....* He strained against the cargo bay wall, but he still could not reach it. His regulator hose snagged on the opening, and the air tank nozzle banged against the outside of the container.

Nahigian pulled back, repositioned the cutter to his fingertips, and tried again. He was close but not quite where he needed to be. He pushed his shoulder as far through the opening as possible; his fingers cramped slightly as he felt the blades barely on the wire. He pushed again. His shoulder and arm muscles stretched to the breaking point. He closed his fingers as best he could but lost his grip. The cutter slipped out of his hand and quickly settled on the bottom of the cargo bay floor.

Argeaux punched in the first three numbers of the fire command, and then paused. He thought about what would happen next. Entering the last three digits would set off a dirty bomb that would destroy all life in the Galeegi River and surrounding marshes. The fallout would completely salt the two islands, rendering them uninhabitable for centuries. Most of the Amoyeli population would die instantly.

Major Zandt masterminded the construction of the bomb. With his recent stint working for Blackwater Security in Iraq and Afghanistan, Zandt had perfected his bomb-making methodology. Argeaux gave Zandt complete access to his medical and chemical facilities, and the Major had little problem in concocting the specialized river bomb.

Chloe Hart was only half right about what was in the bomb. It did contain plutonium oxide in combination with a bio-attaching agent called Aroclor 1254, which is a PCB that would carry the radioactive material down river to the ocean before being sucked into the groundwater aquifer, making the islands uninhabitable. That was the bomb's permanent effect.

But Chloe did not know that the top half of the barrel contained a booster explosive and compacted hydrogen cyanide, which upon detonation, would rain down as a liquid spray across parts of Amoyeli and its marshlands, immediately killing everything it touched.

What Xevioso started, Argeaux would finish. The Legba would be open. It was to be death on a massive scale.

Nahigian unbuckled his weighted dive belt and slipped off his air tank. He could not squeeze through the opening with it on his back. He would have to slide through the opening, retrieve the wire cutter from the cargo bay floor, and finish the job the hard way—holding his breath.

The botono's plan was clever; Argeaux could not deny it. The hated Igbo descendants would be swallowed whole, their payment for generations of overt disobedience. They had ignored their gods and lost their way, and worse, they had treated her and her heritage with disdain. Even her father had denied his connections. It was an abuse of the botono that would no longer be tolerated. At the same time, the descendants of the white masters would be punished for their ancestors having put them with the Igbo cargo for the middle passage, a fitting retribution for the more than three-hundred-year-old sin. And the punishment would be inflicted because he, Charles Argeaux, had failed her.

Argeaux typed in two more numbers, then stood up and looked out through the back terrace doors. If only the summer rain could wash away the madness.

He lifted his glass and downed the rest of the bourbon. He felt no pain now; he felt absolutely nothing. He turned back to the computer, and with his right index finger, he encoded the final number and pressed "enter."

Showers pounded the Galeegi River, yet the black water snaked seaward as usual. At the landing near the bridge, air bubbles rose from the river to meet the rain-pocked surface. Suddenly Phil Nahigian's head burst out of the water, followed by the disabled detonator that he held firmly in his right hand.

"Whoohoo!" he screamed to high heavens. "Somebody owes me a beer!"

7:17 PM

ALL CLEAR! BOMB DEFUSED!
Tyler read the text, slammed the pedal of his Ford

Ranger, and headed for the Argeaux Bridge. Within minutes, the truck slid down the rain-slick road to Poston's Landing and screeched to a halt. Tate, Nahigian, and Chloe were waiting in the Contender next to the concrete ramp. Chloe leaped from the bow, sloshed through the water, and ran up to Tyler.

"It's good? Everything's okay?" Tyler asked.

"We think so," Chloe said with a wet hug. "Phil got the detonator out of the truck. The stuff is still down there, but it's defused. I hope to God there aren't any more like that in the river."

Tate and Nahigian secured the boat, and smiling broadly, both men walked up to Tyler and Chloe. Tyler shook Nahigian's hand. "Thank you, sir. You have saved a lot of lives."

"No, you and Miss Chloe are the lifesavers. I'm just a dumbass who enjoys swimming in bomb-infested waters."

Tyler laughed and turned to his uncle. "Well, that takes care of the bomb. What now?"

Tate looked back at the river as the rain was letting up, then turned back to Tyler and said, "Our serial killer has been protected through all of this, and that required lots of power and money. I think your suspicion of Argeaux might be correct."

"Maybe, maybe not," Tyler said as he reached into his pants pocket and pulled out a small plastic bag.

"What is it?" Chloe asked.

"Possibly some more evidence." Tyler showed the bag to his uncle. Inside was the bloody handkerchief. "And if it is, then there are more people involved than just Argeaux."

"Okay," Tate said wearily. "I think it's time to have us another powwow. First let's get cleaned up then meet at the station in two hours. And don't tell a soul what has happened."

"What about the cargo truck?" Chloe asked. "It's still a danger. One of the barrels is ruptured."

"If I may..." Nahigian broke in. "I know a couple of old grunts who could yank the truck off the bottom and have it on dry land before sunrise."

"Can they be counted on to keep it quiet?" Tyler asked.

"We're talking about former members of the Marine's Expeditionary Viper Unit, son. They've seen more and know more classified info than the past four presidents combined. They won't talk."

There was a brief silence and all eyes drifted to Chief Tate. He tossed his cell phone to Nahigian. "Give 'em a call. Get this done."

Tyler and Chloe headed for the Ranger. Tate walked back to the boat, got in, and moved behind the wheel.

"Ain't you forgetting something, Fletch?" Nahigian called out from the shore. Tate looked up from the Contender's console wondering what else he could have possibly missed. "You still owe me that beer, and these fellows who are coming will be mighty thirsty too."

Tate smiled back as he fired up the Contender's engine. "Phil, if you and the other jarheads pull this off, I'll personally sail a tanker up here filled with the coldest brew in town."

8:17 PM

Chloe stripped off her wet bathing suit and t-shirt and stepped into Tyler's shower. The hot water washed away the chill of the rain and the brine of the river. The steam opened her pores and softened her skin. An overwhelming sense of relief followed. She would have a lot to explain to the government, the EPA , and especially David. But she knew she had done the right thing. She had made a lot of the right choices in the past few days, and she knew it. All she needed now was the pulsating water of her soothing shower.

That and perhaps one more thing.

The shower door opened on cue, and Tyler stepped in behind her. There were no words; but as before, none were needed. He rubbed the back of her neck and shoulders deeply, in a circular motion. Turning to face him, she wrapped her arms around his shoulders and pressed her body against his. Their lips met as the hot water enveloped them, paving the way for the human touch to follow.

Thirty minutes later, Tyler was laid out on the flat of his back in his bed catching his breath. He reached over and touched Chloe's hand. They said nothing. It was the same as after the night on the beach. The more they were together, the more they loved each other, the harder it would be to say goodbye.

Tyler looked over at the alarm clock. "We should get going. Uncle Fletcher will be waiting."

Chloe leaned up to look at the clock as well. "Yeah, okay. I guess I need to take another shower."

"Yeah, me too."

"One at a time this time," she said with a laugh. Chloe hopped out of the bed and ran naked to the bathroom.

Tyler watched as she closed the door. He clasped his hands behind his head and looked at the ceiling fan, thinking about her. She was perfect—brave, smart, intuitive, resourceful. He knew he would never find another woman like her.

Tyler sat up, looked over to his dresser at his pistol in its holster, and thought about the man he killed. *Most cops go their entire careers without ever killing anyone. I did it in only two weeks.* He didn't want to do it, but the reality was he had no choice. It flashed again in his mind, the bullet splitting open the man's head—his subsequent fall into the river. The memory of the kill shot then blurred to one of his father lying in that hospital bed, suffering—the disease ravaging him to the bitter end. *The effect is the same. Death is death. The end is the end, by my bullet or God's will.*

Tyler rubbed his forehead. This had been such a surreal time in his life. So many unexpected twists and turns. So many life and death questions. And it had all happened so quickly. He contemplated it for a moment more and then stood next to his bed, resolved.

Enough of this. Get back to work.

9:22 PM

Dr. Yolanda Chabari had returned to the shelter, and after a brief meal, she began speaking quietly with some of the older islanders. She mentioned the Fon names to them, but no one said anything about the family until they were retiring for the evening. Suddenly, Tattiana approached Chabari and took her by her hand. She ushered the younger woman outside to a tree far enough away so no one could hear them.

"You have something to tell me, Sister Tattiana?"

The rail-thin woman with straight grey hair nodded, but said nothing. She lifted her hands to her face and covered her mouth like an embarrassed child.

"It's okay, Tattiana. Tell me when you are ready."

The woman just looked at her, continuing to hold her

hands in place and said nothing. Chabari waited for a moment more, smiled, and turned to go.

"Wait," Tattiana said. "There is something." She immediately put her hands back to cover her mouth.

Chabari reached out and took the woman's hands in hers, pulling them to her side. "What is it you have to say, Sister?"

Tattiana turned her head away. "Imarogbe...two daughters he had. Two. One died of the sudden breath-taking. She was very young. I remember."

"And the other?"

The old woman tried to draw up her hands, but Chabari wouldn't let her. She stood quietly for a moment shaking her head. "Imarogbe could not handle her. He sent her away."

"Where did he send her, Sister?"

"Away. To white folk."

"Which white folk, Tattiana?"

The old woman said nothing and turned her head away, struggling to break free. Chabari hardened her grip and held tightly.

"Tattiana, please, this is very important."

Again the woman struggled as if it were causing her great pain. "I do not know."

"Why did he send her away?" Chabari demanded.

"She...conjurer. She...Vodun caster."

"She was botono?" Chabari asked.

Tattiana gave a desperate nod as if she had said too much. Chabari let go, and the old woman ran to the shelter.

It made sense now. Jaja's mother was the botono. She had inherited the ability from her ancestor. Her father sent her away, sold perhaps to a white family. There would

241

be hatred there, resentment. And she would have had the motive to call upon Xevioso. To have asked for justice after her son was killed.

Chabari looked out into the darkness. She sensed her now. She felt the botono's control, her hatred for this place and these people. She was out there, and she was very close.

10:05 PM

Tyler and Chloe entered the police station and hurried through Control Central to Tate's office, the only room with a light on. The Chief sat at his desk looking at a map of the islands.

"Are we alone?" Tyler asked.

"Yeah. I told Sarge and the on-loan officers I would handle night duty tonight. I sent them all home."

Tyler and Chloe sat across from the desk. "Good. The fewer people around here the better," Tyler said.

"Tell me about what you found," Tate directed.

Tyler pulled the handkerchief in its plastic bag from his back pocket and pushed it toward Tate. "I don't know if it's significant or not. We'll have to have it tested."

Tate held up the bag. "I can get that done without too much trouble. Where did you get this?"

"The Rutherford plantation, while staking out the bridge. I saw a man making his way through the marsh in a small boat. He tied up near the house. I followed him until he went inside. I went to his boat and saw the handkerchief on the floorboard."

"What man?"

"Don't know; a white male around forty years old, short, grayish-brown hair. I wouldn't have given him a

242

second thought except he was the same man who spied on me and Chloe the other night at the restaurant."

"Was it Collin Rutherford?"

"I don't know. When I confronted him at the restaurant, he was obnoxious and reeked of alcohol and cigarettes."

"Sounds like Collin. Could this blood be his?"

Tyler shrugged his shoulders. "I guess, but I didn't see an injury as he rowed in or any blood in the boat. No fishing gear or nets or anything like that."

"Was he just out rowing in the marsh?"

"I have no idea what he was doing out there. He looked beat. Sunburnt. It was obviously not a pleasure cruise."

Tate ran his finger along the map. "Beyond the marsh there's not a whole helluva lot out that way. He couldn't have come from down the river or we would have seen him at Poston's Landing."

"What about St. Agnes?" Chloe asked. "I remember when I was mapping out the Galeegi that the tiny island is over that way."

"I don't know," Tate said. "St. Agnes is a good piece away from the Rutherford place. Besides, he would have had to time his way through with the tide. During all but just a few hours of high tide, the marsh on that side is exposed pluff mud. It's a small window. A trip there and back in a boat like that would take you through the tide cycle—several hours at least."

"I've never been to St. Agnes," Tyler said. "Anything over there?"

"Not much," Tate answered. "It's a dry island with little to no beach. Besides the marsh pass there are no good landing spots. History has proven it not to be the most hospitable of places."

"What do you mean?"

"In the early '40s, I think, some Benedictine monks built a small monastery there. It was supposed to be an island of retreat and solitude for them, but the well they dug quickly dried up, and they left. In 1958, a man named Ben McCreight tried to make the place over as a tourist attraction. He was going to showcase the reptiles of the Carolina coast with all kinds of snakes and gators in cages and sunken pits. The South Carolina Serpentarium he called it. He put a ton of money into it. Even had a quarter-mile bridge built from Pavilion Beach and water piped over from Galeegi."

"What happened?" Chloe asked.

"Hurricane Gracie hit in 1959. Destroyed the bridge and the pipes. Ol' Ben took it as a sign and moved on."

"Who owns it now?" Chloe asked.

"After the hurricane, the island of Galeegi annexed it. They took down the bridge supports and just left the place to the birds."

Tyler got up, moved around to Tate's side of the desk, and looked at the map. "So there is a structure there. A building of some sort."

Tate nodded. "About dead center of the island. You can't see it from the marsh, but when you approach ocean side, you can make out the roof of the primary building."

"Sounds like a place to check out. Isolated but close by," Tyler said. "Did the FBI investigate it?"

"Initially after the Witch Doktor incident, but they didn't find anything."

"Maybe we should pay another visit," Tyler said. "I could head out there tomorrow morning."

"It's a long shot, sport. May turn out to be nothing."

Tyler looked at Chloe and back to his uncle. "After the past few days, a little nothing might be just what we need."

JUNE 11

As the sun rose over Galeegi Island, waking residents had no idea how close they had been to disaster. Although the serial killer had most islanders on edge, the only evidence they had of the night's near-catastrophic events was an unexplained, empty cargo truck covered with mud and abandoned on the ramp at Poston's Landing.

On Amoyeli Island, tensions remained high. The Igbo descendants knew of Hammie Swantou's death and the sign of the Legba left behind. Most woke waiting to hear of death on a massive scale, some terrible carnage that had happened during the night, but as light washed over the island, news spread that everything was okay. The Guard patrols, SWAT teams, and the FBI reported that no new killings had taken place.

No one was more shocked at the news than Xevioso himself. The thunder god, the god of justice, knew what should have taken place. As he roamed Amoyeli, he became more and more incensed that the Igbo had not been dealt their final blow. And he knew only one person was to blame—Charles Argeaux.

7:55 AM

Tyler piloted the confiscated Baja Performance speedboat out into the Atlantic. The morning breakers approached with increasing ferocity; however, the boat comfortably cut through the frothy waves.

Tyler planed out the boat and headed to St. Agnes. He

stood behind the wheel with Chloe seated in the cockpit next to him. It felt strange to be riding in the boat that just two days before was used to hunt them down, but as this was unofficial police business, it seemed to make more sense than taking the Contender. Besides, the Baja was much more fun to drive.

But Tyler was more concerned about Chloe. She needed to head back to Washington. She had not returned the dozens of messages the EPA had sent her, but Tyler didn't want to press her on it. He was glad she wanted to stay.

Tyler carefully considered the dangers of taking her to St. Agnes. He didn't want to put her in harm's way at any cost, but she made a compelling argument that, as a research biologist, she could help him make immediate tests for blood if need be. That and the fact that he hated to spend a second without her skewed his reasoning.

He looked over at her. She had her head slightly turned, and she watched the shoreline as they sped past Galeegi. The wind was wildly throwing her dark hair behind her. She was beautiful. *Perfect, as always.*

He would dare not say it aloud, but Tyler finally admitted it to himself. Without a question, without a doubt, he knew he was in love with Chloe Hart.

8:34 AM

At the shelter in Amoyeli, Miller Kasko finished passing out the day's assignments. He admonished the men and women under his command that there was still a need for vigilance. They went over the latest satellite images, reconnaissance reports, and weather updates to prepare everyone for the day.

After the law enforcement agents dispersed, Kasko was

alone in the shelter's back room. He sat on the conference table rubbing his hands together, hoping for a miracle.

He got one.

The phone rang. "Kasko," he answered.

"Donovan here, sir. We may have something."

"Talk to me."

"We checked the names you gave us with an employment commission census on the island. We looked for variations against the name "Irawagbon." Crossing them with gender, approximate age..."

Kasko interrupted. "Don't give me the how, Donovan, just tell me what you found."

"Yes, sir. We located an Ira Rigby who works on Galeegi Island. Female, approximately seventy-five years old."

"What are her bona fides?"

"She doesn't have any. That's what raised the red flag. Everyone else on the employment record checks out. She's the only one with a created I.D."

"Driver's license? Social Security?"

"No license; SS number's false. Fairly elaborate cover."

Kasko mulled it over. "We'll need some form of confirmation that she is originally from Amoyeli."

"I've got better than that. I've got visual corroboration that she is connected to Jaja: a 1968 picture of her coming out of the courthouse during his trial. I'm looking at a side-by-side comparison right now. It's the same woman, sir. No doubt about it. "

Kasko slid off the table and headed for the door. "Fax me the info, Donovan. You got an address on her now?"

"617 on the Island Highway. The Rutherford plantation."

8:45 AM

Tyler cut the powerful engine on the Baja about one hundred fifty yards from St. Agnes's angular shore and drifted in. From this distance, the red tile roof of the monastery was clearly visible. Chloe slipped out to the bow and wrapped a rope around her wrist, awaiting the waves and momentum that would push them ashore. She soon jumped feet first into the knee-deep water, pulled the boat onto the narrow beach, and tied it to a downed water oak half-buried in the sand. The immediate rise of a fifteen-foot bank cropped St. Agnes's thin beach habitat. A jutting land mass ran directly above the beach, drowning it with hanging vegetation. Chloe immediately understood why St. Agnes never made it to the real estate development stage.

"See a way up?" Tyler asked.

Chloe craned her neck to look as she popped down the right side of the beach. "No, not yet. Let's try this way."

Tyler strapped on his service revolver, grabbed Chloe's backpack, and hopped into the ankle-deep water. He followed Chloe as they made their way down the heavily eroded shoreline. They soon came to a dip in the high bank. Tyler crawled to the top, lay on his stomach, and offered Chloe his hand. She made a running leap and grabbed hold of it. He braced himself and pulled her up beside him.

"Which way?" Chloe asked as she dusted the sand from her shirt.

Tyler surveyed the dense maritime forest and then pointed toward a group of oaks and pines. "There's an opening."

Chloe strapped on the pack and followed Tyler into

the woods. The tree limbs and undergrowth made the going difficult; clusters of thorny devil weeds shot up from under the tree line and nicked their exposed legs. In several places, the growth was so heavy that they had to backtrack and find other avenues.

"Are we getting close?" Chloe called out.

"I can't see the building anymore, but we are still heading in. We should find out soon enough."

After fifteen more minutes of searching, they came to a trail. Tyler stood in the middle of the overgrown path, looked in both directions, and pointed north. "I think this leads to the back of the island, the marsh area." He indicated the opposite direction. "Let's try this way."

"Not much of a trail, but someone obviously has been using it," Chloe said.

Tyler wiped the sweat from his face. "Yeah. No telling who. Let's head on."

Tyler stopped suddenly and did not move. Chloe froze, thinking he had seen a snake perhaps. He put his left index finger to his lips and pointed with his right in the direction of the marsh. Chloe strained to hear and made out the sound of footsteps. Someone was coming up the pathway.

Tyler took hold of Chloe's hand as they slipped off the trail into a thicket. He pulled his Glock and released the safety. Chloe heard the footsteps getting closer until the person stopped directly across from where they hid. Her heart beat wildly, and she saw Tyler's chest bumping as well. The person was so close she could now hear breathing. And then she heard another, more dangerous sound, that of a round sliding into a gun's chamber.

Tyler looked sternly at Chloe as he cupped both hands around his weapon. He bit down on his lip as he sensed the person moving towards them. Tyler took one more deep breath and leapt out from behind the thicket.

9:22 AM

Kasko stood several yards beyond the twirling blades of the Huey transport. A National Guard jeep pulled up, and Dr. Yolanda Chabari hopped out, heading for Kasko.

"You have found her, Agent Kasko?" Chabari asked over the noise of the helicopter.

"We think so, Doctor. I'd like you to come along. Help us verify."

"Of course," she said, before heading for the chopper.

Dan Sheridan walked up behind Kasko and put a hand on his shoulder. "Got several of my deputies en route there now; SWAT and Galeegi Police, too. I'll stay here and help keep watch."

Kasko cut his eyes to the horizon. "What about SLED? Where's Dupree?"

Sheridan shrugged his shoulders. "Don't know. The other SLED officers haven't seen him since early this morning. He's not answering his radio or cell."

Kasko frowned. "Okay, when you do see him, tell him to get over to Galeegi and make it quick." Kasko turned, walked to the helicopter, and climbed aboard.

Sheridan backed away and watched as the Huey lifted with a thunderous thrust of power and headed off into the morning's blue sky.

9:29 AM

"Freeze!" Tyler yelled as he stood in firing position, holding his pistol with both hands. Then he angled the Glock upward and eased off on the trigger. "Jesus! Man, I almost shot you."

Howard Dupree lowered his revolver and smiled. "Same here, Patrolman. Same here."

Tyler holstered his weapon and turned to Chloe. "It's okay. Come on out."

Chloe poked her head above the thicket.

"Lieutenant Dupree, this is Chloe Hart," Tyler said. "Chloe, Howard Dupree of the State Law Enforcement Division."

Dupree and Chloe acknowledged each other with mutual nods.

"What are you two doing out here?" Dupree asked.

"We thought we might be following a lead, but I don't know now. You?"

"FBI sent me over to re-scout the island," he said quickly. "What lead were you following?"

"A blood trail, and I mean that literally."

"Tracked to here?"

"It's a long shot," Tyler said. "More like a real long shot. But there's a possibility the source came from this island."

"Did you call it in to the FBI?"

Tyler glanced at Chloe. "Not yet. We were going to wait to see if we could verify anything first."

Dupree nodded. "That's probably smart. Come on. The building is not far away. You can fill me in on this blood trail thing along the way."

"Sounds good," Tyler said. "We could definitely use another pair of eyes."

"Yeah," Chloe added. "And to be honest I feel a whole lot better having another cop on our side."

The Huey circled the Rutherford compound before landing on the semi-circular drive in front of the mansion. Kasko jumped out. He took note of members of the SWAT team, already in position with high-powered weapons trained on the doors and windows from various angles.

As the blades of the Huey began to wind down, the rest of Kasko's team emerged with Dr. Chabari the last to exit the cargo doors. "Wait here with Agent Nettles," Kasko told Chabari. "We'll call you in when everything is secured."

Chabari could only nod.

As Kasko headed for the doors, Chief Tate and Sergeant Johnson joined him. "We got your call, Agent Kasko. What's this all about?" Tate asked.

"We think we may have found the woman responsible for calling in Xevioso—Ira Rigby."

Johnson laughed. "Ira? The Rutherford's maid? Are you kidding me?"

Kasko looked sternly at Johnson. "She's here under false pretenses, Sergeant. She's got an alias; she's connected to Xevioso and to Jaja Nayu."

"Jaja?" Tate asked. "What's this got to do with Jaja?"

"She was a practicing Vodun botono priestess, and Jaja was her son. His death may have been what triggered this whole mess."

The chief and the sergeant shared a puzzled look as they followed Kasko and two other agents to the door. Kasko knocked only once. "FBI," he called out.

No response.

He turned and nodded to the other agents. They drew their weapons, and one of them opened the door. Kasko glanced back at the Galeegi policemen. "Watch your backs."

All five men entered into the circular foyer, which was huge and ornate with several oil paintings of Rutherford ancestors, elaborate tapestries, and a twisting staircase that began near the entrance and circled up around the entire room. With a wave of his gun hand, Kasko signaled to the two trailing FBI agents to check out the upstairs. He, Tate, and Johnson quietly searched the first floor.

They peeked inside the dining and sitting rooms, all of which appeared to be rarely used from the smell of mothballs and number of slipcovers. They entered the large library at the end of the hall.

Tate was the first to see her. Emil Rutherford was slumped over in her favorite Queen Anne chair. "Mrs. Rutherford?" Tate called out.

She did not respond.

Tate leaned over her, held his hand under her nose, and looked up at the others. "She's dead."

Kasko nodded. "Look at the bruises on her neck."

"Christ. Somebody's choked the life out of her," Johnson said. "You think her maid did this?"

Kasko pulled a walkie-talkie from his belt. "Elliott, anything yet?"

"Got a white male, about forty-five. He's in one of the bedrooms out cold."

"Probably Collin Rutherford, Emil's son," Tate said.

"Can you rouse him?" Kasko asked.

"I'll try. Looks like he went through a liter of scotch, and there are some other kind of empty vials here on his nightstand."

"Do what you can. Throw his ass in the shower if you have to. We need to talk to him."

"Yes, sir."

"Agent Kasko," another voice cut in over the walkie-talkie. "Palmer here, sir."

"Whatcha got, Palmer?"

"I'm in the bedroom at the end of the third floor. Has to be our botono's."

"What did you find?"

"Not easy to explain, sir. I think you need to check this out yourself."

10:11 AM

Dupree led Tyler and Chloe around the side of the old monastery. Chloe marveled at the building's architecture with its simple, yet elegant, design. Even after years of neglect, there was still a certain aesthetic to the old stone-brick building.

As she worked her way through the overgrowth of the courtyard, she wondered why the monks set up shop on such a bleak island. It seemed so isolated, but maybe that was the point. They probably felt it offered that sense of ultimate communion—only God could hear one's prayers so far out here.

"So you think this Rutherford man had been out on this island?" Dupree asked Tyler.

"Just a guess, Lieutenant. But there's little else out this way."

"The blood may have come from any number of sources," Dupree reasoned.

"Yeah, but that handkerchief was soaked in it," Tyler said. "This wasn't some little nose bleed."

"Okay, then. We'll start on the inside and work our way out. Maybe we'll get lucky."

254

As they rounded the corner, they came to huge stone steps that led to the columned entrance. It was a strange sight. Above the wooden doors of the monastery, Ben McCreight had cleverly constructed a giant, concrete water moccasin's head with piercing, slanted eyes. The two columns of the old entrance now appeared to be the snake's fangs jutting from the roof of its opened mouth. The paint on the snakehead had long since faded, and portions had been chipped away, but it struck a menacing pose nonetheless.

A stone block kept the left panel door of the entrance from closing. Tyler noted that much of the heavy oak doors' original beauty had been worn away with time and exposure to the salty air. Dupree briefly scanned the entrance and then took hold of the door with both hands. With great effort, he pried open the door.

"Doesn't look like anyone has used this entrance in quite a while," Chloe said as she pushed away fragmented cobwebs and followed the men inside.

The interior was dark, but with the door opened and holes in the roof and cracks in the walls, there was enough sunlight to see. The trio moved through the entranceway to the main sanctuary. It was a plain, square room. All crucifixes and other symbols of the order had been removed.

"It doesn't appear that McCreight made a whole lot of structural changes to the interior of the building," Tyler said.

Dupree pulled a Maglite from his belt and scanned the darkened recesses of the room. "From what I was told, the hurricane hit before many of the planned changes for the reptile center could be made. The man lost all he had invested at that point and just took off."

"Why don't we split up," Tyler said, pulling his flashlight from the backpack. "Chloe and I will take the hallway on the left. You check those rooms to the right."

Dupree agreed.

"And if you find anything that you think might be blood, holler. We have a test kit in our pack," Tyler said.

"Will do," Dupree said as he disappeared into the shadows.

Tyler handed the light to Chloe and slung the pack around his shoulder. "Shall we?"

They made their way down the darkened hallway, which turned at a right angle toward the back. Chloe moved at a snail's pace, using the light to scan every square inch. Except for a few, small trash items left behind by some of the island's past explorers, they found very little that shouldn't be there in the old building.

They eventually came to another light source. It was a side door. The sunlight streamed in through every angle of the frame. Tyler leaned into the door and opened it with ease. They stepped outside onto a rickety, wooden veranda. Vines and other undergrowth reached up through the flooring and wrapped around the wobbly porch rails.

"I'll bet this was the entrance from the monastery's well and garden area. And look over there," Chloe said, shielding her eyes against the sun. "I think that's the path we came up on earlier."

Tyler looked all around then checked his watch. "Let's keep searching."

Tyler led Chloe back inside. As they continued down the hallway, they noted puddles of rainwater on the floor where a portion of the roof had caved in. Chloe shined the light on the ceiling, following the severe crack. She stumbled, and Tyler extended his arm to catch her. "Watch it."

Chloe turned back around—the flashlight now directed on the bump in the floor. "What was that?"

They both knelt down to inspect it closely. Recessed into the hallway was a two-foot-square slab of the stone flooring. The front edge of it was at a slight angle, enough of a rise to have caused Chloe to trip. Tyler traced the square with the light. "Looks like it was designed to be removed, a covering of some kind," Tyler said. He handed the flashlight back to Chloe, grabbed the lip of the covering, and raised it about an inch. "It won't budge past this point." He yanked at it again and heard a metallic rattling sound. "I think it's chained down."

"From underneath?" Chloe asked.

"Yeah," Tyler said as he scanned the hall again. "Has to be a release somewhere."

They looked around the hall for a few moments. "Look at this, Tyler," Chloe said. "There's no mortar around this block." Chloe kneeled down and inched her fingers onto the sides of sizable brick, pulling it out into the hallway.

Tyler got down on his knees and aimed the light inside the hole. "That's it," he said as he examined a rusty metal chain attached to the wall that ran back under the flooring to the square covering. "It's an old-looking chain but with a relatively new combination lock."

"Can we open it?" Chloe asked.

Tyler reached in and pulled on the lock and then the chain but to no avail. He stood and cupped his hands around his mouth. "Lieutenant Dupree! Lieutenant Dupree! We need you down here!" His voice echoed throughout the old building.

Tyler shined the flashlight up and down the hallway again.

"What are you looking for now?" Chloe asked.

"Something we can use to pry off that cover. We might be able to break it from that chain if we apply enough force." Tyler turned back to the hallway. "Dupree!" he shouted again.

"Would a porch banister work?" Chloe asked. "That top railing didn't look very secure. We could use it against the lip of the covering like a lever, maybe pop it right off."

"Good thinking, Dr. Hart. I'll be right back." Tyler handed her the flashlight and walked down the hall. Stepping out onto the veranda, he grabbed a section of the banister and worked it loose. It was heavy, curved and ornate, obviously hand-carved by those monks long ago. Within a few minutes, he freed it from the railings and brought it back inside. "See anything of Dupree yet?" he asked Chloe.

"No. He must have stepped back outside." She strained her eyes down the darkened hallway. "Apparently, he can't hear us wherever he is. You think you and I can do it?"

Tyler shrugged. "Yeah, why not?"

Tyler put one end of the banister under the cover opening and wedged it against the lip. He got on the opposite side of Chloe and grabbed the banister at the top and pushed. Chloe put her hands just under his and pulled toward her. They pushed and pulled together until they were exhausted.

"Let's give it one more try," Tyler said.

He leaned into it and gave it a powerful shove. This time the banister arm gave way, splitting in half. Tyler tumbled forward, landing on top of Chloe, who fell hard against the stone floor and banged her head.

"Chloe! Are you okay?"

Chloe winced. "Yeah...yeah, I think so."

Tyler crawled over and examined the back of her head. "Nasty bump. You sure you're okay?"

"I'm good. No brain damage," she said, trying to laugh it off.

Tyler helped Chloe, and they both stood up. He shined the light around the covering.

"Hey look, one of the chain links broke. We did it!" he said.

"Good. Then it was worth the pain," she said as she rubbed the knot on her head.

She watched as Tyler lifted the covering and tossed it aside. He leaned into the opening and streamed the light into the hole. "Stairs."

He looked at Chloe. "You coming?"

"As long as you're with me."

Tyler smiled, shouldered his backpack, and together they descended into the darkness.

11:10 AM

Agent Nettles escorted Dr. Yolanda Chabari up the three flights of stairs, down the hall to the door of Ira Rigby's room. Chabari entered first. The first thing she noticed was a sharp, unfamiliar odor, something acrid mixed with something burning.

Kasko walked over to her, and several other officers followed. "She's back there, Doctor," he said, pointing to the bathroom. "Better prepare yourself."

Chabari moved past the gathered policemen and walked into the small bathroom. There in the clawfoot bathtub was the charred body of Irawagbon; one of her

259

arms was hanging over the side. The odor of burned flesh filled the room. Next to the tub were a cigarette lighter and a half-empty kerosene can.

Kasko entered the bathroom behind Chabari. "Doctor, are you okay?"

Chabari held up her hand. "I am fine, Agent Kasko. This was to be expected."

"Expected? What do you mean?"

"The burning. It is the *boule zen*, a ceremony in which the botono has released her *ti-bon-ange*, her spirit. She may be seeking her final destination, or more likely, she seeks to conjure the *duppy*."

"The duppy? What the hell is that?"

"A different entity. A different way of being. She hopes to transform her life force; to be able to do some form of evil or physical harm from within the spirit world."

Kasko shook his head. "She's toast, Doctor. The only harm she can do now is to our nostrils."

Chabari turned to the FBI agent and looked into his eyes. "There is so much you do not understand, so much you miss because you are unwilling to open your mind to other worlds, other possibilities. You're a great seeker, Agent Kasko, but you remain woefully unprepared to handle the complexities of these islands and these people."

"You're right, Doctor. I don't believe in all the hocus-pocus. Never have. I'm a facts man. What you can see, hear, and shoot." He laughed his concession. "Of course, I'm glad you believe."

"It is not so much a matter of belief as understanding. These ways are ancient, mythical, but very real to the people who believe in them. This was meticulously planned by the botono. Her work here in her earthly form was finished."

"And what about Xevioso? Is he still around? Or did she take him with her to the spirit world?"

Chabari paused for a moment and then said, "She may have orchestrated this whole affair, and she may have used Jaja's death as a pretext to unleashing her hatred against those who wronged her. But someone else is responsible for wielding the Oshe. Someone else has committed these awful crimes. And yes, Agent Kasko, I believe that person is very much still with us."

11:22 AM

Tyler directed the flashlight around the small room at the bottom of the stairs. "What is this place?"

Chloe rubbed her arms. "Damp and cool. Storage room? Wine cellar?"

"Could be. Monks do like their wine." Tyler ran his hand along the brick wall. "Odd they were able to construct a basement like this without heavy machinery. Especially on an island."

They ducked under a low overhang and entered an even smaller room. It was pitch-black. Tyler directed the light into all corners of the room. It was empty with a dirt floor and walls made of the old monastery brick that ran deep into the ground.

"End of the line," Tyler said.

"You sound disappointed."

Tyler laughed. "I was hoping for at least a half-empty cask of port or something."

Chloe was smiling her agreement when she spied an oddity in the streaming light. "Let me see that flashlight for a second." She focused the light on the right side of the room five feet above the base of the wall. Several of the stone bricks had been chipped away, leaving a narrow hole just big enough to squeeze a person through.

"Well, there's something," she said as she walked over to the hole, got on her toes, and peered through. "Looks like a crawlspace under the upstairs flooring. What do you think?"

Tyler moved beside her. She handed him the light, and he shined it inside. "Yeah. And it looks like something or someone crawled through there recently. Must lead somewhere."

Chloe took a deep breath and confessed. "I guess I should tell you that once I went cave diving with my father in Manatee Springs, and I got turned around in one of the cave's restricted sinkholes. I almost ran out of air before he found me and got me out. And let's just say that as a result, I've developed a *slight* phobia to enclosed spaces."

Tyler smiled. "You can stay here if you want. I promise I'll be right back."

Chloe reached out and held his hand. "Are you kidding? I'm even more afraid of the dark. You just go first. I'll follow."

Within minutes they had scaled the wall and were crawling around the stone supports of the top floor. The ground felt wet and cold on their exposed skin, and it smelled old, earthy—like the inner chambers of an ancient catacomb. Periodically, as they inched along, Tyler stopped and shined the light ahead of them. Chloe tried not to think about how dizzy and suffocated she was beginning to feel.

Eventually the path led them through another broken wall opening, and they dropped down into yet another small room with a low ceiling and a heavy-planked wooden floor. Tyler figured they had to be close to the center of the old monastery by now. He entered first and helped Chloe through the opening. Once inside, they both stood and dusted themselves off. Chloe breathed a little easier and took a look around.

"What's that?" she asked, pointing across the room.

They saw a candle, still lit, its flame flickering. "My God, someone has been down here," Chloe said.

They walked to the center of the Hounfour, the teakwood floorboards creaking beneath them. Tyler swung the light around the odd center pole and the heavy support beams that crisscrossed the eight-foot ceiling, and then to the altar before them. Two skulls, halved at the mouth, were ominously placed on each end. They saw twelve extinguished black candles along with the one that was still burning.

Tyler nodded. "Vodun, I imagine. We may have hit the jackpot."

Next to the lit candle was a clear glass vial containing an amber-colored liquid. Chloe poked the glass with her finger and eyed it closely. "A medical vial," she said.

Tyler reached past Chloe, opened an oddly shaped container beyond the candles, reached in, and removed a black cloth covering. He held it out in front of him as its length unfolded to the floor. "What's this?"

"It's called the *drapeaux*," a deep voice in the darkness said.

Tyler and Chloe spun around as Dupree stepped out of the shadows, his pistol aimed at Tyler's chest. "It is the flag of the storm, of the ram. It is used as the sacred covering for the Oshe."

Tyler and Chloe stood motionless as Dupree moved closer. He had the battle-axe in his left hand.

Tyler turned his head from side to side, trying to take

in the scene and fully process all that was happening. "Dupree? How'd you get in here?" he refocused on the man and specifically on the weapons in his hands. "What the hell are you doing?"

Dupree laid the Oshe against the altar, leaned over toward Tyler, pinning him against a wall so that he could not move. Dupree then removed Tyler's Glock 22 from his holster. He pulled out the clip, slipped it into his pants pocket, and tossed the empty pistol to the other side of the room, rendering Tyler defenseless. It landed with several rattling clunks against the floor. "It's called justice, Patrolman, a justice of which you have no understanding."

Chloe's heart raced as she stepped closer to Tyler. She sensed the maddening, cold chill of imminent violence.

"You killed all those people?" Tyler asked.

Dupree shook his head. "I am a *cheval*—only a vessel for the god, Xevioso. He seeks justice for the committed sin."

"What sin?" Tyler asked. He paused, searching Dupree's eyes. "Who are you?"

Dupree smiled as he stuck his pistol in his waistband. He grabbed at the vial, snapped it open and drank the contents. He closed his eyes momentarily as the drug entered his system.

When he opened them again, he was no longer Howard Dupree.

Collin Rutherford sat practically naked at the end of his bed. He wore only black socks. He covered his genitals with his hands as FBI Agent Riley Elliott poured another pitcher of cold water on his head.

"That's enough! I'm awake. I'm awake!" Collin spit out the water streaming into his mouth and glared at the FBI agents.

Elliott looked at Kasko, who was leaning against the bedroom door.

"You ready to talk, Mr. Rutherford?" Kasko asked.

"What? Yeah, yeah, whatever. Just no more damn water."

Kasko straightened up, walked over, and sat on the edge of the bed next to Collin. "You've got a lot of explaining to do, Mr. Rutherford."

Collin swallowed his nausea and then blew out a scotch-soaked breath. "Explain what? What do I have to explain?"

"Well, your mother for starters. She's downstairs in the library. Dead. What happened?"

Collin looked at Kasko. "She's dead?"

"Someone choked the life out of her. Wasn't you, was it?"

Collin Rutherford shrugged his shoulders. "I don't...I don't know."

"Mr. Rutherford, what's your relationship with Ira Rigby?"

He looked around his room at Dr. Chabari, Tate, Sarge, and the others. "Who are all these people?"

"The law, Mr. Rutherford. My name is Special Agent Miller Kasko of the Federal Bureau of Investigations.

You're in serious trouble, sir. At this point, you might consider a call to your attorney."

"It doesn't matter. It doesn't matter anymore."

"What doesn't matter?"

"Everything. I'm a dead man. He will come for me now."

"Who? Xevioso?"

"Yes. He will punish me for my failure. He will punish us all."

"What do you know of Xevioso?" Kasko continued.

"He is the sky god, the god of justice."

"I know all that, slick," Kasko said. "I want to know who Xevioso really is and where we can find him."

"He'll kill me."

"And I'll kill you if you don't speak up, you sorry bastard," Kasko said firmly as he reached inside his coat pocket.

Collin slowly raised his hands to his eyes and began to weep. "I can't."

Kasko pulled out his Glock 23, cocked the pistol, reached over, and pressed the barrel to Rutherfold's crotch. "I'm about two seconds away from making you have to squat to piss."

"I don't know who it is. I swear to God," Collin stammered. "I am just a *bossale*, a slave of the botono. She would not let me know the cheval. That is beyond the bossale. I only tend to his needs. I bring him his elixir, clean the Oshe, maintain his temple."

"His temple? What the hell is this wacko talking about?" Hank Johnson piped in.

"Of course, the temple of Xevioso, the Hounfour," Dr. Chabari said. "It's a place of transformation; where the cheval, the human host, embodies the spirit of Xevioso."

Kasko lifted the Glock, stuck the barrel under Rutherford's chin, forcing his head up. "Where is this temple, Rutherford?"

He took several short breaths and cut his eyes over to Kasko. "On St Agnes; inside the monastery."

"My God," Tate said, his face growing pale.

"What?" Kasko asked.

"Tyler."

11:46 AM

Tyler kept Chloe behind him as they moved backward in unison, matching each step that Xevioso made toward them. The thunder god took his time, twirling the Oshe in his hands, feeling its weight and power. Tyler had had enough, but he saw no way to escape. Trying to leap up the wall and crawl back out of the opening was not an option. Dupree's revolver was still stuck in his waistband, but he wasn't about to let Tyler get that close. And Tyler's own weapon was useless without the clip. He thought about rushing him and grabbing the axe, but if he failed that would leave Chloe vulnerable. One false move, one mistake, and it would be all over.

He felt Chloe holding a death grip onto the back of his shirt. They both breathed hard, excited breaths. No time to plan. No time to think. Xevioso swung the Oshe with both hands at the pair—once, twice, three times—backing them into a corner of the room. Xevioso's eyes suddenly rolled back into his head, only the whites of them showing, and he swung again. Chloe tried to pull Tyler back, but the razor sharp blade slashed through his shirt and sliced open his chest. Tyler looked down at the gash as blood poured down across his stomach and onto his pants. He held his right hand over the wound and dropped to his knees.

"Stop this!" Chloe screamed as she stepped in front of Tyler and looked the madman in the eyes. "Leave us alone! Please, please let us go!"

Xevioso, his hulking frame outlined by the light from a single candle on the altar behind him, slowly raised the axe to shoulder height. "I will not withdraw. Justice must be done," he bellowed.

11:59 AM

"Can you set her down on the island?" Kasko shouted to the pilot of the rescue helicopter.

"Too much growth, sir. Nowhere to land."

Kasko looked back at Tate, then out the shaking cockpit window. He pointed to the marsh on the inland side of St. Agnes. "Over there. Get this thing down low. Drop us there in the marsh."

The chopper swept over the monastery and hovered low just over the marsh. The tide was up, and the water covered the grass and mud. Two SWAT team members jumped from the side door feet first and landed in the pluff mud. Agents Elliott and Palmer were next, followed by Kasko and Tate. All six men sloshed through the marsh to the island then ran single file along the path toward the monastery.

12:03 PM

Tyler was doubled over in pain. He sensed Chloe's grip on his arm. He knew she was in front of him, protecting him. He looked past her as Xevioso stepped forward with the raised axe above his head, his flexed arm muscles rippling in strength. For just a fraction of a second, Tyler looked up at the cracked, wooden beam that ran above her and then quickly back into her eyes.

Xevioso brought the mighty Oshe down intending to split the woman in half, but Chloe acted on Tyler's unspoken warning and leapt for the wooden beam. She had just enough in her as she caught hold of the top of the support and swung her body forward. She pulled up and pushed out in the same motion; her legs stretched over Tyler's head. The Oshe missed its mark and landed with a *thwack!* The razor sharp blade combined with the powerful thrust of the swing allowed the axe to penetrate deep into the swollen teak board where it promptly became stuck. Xevioso strained to relieve the Oshe, but it wouldn't release.

Tyler summoned enough strength to stand. He threw himself at Xevioso, splattering the crazed man's midsection with blood. Xevioso stumbled backward but stayed on his feet. He reached down, grabbed Tyler around his neck, lifted him off the floor, and heaved him at Chloe. Tyler fell on top of her against the back wall.

Xevioso turned to the Oshe and worked the handle back and forth numerous times until it was free from the floorboard. Xevioso, axe in hand, headed for Tyler and Chloe. "Justice will be served," he vowed.

Tyler, with blood oozing from his chest wound as well as his nose and mouth, regained his footing and whispered, "Yes...it will." He lifted his arm and in his hand was Dupree's revolver. "But not by you."

Xevioso's eyes grew wide. He let out an intense scream of hatred as he swung the Oshe violently toward them.

Two shots rang out and blood gushed into the madman's

face. One of the rounds ripped through Xevioso's throat, severing his carotid artery. He dropped the Oshe and grabbed his neck, then fell to his knees.

Tyler fired three more shots—all three slamming into Xevioso's chest, knocking him backward onto the floor. Dupree's gun fell from Tyler's hand as he staggered back against the wall, lost consciousness, slid down to his knees, and collapsed onto his right side.

Chloe scrambled over to Tyler and held her hands over his bloody chest. She ripped off a part of his shirt and stuffed it into the wound as tight as she could. "No, Ty. Please don't do this. Stay with me. Don't give up on me," she said.

Tyler's breathing became quick, shallow; his skin grew cold to the touch.

She knew she had to act quickly. Chloe made Tyler as comfortable as possible and then stood. She stepped over Dupree's body, picked up the flashlight and scrambled into the hole in the wall. She made quick passage through the dirt to the other side, never once thinking about her claustrophobia. As she emerged into the outer room, she heard the steady *thump, thump, thump* of the rescue team running down the hallway. "Down here!" she yelled. "We need help down here!"

Within seconds, a beam of light illuminated the stairway, and Kasko was standing there, both arms outstretched, his Glock 23 cocked and ready to fire in both of his hands.

"Don't shoot, don't shoot!" Chloe shouted. "We need help!" She held up her hands as Kasko descended the stairs.

Kasko lowered his weapon and said, "FBI," as the other men stepped inside behind him.

"Tyler Miles—he's been hurt," Chloe said, "he's through that hole in the wall. It's a tunnel. He's in a room on the other side. Please hurry."

Kasko scrambled into the tunnel followed by four of the others. Tate was the last one down the stairs.

"My God, Chloe, are you all right?" Tate asked as he held his hands on her shoulders.

Chloe squeezed her eyes shut and gave a shaky nod. "Tyler's hurt, Chief Tate. He's hurt bad. We've got to get him to a hospital."

Moments later a member of the SWAT team, covered in sweat and dust, crawled out of the tunnel. He had a rope clipped to his chest harness. "Quick, Chief. Your nephew is on the other end. Help me pull him through."

Tate and the other man slowly dragged Tyler through the tunnel and feet first onto the floor of the outer room. The other end of the rope was secured to Tyler's boots. Three more members of the team crawled out as Tate lifted his nephew and carried him up the stairs. They carefully maneuvered Tyler through the darkened monastery. Once outside, one of the team members lifted Tyler by his feet while his uncle held him under his shoulders. They quickly carried Tyler down the path into the marsh. The pilot maneuvered the chopper over the men and a crewman lowered the rescue basket. Tate secured his nephew in the basket and signaled for the pilot to lift it. Seconds later the helicopter whisked him safely off to the mainland.

Meanwhile, Kasko remained behind in the Hounfour. He held the flashlight on Dupree's blood-splattered face as a million questions ran through his mind. The FBI agent knew that connecting the dots of this bizarre case would come later, but for now at least, the larger part of the nightmare was over.

Kasko stood and walked in front of the Vodun altar. He looked at the skulls and wooden idols, and the candles. For just a moment, Miller Kasko was a young boy again, dressed in the uncomfortable robes of the acolyte, tending the altar of his mother's church. At the time, the crucifixes and rosary beads seemed as foreign and dangerous to him as these odd artifacts. He just never got it and had abandoned faith a long time ago.

He leaned over the burning black candle. He then turned and took another glance at Dupree's fallen body. Kasko thought briefly of the sheriff's analogy once again—these islands and the Garden of Eden. He wasn't sure if the metaphor was appropriate anymore.

How could it be when the protective angel was really the serpent in disguise? Paradise never stood a chance.

Kasko turned back to the candle, and with a quick breath, plunged the Hounfour into complete darkness.

7:17 PM

Two Galeegi police cruisers raced down the front drive and slid to a stop at the steps of the Argeaux mansion. Kasko, Chief Tate, Sergeant Johnson, and Agents Palmer and Elliott got out of the vehicles. Sergeant Johnson grabbed Kasko's arm and said, "Agent Kasko, this is wrong, and you know it. This is completely unnecessary. It's gotta be a mistake. Mr. Argeaux would have nothing to do with all this."

Kasko headed for the front door as Johnson and the others followed.

"This is Charles Argeaux for crying out loud. You don't

just barge in on a man like him and make these kinds of accusations."

Kasko, ignoring Johnson, walked up the front steps and stopped at the top. "What the...?" he started to say. Fresh blue paint covered the walls around the massive front doors. He pulled out his gun, kicked open the doors, and walked in, gun raised, as the others followed suit. Kasko tracked paint-stained footsteps down the hall to the study. He slowly turned the door handle, but it was locked.

"Stay away from me!!" Argeaux yelled from inside.

"Charles Argeaux? Special Agent Kasko, FBI."

"Nobody comes in here, or I swear to God I'll start shooting!"

Kasko looked at Agents Palmer and Elliott and whispered, "Circle around back. See if there's another way in." He then pounded on the door and said, "Mr. Argeaux, we have a warrant. We need to speak with you now."

"Step one foot in here, and I'll blow you away! Leave me alone!"

Kasko looked at Tate. "Can you talk some sense into him?" he asked.

Tate glanced over at Sergeant Johnson, who took a step back and shook his head dismissively.

"Mr. Argeaux? This is Chief Tate. It's over, sir. Come on out and let's talk."

There was a long pause. "Mr. Argeaux? We know all about the truck bomb. It's been traced back to your..."

A shotgun blast ripped through the door and rattled the hall. The lawmen hit the floor, rolled over, and pulled out guns. Kasko, his back against the wall next to the door, chambered a round and slicked back his tussled hair with the fingers of his left hand.

"Go away, goddammit! Get the hell out of my house!"

Kasko whispered into the walkie-talkie attached to his shoulder strap. "Palmer, Elliott. Report."

"We're on the terrace in position. I have a clean shot at the target," Palmer said.

Kasko paused for a moment, then said, "Argeaux, there's no way out. We have agents in position all around you. Give it up before it's too late."

"That's what you don't understand. That's what none of you understand. It's already too late." Argeaux said—his voice shaky, desperate.

Kasko slowly leaned over, peeked through the hole in the door and saw the barrel of a 12-gauge shotgun sticking straight up from behind an antique desk. "Palmer, in 30 seconds, give me two shots in the air but stay the hell away from those terrace doors," he said.

"Yes, sir."

Kasko looked at the others. Each nodded. Moments later, two shots rang out.

Argeaux jumped from behind his desk and discharged two blasts from the shotgun, tearing away glass and wood from the exterior French doors. Before he swung back around, Kasko burst into the room and leaped toward him. He caught the old man mid-waist and tackled him onto the desk. Another shot fired straight up brought ceiling fragments raining down on top of them. As Kasko pinned him to the desk, Tate fell in next to them and wrestled the shotgun out of Argeaux's hands.

The room was secure. It was over.

Kasko stood in the hall of the mansion with his hands on his hips, waiting. Palmer and Elliott bounded down the stairs. "The rest of the house is clear," Palmer said. "No signs of struggle in any of the other rooms."

Kasko nodded. "Find the wife. Tell her to gather up the family and servants. I want to have a word with them."

"Will do," Elliott said.

As the two agents left, Kasko turned and went into the study. Charles Wesly Argeaux sat in his leather-backed desk chair. Streaks of haint blue paint ran down his face and hands. His white hair was splattered with it as well. Tate and Johnson stood on each side of him. The master of Galeegi looked like a broken man on death row. Kasko plopped down on the edge of the desk and studied the old man's face.

"Mr. Argeaux, I'd read you your rights and haul you off to jail right now, but to be honest, I'm too damned tired. This case has whipped my ass in every way possible. So speak up. Tell me everything you know. This is your day of reckoning, sir."

Argeaux looked up at Kasko. "She will do far worse to me than you ever could, Agent Kasko. So do me a favor—shoot me; blow my brains all over this room. I don't care. If it was just about my life, then I would have taken it myself a long, long time ago."

"All right, then, what is it? What is this hold that Ira Rigby has over you? What could she possibly do to you to make you want to destroy these islands and everybody on them?"

He shook his head as if there was no real way to explain, and then said, "My soul, Agent Kasko. My eternal soul. She has condemned it. I am forbidden entry to *Yesunyime*. I have no future. I am to be...eradicated."

"I don't understand," Kasko said.

"I have failed her so there is no hope for me. Everything—my family's past, my power, my future...my very essence—is gone forever. "

Kasko crossed his arms over his chest and thought for a moment. "You do realize that Ira Rigby is dead. She torched herself a couple of hours ago. She can do you no harm."

Argeaux sneered. "Fool. Don't you get it? Ira—Irawagbon—awaits my death now. She will send Xevioso, my judge and my executioner. I deserve death. That I can accept. But she will take my ti-bon-ange, my spirit, and I will be cast off into nothingness."

Sergeant Johnson shook his head and said, "Mr. Argeaux, surely you don't believe all that? That's colored folk talk. Voodoo, hoodoo, horse shit."

Argeaux said nothing.

"You're a Christian for God's sake. We go to the same church. Please tell me you don't believe all that chicken blood and black candles crap."

Argeaux stared straight ahead, and then replied, "There are worlds far beyond your vision, Sergeant Johnson. I have seen its power, and I know the consequences. It's why I am who I am. I am a destroyer, more powerful than anyone can possibly imagine. If not for the one unforgivable mistake I made, my power would have been eternal. I would have lived forever."

"What mistake?" Kasko asked.

"Jaja," Argeaux said.

"He killed your daughter," Johnson said, "No one would blame..."

"No," Argeaux interrupted. "Jaja did not kill Katherine."

"Of course he did, Mr. Argeaux. He raped her, and then he beat her in the head. Everybody knows that."

Argeaux said nothing. Tate swung Argeaux's chair around to face him.

"If it wasn't Jaja, then who? Who killed Katherine?"

Tears welled in Argeaux's eyes.

"Tell us, Argeaux," Kasko said. "Tell us what really happened that night."

Tears streaked Argeaux's cheeks, and then he spoke. "I went out looking for Katherine soon after dark. I called out to her to come home. But there was no answer, so I walked down to the dock. She often went down there during the evening hours. She loved the river at night. She said that's when it came to life." He paused as he pictured what he discovered there. "And that's where I saw them. Together."

"They were intimate?" Kasko asked.

"Yes. And I couldn't allow it. Katherine and Jaja. I could not allow it."

"No white man in his right mind would stand for that," Johnson said.

Kasko watched the old man's reaction, rubbed at his chin in thought, and then said, "But that's not the reason, now is it, Mr. Argeaux? This was never about race. Your connection to the botono runs much deeper than that."

Argeaux leaned over and put his face in his hands as the painful memory soared.

Johnson looked over to Kasko. "I don't get it."

"He did it, Sergeant. Charles Argeaux killed his own daughter. He killed his daughter because of some pact he made to protect his other child. Isn't that right, Mr. Argeaux?"

"What other child?" Johnson asked. "Charles Argeaux didn't have any more children."

Tate too shook his head and asked, "What exactly are you saying, Kasko?"

Kasko stood up, walked over in front of Argeaux and looked down on the old man. "They say blood is thicker than water, but for Argeaux, power is thicker than blood." He looked back at Tate and Johnson. "I think we'll find that Charles Argeaux killed his daughter that night to protect the child he created with the botono—his own son Jaja."

11:07 PM

Tyler batted his eyelids open and immediately felt the searing pain. He gently drew a finger across his chest and felt the hard line of skin and sutures. He could hardly breathe.

He focused on his surroundings—the low-lit overhead light, the white sheets, railings, IV bag, and monitors. He turned his head just a little and saw Chloe asleep in a chair next to him. After all they had been through, she was still there with him, still by his side, keeping watch, keeping vigil.

Her eyes opened, and she slid over to him. She pulled his hair back from his face. "You okay? Need anything?"

Tyler smiled. "No, just you. You okay?"

"A few bumps and bruises, but I'll be okay," she said, returning the smile. "You saved my life."

"You saved mine. I'd say we're even." Tyler coughed a little, which caused him to wince in pain. He closed his eyes, held still for a second, and then looked back to Chloe. "How'd we get here?"

"Your uncle and the FBI arrived just in time." She looked up and briefly checked his IV line. "You lost a lot of blood."

"Where is Uncle Fletcher?"

"He went with the FBI to arrest Argeaux. Put this whole ugly mess behind us," she said. "Of course, he waited until the doctors had you stabilized first."

Tyler leaned his head back on the pillow and tried to get as comfortable as possible. "So, it's over now." He blinked his eyes. "I just can't believe it. A man like Dupree."

"Nobody could. I heard some of the cops talking earlier. They said he had been with the Beaufort Police for twenty years before joining SLED six years ago. Nobody knows how he got so involved in all this," she said.

"I'm sure they're checking all angles now. Has to be some logical explanation." He thought about it for a second. "How did he get down in that altar room before us?"

"They found another passageway, an older set of hidden stairs that descended from one of the rooms upstairs. They believe that lower level was originally used as the monks' special prayer room." She paused. "Dupree apparently had all this planned out for some time, waiting for the right moment to strike."

"Unbelievable," Tyler mumbled.

"It's like a nightmare," Chloe said as she weighed the whole scenario. "All this death and destruction."

Tyler turned slightly toward her again and studied her face. "I'm sorry, Chloe. I'm sorry I involved you in all of this. I should have never put you in such a dangerous situation."

Chloe reached out and squeezed his hand. "I don't blame you at all, Patrolman Miles. I'm just glad you were there with me."

She leaned over and held him with a long kiss.

JUNE 12

K asko leaned back in his metal chair inside the makeshift conference room at the shelter and said: "Okay, here's what we know about Mr. Charles Argeaux IV: He was born in 1930 at the family home on Galeegi. His father, Charles III, and his mother, the former Miss Ali Louise Baker, raised him like all the Argeaux men before him—to run their vast empire. Private tutors, specialized training, finishing schools. He was given all the silver spoon advantages."

He flipped ahead through his notebook.

"In 1948, they sent him to Princeton to study business and perhaps to color his blood just a little bit bluer. It was during the summer of his sophomore year when he met Ira Rigby. She was only fourteen, but she was working as a full-time maid at the Rutherford plantation. They developed, shall we say, an unusually close relationship. At any rate, as they spent more time together, she exposed him to Vodun and her power as a botono. He kept it secret from family and friends, but he obviously became committed to its practices and beliefs."

Across the table, Dr. Yolanda Chabari was sipping coffee from a Styrofoam cup. Kasko and Chabari had agreed to get together and share their summations.

Kasko continued:

"It was in the spring of Charles's junior year that Jaja was born. The young mother sent the child to live with his grandfather, Roger Nayu, who became the caretaker of the Amoyeli lighthouse. But she also demanded that

Charles Argeaux be Jaja's special protector for the rest of his life."

"The *Joto*," Chabari said.

"What's that?" Kasko asked, turning an ear as if he missed it.

"In Vodun, the Joto is the ancestral protective force of a child. The protector is charged with shielding the child from all corruptive influences. When the Joto manifests itself in human form, that person must protect the child at all costs—to keep him alive, well, and pure."

"So you think Charles killed Katherine, his own daughter, to keep Jaja pure?" Kasko asked.

"Yes. I imagine Irawagbon believed that her child with Argeaux was special—divine. I'm sure Jaja was not to be confined, influenced, or harmed in any way. It was Argeaux's responsibility as his father and Joto to keep him that way. When Charles Argeaux saw Jaja and Katherine together, intimate, that night down by the dock, he decided then and there that she must be destroyed. She was corrupting Jaja, and that could not be tolerated."

"But to kill one's own daughter," Kasko said. "I still find it so hard to believe."

"Agent Kasko, as I tried to tell you before, the tenets of Vodun are as stringent as they are strange. It is a source of great comfort and joy for believers, but when the rules are abused, the punishment is severe."

Kasko reached into his pocket and removed a clear glass vial full of amber liquid. He leaned forward and placed it on the table. "We found several of these in Mr. Rutherford's room, and several empty ones in that dungeon over on St. Agnes. It's a pure blend of heroin and methaqualone. Ever hear of this associated with the practice of Vodun?"

Chabari picked up the vial and examined it for a moment. "No, not that particular combination. I have heard of drugs being used to initiate a transformation, when one embodies the spirit of another, for example. I imagine the cheval used this to help him embody Xevioso."

Kasko nodded again. "It's quite the fireball. Very powerful stuff. Very addictive. Expensive too. We think not only the cheval, but also Collin Rutherford, the bossale, was also hooked on this stuff, which goes a long way to explaining his actions."

"So Rutherford was also the drug supplier?" Chabari asked.

"Yeah, we think so. Apparently he had gone through his entire trust fund and then some. He owed money to just about everyone in Galeegi. Irawagbon must have kept him afloat. At least enough to have him do all the slave details."

"And her money came from Argeaux?"

Kasko shrugged slightly. "We're checking her records now. But that would be my guess." Kasko laughed in disbelief. "Who would have thought a simple island maid would have had two of the most powerful families on the Carolina coast eating right out of her hand?"

"Not simple at all. She was a very complex woman, very skilled in the art of manipulation. And she had help." Chabari raised her head in thought. "Speaking of which, is there any word on the cheval?"

Kasko finished his coffee and slammed his empty cup on the table. "Howard Dupree was raised down the road in Yemassee. He was adopted, although the details are sketchy."

"Ewansiha?" Chabari asked.

"I hadn't thought of that," Kasko said. "But it makes

sense. If she did have a second son, she may have given him to the Duprees to raise, then contacted him later, after he became a cop down in Beaufort."

"Being a botono runs in the blood," Chabari said.

"So does heroin," Kasko quipped. "Whatever the reason, Dupree went over to the dark side. He became very skilled in his work. What I still don't understand is why he had to kill the twelve Igbo in the first place. Why do that when they were planning to destroy the islands with the dirty bomb anyway?"

"According to Vodun myth, the Legba, the gate of destruction, could only be opened by a god—in this case Xevioso," Chabari said. "And according to legend, the Legba has twelve locks. Apparently, Swantou was number twelve. His death was the signal for Argeaux to activate the bomb."

At that moment, Agent Nettles walked into the conference room, removed his sunglasses, and said, "Excuse me, sir. The doctor's helicopter is ready."

"Tell them she'll be right there," Kasko said. Nettles nodded and left.

"Well, Dr. Chabari, I guess this is it. Thanks for your help. The people of this island and this state owe you a debt of gratitude. As do I."

Chabari stood up, gathered her papers and slipped them into her leather satchel. "As I said before, Amoyeli is where I was born. Gullah is my culture. Africa is my home. This island, Agent Kasko, is a living, breathing museum—a testament to my people. I would do anything to protect this beautiful and sacred place."

She smiled, shook Kasko's hand, and turned to leave. She stopped at the entrance and turned back around. "One thing further, Agent Kasko. If Charles Argeaux is the father

283

of Jaja, and he was sworn to protect him at all costs, who was it that shot Jaja that night?"

"I don't know, Doctor," Kasko said. "He truly may have killed himself."

Chabari stared at Kasko for a second. "No. Someone else shot Jaja. Someone killed him and set into motion the whole sordid process. It was done for hatred's sake."

"It's an unfortunate side of humanity that I deal with all too frequently. I guess the only way we're ever going to get past it is to recognize and appreciate our differences. Simply not let hatred enter the equation," Kasko admitted.

Chabari gave the haggard FBI man a relenting smile. "Yes, you are correct, Agent Kasko. It would make for the world a better place. But, apparently, we still have a long way to go." She closed the door behind her.

Kasko turned to collect the assorted files and papers spread out on the table. The photograph of Xevioso's morbid symbol slipped out from one of the folders. He picked it up and briefly studied the blood veve of the ram and the Oshe.

"Yes, ma'am, a long way to go, indeed," he whispered.

OCTOBER 23

6:03 AM

Tyler pulled his Ford Ranger 4x4 into his space at the Galeegi Police Station. He grabbed his coffee mug and morning paper, got out, entered Control Central, and flipped on the lights. The room was empty, as it usually was during the nights of off season. He checked the station's messages and went to his desk. He sipped on his coffee and unrolled *The Post and Courier*. He scanned the headlines, looking for a follow-up on the Galeegi tragedy. Nothing had been written for months, but the events of early summer still haunted him.

The weeks following the case passed. Eventually the professional investigators wrapped up all the details and gave charge of the islands back to Chief Tate and the Galeegi Police. But the effects of the murders would mar the small island chain with an interminable stain. Many of the Galeegi locals had a hard time getting over the role that the island's two most prominent families had played, with Charles Argeaux's admittance of guilt in his daughter's death being the bitterest pill to swallow. The list of charges against Argeaux ran long, and his quick confession of these crimes ensured an agonizing wait for him in prison. Tyler heard that he would just sit in his cell, torturing himself, forgoing sentencing appeals, awaiting the end of his days, believing that the botono and oblivion would be there to greet his death.

Collin Rutherford faced many charges as well, but he was still at the G. Werber Bryan Psychiatric Hospital in Columbia. He had been sent there for a stability evaluation and also to get aid in overcoming his various addictions. Collin helped the FBI frame the story and fill in the missing details. He hoped his collusion with the FBI and the state solicitor's office would help with his later sentencing.

Howard Dupree remained an enigma to Tyler and just about everyone else. His service record with the Beaufort Police Department had been spotless, and Richard Hinton, SLED's director of its southern branch, echoed those same sentiments. The DNA analysis did show he was the son of Irawagbon; his father, however, remained unknown. Most of the FBI behavioral analysts believed he had been conceived just for the sole purpose of becoming the muscle behind Ira's madness. But that somehow didn't seem enough to explain his behavior. Those who knew him attributed much of his Jekyll-and-Hyde persona to his addiction to the methaqualone and heroin combination, which alters even the most benign of personalities. His involvement with such a heinous plot still bothered Tyler as much as their inability to solve Jaja's death, which, even today, remained an open case.

Tyler looked around Control Central and then to his uncle's dark office. The senseless deaths had strained Fletcher Tate. As the summer wore on, Tate became less and less involved in the station's daily operations; the magnitude of the case had worn him thin. He spent most of his time at home with Marie, giving Tyler and Sergeant Johnson more responsibilities. He would come in for a few hours and then leave early to go shrimping or to work on his catamaran.

Tyler struggled with his own battles daily. After he was discharged from the hospital, Chloe finally gave in to the pressures of work and made plans to return to the EPA. Tyler wanted to talk her out of it, but he didn't. He knew it was her life, her calling, and she had to move on. They promised they would stay in constant touch, but weeks later, the emails and phone calls became less and less frequent. As he looked at his desk calendar, he realized it had almost been two weeks since he had had any contact with her.

That didn't stop him from thinking about her though. He could still see her beautiful blue eyes and that jet-black hair. The way she moved and smiled. He thought about the last time he saw her at the airport in Charleston. He leaned over and kissed her, and they both had tears in their eyes when they pulled away. He then watched her as she turned and disappeared down the tunnel connector. He felt a gnawing in his gut from his regrets...not saying the words—not telling her that he had fallen for her and wanted her to stay in his life forever.

And now, he knew, he never would have that chance.

10:17 AM

The station grew busier as the morning wore on. Both Robbie Cone and Sergeant Johnson were working diligently at their desks. As Tyler stood to get his third refill of coffee, he noticed Johnson filing his own papers. For once, he wasn't trying to shove it off on Tyler or anyone else. He smiled. He wasn't sure which had a greater affect on Hank Johnson's change of heart: his idol, Charles Argeaux, turning out to be a Vodun disciple, or Tyler's threat to "kick the fat out of his ass" if he ever bothered him again. Either way, Tyler felt Johnson's change in attitude was long overdue. It sure made working at the station easier.

The phone rang, and Robbie was quick to answer it. He

listened briefly and looked over at Tyler. "It's the chief for you. Line one."

Tyler nodded and took the call at his desk. "This is Tyler. Morning, Chief."

"Hey, Ty. Wonder if you would do me a favor? I've got some mail spread out on my desk that I need, and I'd like you to bring it over to my house, if you don't mind."

"Not coming in today?"

There was a long pause. "No. Not today. Just ain't up to it."

Tyler glanced over at the activity board. "Sure. Not much going on now anyway. I'll see you there in a few minutes."

Ten minutes later, Tyler had Tate's mail beside him as he drove down Old Safari Road, heading toward the chief's house. He thought it unusual that his uncle needed the information delivered to him immediately. He didn't mind the task; it just seemed as though the mail wasn't that big of a deal in the first place. He took another look at the stack. Most of it was just his office junk mail: police unit catalogues and training seminar brochures. There was only one official looking letter, and it had already been opened. Tyler flipped it around so he could read the return address. It was from the South Carolina Preservation Society. He pushed it aside and continued down the road.

And then something dawned on him. He slowed his truck down, pulling off onto the shoulder. He picked the envelope up again and held onto it for just a moment. Curiosity got the better of him. He reached into the envelope, pulled out the letter, and began to read. After only few lines, he looked up.

Oh my God....

Tyler walked into his uncle's house unannounced. He heard commotion in the back of the house and followed it into the kitchen. Marie stood at the stove with her back to him—a frying pan heating up on one of the eyes. She was barefooted, dressed in cut-off jeans and an old Cooper River Bridge Run t-shirt.

"Marie?"

Marie spun around. "Well, hey there, Ty. I didn't know you were coming over."

Tyler attempted a smile. "I just brought some stuff over for Fletcher."

"Oh, he's out back right now. I think he's working on that boat of his."

Tyler made a quick move towards the door. "Okay, I'll just run these on out to him."

Marie called out. "Why don't you stay over for lunch? We're going to have BLTs."

Tyler didn't respond as he was already past the sliding glass doors, making his way across the deck. At the top of the deck stairs, Tyler paused, looking into the backyard. He saw his uncle working with a sander underneath the suspended catamaran. He placed the catalogues and brochures on the deck railing but held onto the letter. Tyler then slowly made his way down the steps and across the yard. He felt weak, wobbly, like his legs were made of Jell-O.

Fletcher Tate looked up from his work and watched Tyler approach. He saw the open letter in his nephew's hand and the sickly pale look on his face. Tate shut off the sander. He reached over onto a worktable and picked up a plastic cup filled with ice water. He kept his back to Tyler while he downed the entire drink. There was an agonizing minute of silence between them before Tate finally spoke.

"I loved her, Tyler," he said. "I always did." He swung around to face his nephew. "She was rich, sophisticated, way beyond a boy like me. I knew that. I was just some kid from the other side of the island. But she was the most incredible girl I'd ever known." He paused, remembering it as if it were yesterday. "We were in high school together, both around sixteen. We started out just exchanging looks in the hallway; and then, eventually, we got to be friends." He bit down on his lip. "She led me to believe we were more than that, more than friends. We became close, you know?"

He momentarily closed his eyes. "She was so beautiful, soulful. I never knew anyone quite like Katherine Argeaux. She had such a lasting hold on me."

Tyler didn't know what to say. He rubbed the opened letter between his fingers. Tate noticed.

"I wanted you to know. I wanted to explain it to you."

"Why? So you could justify what you did? Justify murder?" Tyler asked—his voice brittle yet damning.

Tate looked at him with pleading eyes. "He killed her. Don't you understand? Everybody said that he killed her. There was no doubt, Tyler. He raped her and killed her and then got away with it. She was only sixteen. And he got to live a lifetime after. It was so unfair. It was so fucking *unfair*!"

Tyler trembled. He had never heard his uncle yell before, much less act like this. Tate was coming unglued, coming apart. Tyler offered the only words that came to his mind. "But he didn't kill her."

"Don't you think I know that now?!" Tate screamed. He ran his hands through his hair like a madman, wildness enveloping his eyes, and he clenched his teeth. He stared straight ahead with that pained look for a moment as if he were watching what he did to Jaja all over again. He massaged his temples, trying to calm himself.

"Don't you think I know?" he repeated softer, more in control. "I killed Jaja Nayu because I thought he had gotten away with murder. How dare he come back to these islands? How dare he live a life when she had none to live? Especially here. Especially in Galeegi." Tears shot down his face. "How was I supposed to know her own bastard of a father killed her? It was so clear back in those days. That black boy from the islands had raped her and killed her. Everybody said so. Everybody. They all said he deserved to die, Tyler. I listened to them. They talked about justice. I heard them. I believed them. I built up such a hatred for that man. And I carried it around for forty years. I kept it to myself. I hated Jaja Nayu. Don't you see, Tyler? I swallowed the lie whole. I believed he had taken away the first girl I ever loved."

The tears came faster now. "I killed an innocent man. I punished him for a crime he didn't commit. I did, Tyler— me, Fletcher Tate—Chief of Police." He paused as the weight of his actions overwhelmed him. "God, forgive me. I started all this. I killed Jaja and unleashed the hell that followed. I was sworn to uphold the law, protect each and every citizen. Yet I let the botono have her day. I set Dupree upon our islands. I let Argeaux nearly destroy everything. You and Chloe were almost killed for Christ's sake. I caused this pain and suffering. I did, Tyler. I did."

"You couldn't have known," Tyler whispered to him.

"No, but I did kill him. I'm ultimately the one responsible."

Tyler stared at his uncle blankly then looked down at the letter in his hand. "You wanted me to know. You wanted me to find this letter. To find out about the new caretaker of the lighthouse. That the Preservation Society had to have the local authority know of any new caretaker stationed on Amoyeli."

"Yes," Tate answered. "It was just a cautionary procedure that the Preservation Society used. More of formality really. But it's how I knew Jaja was returning. I knew to be waiting on him that night. When I saw his name on that letter, something inside me just snapped. I felt that rush of hatred that I carried with me for all those years."

Tate paused for a moment. "I wanted you to know, Tyler, because I want you to tell everyone. You're smart. You have insight. I want you to explain everything to everyone." He looked at the house, dropping his voice to a whisper. "Especially to Marie."

During the next few moments, everything moved in slow motion for Tyler. He watched as his uncle reached up into the hollow pontoon of the catamaran. He withdrew a handgun, a black .38 revolver. Tate turned the gun on himself and placed the tip of the barrel in his mouth. Tyler sensed the air escaping his lungs. He moved forward, raising his arm out toward his uncle, yelling for him to stop. But Tyler could do nothing. Tate had made up his mind.

The shot rang out, jolting Tyler to a stop. He watched Tate fall to the ground—lifeless. Tyler dropped to his knees, immediately shaken, broken; his breaths were short and quick. It was if he had been shot himself. He kept his head down, daring not to look upon his uncle's final act.

He heard the glass doors opening behind him. A shiver ran out his spine at the pitiful wail that followed. He felt Marie running past him, screaming and crying. But Tyler just stayed on his knees, keeping his head down, hoping it would go away, wishing he could wake up from this very bad dream.

OCTOBER 27

12:45 PM

Tyler parked on the side of Pavilion Avenue and climbed out of his truck. He still had on his coat and tie from the funeral, but the morning storm that had socked Galeegi during the services had moved on, so he left his raincoat in the cab. He had just left Marie at her house. She had friends and other family members with her now, and he felt comfortable enough to leave her for a little while. He would go back over there later in the evening, but right now, he needed his own quiet time—his time for reflection.

The service had been difficult enough. There was very little the Methodist preacher could have said at this point to help ease the pain, and Tyler didn't pay that much attention to his words anyway. He held Marie's hand the whole time, holding her up, keeping her steady. Periodically, he turned his head to look at those gathered. The small church was packed with those who had come into contact with Fletcher Tate during his life—friends, family, fellow lawmen, former Marines. He noted the familiar faces of Manu Ando, Sheriff Dan Sheridan, and Phil Nahigian. Even Miller Kasko returned from his Atlanta office to pay his respects.

Tyler scanned the crowd looking for Chloe, but he did not see her at the church or at the graveyard services. In the rush of the past few days, he had tried in various ways to get her the message. Her office relayed that she had been sent out of the country on some assignment for the agency, and all attempts to her cell phone and email failed to generate a response. It was very disconcerting for Tyler. He needed Chloe's support.

He walked away from the road past the tall palmettos and underlying palms. He passed the washout area and made his way along the creek. Once he crossed the giant dune, he moved down onto the beach area.

The morning storm had been a fierce one and left Galeegi with overcast skies and cooler temperatures. It was low tide now and the ocean had cleaned the beach into a wide band of hard, smooth sand. The receding waves left tidal pools at its lowest points. Tyler stood with his hands in his dress suit pockets; the beach wind played with his tie. There was a sense of desolation now about the beach—an emptiness that ate right through his soul.

Tyler took several steps toward the water. He watched the Galeegi as it slammed against the Atlantic. Turbulent. Torrid. Unforgiving.

He looked further over the bounding waves. Amoyeli stood there at a distance like a tiny speck. The small island had never seemed so isolated, so far away. As Tyler shifted his eyes to the tidal pool at his feet, he thought he could hear the island's old root doctor, Hammie Swantou, whispering in his ear. *Look to what the tide leaves behind. You find your answer there.*

Tyler bent down to take a closer look. The ocean breeze laid a ripple upon the odd shaped pool. He saw the tiny ghost crabs and other finite creatures crawling about the temporary habitat, longing for the ocean's return. But that was it. There was nothing else—no message—no sign.

Nothing. There's nothing here for me, Tyler thought. He picked up a loose shell and flipped it in the shallow water.

But then as he stared at his blurred reflection,

something caught his eye. Someone was standing behind his right shoulder. He stood and turned inquisitively.

On a cool, October day, on a wind-swept stretch of beach, in an oddly shaped tidal pool, Tyler Miles finally found his answer.

ABOUT THE AUTHOR

Born and raised in the palmetto state, Lawrence Thackston is a writer of Southern tales of mystery, suspense, loss, and redemption. His first novel, *The Devil's Courthouse*, was well-received by critics and has generated a faithful following among his readers.

An English major at the College of Charleston, Lawrence received his teaching certificate and Masters Degree at South Carolina State University. He has been a teacher in Orangeburg District #4 for nearly twenty-five years and has taught everything from SC History to Latin to Creative Writing to American and British literature.

Lawrence lives with his wife and three children on their quiet family farm where the road ends and the river turns.